P9-BZG-662

Praise for J. P. Smith

"I love a story with a touch of paranormal, and *The Summoning* delivers in a suspense novel starring Kit, an out-of-work actress who survives by faking séances for family members of 9/11 victims…until the voices of the dead grow real. A dark and murky slow-burn that will take you by surprise."

—Kimberly Belle, international bestselling author of *Dear Wife* and *Stranger in the Lake*, for *The Summoning*

"An overbearing alpha male gets his comeuppance in this smart, creepy thriller."

—*Publishers Weekly*, Starred Review, for *The Drowning*

"Alex Mason has it all: a lavish lifestyle, a beautiful family, a thriving career. He's built his life around the certainty that no one would discover what really happened twenty years ago at an idyllic summer camp. He's wrong. *The Drowning* is an edge-of-your-seat read."

—Kaira Rouda, bestselling author of *Best Day Ever* and *The Favorite Daughter*, for *The Drowning*

"Smith has hit this one out of the park. Great characters, a plot that will draw you from the first to the last page and destined to be a must-read book."

—*The Strand Magazine* for *The Drowning*

"Part love story, part exploration into the difficulties of marriage and part psychological thriller, Smith's latest masterpiece dazzles and delights with plot twists and turns down to the very last sentence. Literally. Smith's latest novel will leave me questioning the complex nature of love, crimes and punishments for a long time."

—Traci Medford-Rosow, USA Today bestselling
author of Unblinded, for If She Were Dead

"In clear prose, Smith spins out a sensuous, sinuous psychological thriller that compels attention to the final line."

—Booklist for If She Were Dead

"Smith does a masterful job blending multiple story lines. Readers will find plenty of action, intrigue, and surprises."

—Publishers Weekly for If She Were Dead

Also by J. P. Smith

If She Were Dead

The Drowning

Airtight

Breathless

The Discovery of Light

The Blue Hour

Body and Soul

The Man from Marseille

THE
SUMMONING

a novel

J. P.
SMITH

Poisoned Pen
PRESS

Copyright © 2021 by J. P. Smith
Cover and internal design © 2021 by Sourcebooks
Cover design by Sarah Brody
Cover images © Miguel Sobreira/Arcangel; Araya
Netsawang/Getty; VorontsovaNatalia/Getty

Sourcebooks, Poisoned Pen Press, and the colophon
are registered trademarks of Sourcebooks.

All rights reserved. No part of this book may be reproduced in any form or by
any electronic or mechanical means including information storage and retrieval
systems—except in the case of brief quotations embodied in critical articles or
reviews—without permission in writing from its publisher, Sourcebooks.

The characters and events portrayed in this book are fictitious or
are used fictitiously. Any similarity to real persons, living or dead,
is purely coincidental and not intended by the author.

All brand names and product names used in this book are trademarks,
registered trademarks, or trade names of their respective holders.
Sourcebooks is not associated with any product or vendor in this book.

Published by Poisoned Pen Press, an imprint of Sourcebooks
P.O. Box 4410, Naperville, Illinois 60567-4410
(630) 961-3900
sourcebooks.com

Library of Congress Cataloging-in-Publication Data

Names: Smith, J. P., author.
Title: The summoning : a novel / J. P. Smith.
Description: Naperville, Illinois : Poisoned Pen Press, [2021]
Identifiers: LCCN 2020056322 (print) | LCCN 2020056323
   (ebook) | (trade paperback) | (epub)
Subjects: LCSH: Psychological fiction.
Classification: LCC PS3569.M53744 S86 2021 (print) | LCC PS3569.M53744
   (ebook) | DDC 813/.54--dc23
LC record available at https://lccn.loc.gov/2020056322
LC ebook record available at https://lccn.loc.gov/2020056323

Printed and bound in Canada.
MBP 10 9 8 7 6 5 4 3 2 1

For Cheryl

Somewhere in here I was born…and here I died, and it was only a moment for you…

—*Vertigo* (Alfred Hitchcock, 1958)

1

TURN THE PAGES OF THE BOOK OF THE DEAD, AND in their photos no one's quite there yet. Instead they're always on the verge of something else: making plans, devising plots, hoping for the best. Smiling, waving, sipping a cocktail on a beach called Paradise. And then one bright morning it all comes to an end.

On a table in a corner of Kit Capriol's Morningside Heights kitchen, cluttered with laptop and well-thumbed notebook, several Post-its stuck here and there with phone numbers scribbled on them, a selection of highlighters, and a small framed photo of her daughter, Zoey, playing the piano, was also the latest edition of the *New York Times*'s *Portraits of Grief*, which had been published after 9/11, broken-spined, bookmarked, and annotated. This is where the dead lived, where those who disappeared existed in the half-life of doubt and a passing smile in a selfie.

As she did first thing every morning, Kit turned to the obituary feature of that day's *New York Times*. Her attention moved down the page to the memorials, posted annually or on significant anniversaries—every five or ten or twenty years. *Sorely missed. Still loved. Never forgotten.*

In that small print was her day's work.

She uncapped a red Sharpie and circled the one that caught her eye that morning:

MALONE—Lucy. Born Dublin, Ireland, April 5, 1989. Passed this day ten years ago in New York City. Remembered for her blazing red hair and irresistible sense of humor by her many friends and relatives, most especially her mother Brigid, also of New York. Survivors include her aunt, Delia Burke of Sligo, Ireland, and a first cousin, Sinead Thompson of London, England. A promising career as a ballet dancer cut short.

She highlighted some of it: *red hair*; *humor*; *Delia*; *Sinead*; *ballet*. She entered *Brigid Malone, NY* into Google, and there were eight of them. Three in Astoria, two in Long Island City, one in the Bronx, and two in Manhattan, one in Hell's Kitchen, the other in the East Village. There were twelve others, all over the city, listed simply as *B. Malone*.

She wrote the numbers on whatever piece of paper was at hand. Then she initiated a search for a proper obituary. And found nothing, which wasn't unusual.

She tried the numbers in Queens with no luck, then those in Manhattan. The person who answered the second number in that borough, an older woman, seemed hesitant. Or maybe just suspicious, in the way the elderly sometimes are when a stranger walks into their life.

"Good morning, is this Mrs. Brigid Malone?" Kit said hopefully. "The mother of the late Lucy Malone?"

"Yes?" the woman said after a long pause. "What is it you want?"

Kit guessed the woman to be in her sixties or seventies, still graced with an accent.

"I was so sorry to read in the *Times* of your daughter's passing ten years ago today."

"Ah, well, yes. It's all very painful for me."

"Of course these must still be very difficult days for you. But I believe I can help you get through them. You see, Lucy has been in touch with me. In fact, we've spoken a few times lately."

2

I T HAD BEEN LIKE THIS FOR MOST OF MARCH AND into April, gray days and rain, the fading of the brief afternoon, the sad unpromising nights of early spring. The people Brigid Malone walked past on her way to the cathedral seemed glum and unforgiving beneath their umbrellas.

Although traffic on Fifth Avenue was light at that time of the morning, and she could have crossed at any time, she dutifully waited for the walk sign before she made her slow, solitary way across to the cathedral. Three steps up, she gripped the handrail and paused a moment to catch her breath, tilting her head to look up at the grand façade of St. Patrick's Cathedral.

In Ireland she'd been a smoker, and now it was catching up with her, the shortening of breath, the occasional dizziness her doctor attributed to high blood pressure. When her daughter was taken from her, she fell back into her old habits, adding drink to the mix, whiskey and silence and smoke. Since then she'd given up two of the three.

It was silence that eventually became her refuge, the silence that sometimes came late at night, when she inevitably woke in the small hours. The kind of fragile peace that might carry to her ears the voice of her daughter, or a fading vision of the girl she had lost. *Come to me in my dreams,* she sometimes thought before she closed her eyes at night. But her daughter never did.

Brigid thought that her memory was just too crowded with all the other dead she'd known and mourned: her mother, who died giving birth to her ninth child; her father, who gradually drank himself to death every night at McNeill's pub. There were her childhood friends, most of them gone, as well: natural causes, accidents, murder, suicide. Not to mention all the aunts and uncles, especially her mother's brother Jimmy Clancy, a merry soul and amateur fiddle player, who blew himself up with the bomb he was making in his basement flat in Belfast one fine Friday evening. Locals said that all these years later they were still finding bits of him here and there, caught in a crack in the floorboards, or between the jaws of a pet dog, triumphant with the ankle bone it had dug up in the back garden.

And then there was Brigid's husband, Brendan. Only rarely did he visit her in her dreams, and when he did it was a young Brendan, the man who, as her mother put it, was "courting her" when she was seventeen. Back when he was handsome and strong, and still too reckless in his habits, knocking about from one pub to the next with his friends, making his sweaty way home after closing time, only to spend too much time with his head in the toilet, spewing up all the beer he'd bought with his hard-earned money.

Now he was in St. Fintan's Cemetery, out by Howth, a long bus ride from their home in Dublin at any time of the day. He'd been in the roofing business and had died after he broke his neck and back in a fall. She was told that it was merciful that he was taken so quickly, not even an hour after the accident, as he might have spent the remainder of his life, as the doctor bluntly put it to her, "like a giant turnip in your spare bedroom."

When you lose someone, she used to think, when you've lost everyone else, the best thing to do is start over. And so she came to America, to New York, where she had a cousin, Aileen, who lived in Long Island City and who had been dead now these five years. Brigid lived in Hell's Kitchen, a thought which always put a smile on her face, as though she were a guest in the devil's own home.

Save for three or four people sitting alone in their pews, bowed in prayer and seeking mercy, or lost in contemplation and memory, the church was empty. The organist was practicing in his loft, measures, half phrases, arpeggios, finally settling on something by Bach, pleasant to hear, she thought, just as a church should sound at this dead hour. After stopping briefly to speak to the young woman she'd come to know who worked in the gift shop, she made her way to her favorite pew, three from the back on the right-hand side, on the left by the aisle.

She nervously fingered her rosary, and when she reached her third Hail Mary she nearly jumped out of her skin.

"Jesus, Father, you scared the living hell out of me."

The priest who had suddenly appeared beside her smiled—he was young, she noted, so he'd taken no offense, and in any event the words had come out of her mouth just like that, without her willing them for even a second. Devil's work, people back home might think, and she nearly laughed at the idea of it.

"Father Rizzoli," he said.

She introduced herself. He said, "You'd mentioned to one of the people in the gift shop that you wanted to see a priest. I'm the priest on duty for today. Is there anything I can help you with?"

"Might Father McConnell be lurking about?" She looked around, as though she might catch sight of him scampering off like a thief into the vestry.

Father Rizzoli smiled. "I'm afraid for this morning this young Italian-American priest is about it. Will I do?"

She stood, genuflected, though not as nimbly as he did, and followed him to his office. He seemed overwhelmed behind the huge wooden desk that had probably belonged to the cathedral for decades. He said, "I'm afraid my office is quite small and not very comfortable. This belongs to one of the more senior fathers, Father Carroll. Big guy. Notre Dame, '75. Spending the week in Rome. So how can I help you, Mrs. Malone?"

"It's about—"

"Wait—"

He came around the desk and sat in the chair beside her.

She said, "It's about my daughter. She's been dead and buried these many years, Father. But this woman called out of nowhere. She said she's talked to her. I would do anything in the world to spend even five minutes with her again. Is such a thing possible, do you think?"

He took a moment to gather his words. "Well, the Church does frown upon any kind of occult practices. They can often lead one into some dangerous places, you know. Open up doors better left locked." He smiled a little. "But if it makes you feel any better...? I don't see any harm this time."

"Thank you, Father. It's reassuring to know that I'm not going to be in any trouble for it."

"Just remember, Mrs. Malone—whatever you hear, whatever you see, may be the work of someone else. Someone far more dangerous than this woman who called you."

3

D RIZZLE HAD DWINDLED TO SUNLIGHT, A MIDDAY
sky littered with torn bits of morning overcast, shreds of
paper tossed to the wind. A mist began rising from the same
path Kit ran on two or three times a week in Riverside Park,
and the air carried a fresh briny smell, the honest scent of distant
waters.

Spring would give way to summer; summer to fall. The
season she dreaded most.

Though other runners and cyclists regularly passed her,
she quietly recited a poem by Yeats she'd memorized back in
college,

> *"Though I am old with wandering*
> *Through hollow lands and hilly lands,*
> *I will find out where she has gone,*
> *And kiss her lips and take her hands..."*

And then the Irish accent she once had to learn for a role
kicked in:

> *"And walk among long dappled grass,*
> *And pluck till time and times are done,*

The silver apples of the moon,
The golden apples of the sun."

Once again she would speak for the dead.

4

N EARLY EIGHTEEN YEARS HAD PASSED SINCE HER
husband's death, and Peter had moved on from being a
living, breathing person of substance and warmth to becoming
an abstract memory: a notion, a list of words, a pattern of secret
codes. What Kit remembered most vividly were the things
around him, as though they defined not Peter as he was, but
the outline of his absence.

Mostly she remembered the crows, a tree full of them in
Central Park. When she looked up as they took flight, it was
like seeing ink splashed against the sky, the unreadable print of
some ancient occult text.

That midsummer day she was fresh off a rehearsal for a
forthcoming production of *The Crucible* and took the subway to
Central Park. To leave the world of seventeenth-century Salem
was always a relief. Instead of using the full width and depth
of the stage, the director located most of the action within a
trapezoid, narrower at the back, opening up at the front, suggesting both a chapel and a star chamber. Actors could appear
cornered at its greatest depth, and he used the stage to great
effect, pushing the women back until there was no place for
them to go. The heat under the lights was intense, and at the
end of every rehearsal the actors were dripping with sweat. The

claustrophobia and intensity of the play had already cost the cast one member, who had a panic attack one night after a rehearsal and fled home to Teaneck, never to return.

When Kit reached the bench by the pond, a man was sitting at the other end of it. The day settled on her like a warm breeze, stripping her of the anguish and obsession of the play's dialogue and bringing her back to the life she knew. To breathe, to see sky, to taste something real. Now she'd be in a different play, one she'd been in often before.

The man said, "Nice day."

"So?"

"Just sayin'."

She didn't bother to look at him.

"You look like you have a secret," he said, and now she turned to him, a little disconcerted by the comment.

"That'll cost you," she said.

"Just for the question? I'd hate to hear what the answer is going to run me."

"We all have secrets, don't we?"

"From where I'm sitting, yours looks really good."

"Is it really that obvious?"

He nodded. "Uh-huh."

She laughed. "Actually, I could use a secret, too. A new one."

"If you're trying to get rid of an old one, I'll take it."

She sized him up from her end of the bench. "You sound a little needy, mister."

"Tell you what—I'll tell you mine if you tell me yours."

"I bet you used that line when you were a teenager trying to get into some girl's pants."

"Yeah, well, you're only human once." He held out his hand. "Peter Capriol."

"My mother always told me not to talk to strange guys named Peter. And definitely no one named Capriol."

He began riffing, just as both of them had done ever since they'd been in their college's theater program: "Hey. I'm the guy you sleep with every night, remember?"

She looked at him. "Oh, yeah. There are so many others that I almost forgot. Hello, Mr. Capriol, is it...?"

"Hello, Mrs. Capriol."

She slid over and they shared a quick kiss. He put his arm around her and asked how the rehearsal went.

"Really well. I feel both comfortable in the role and about to leap out of my skin. The whole cast is on edge, which I guess adds the right feeling for this play. Plus I must smell like hell. Lost a few good pints of sweat on that stage."

"You're a woman of many talents and scents."

"And you're an amazing cook. Used to be a hell of an actor, too, back at college. Remember how we met—?"

"Improv class."

"Yup. And we're still doing it, buddy."

"What would you do without me?"

"I'll never be without you."

"I have the afternoon off."

"I know."

"Wow, you're good," he said. "How'd you figure that?"

She tapped the side of her head. "Sixth sense."

"You see dead people?"

"You don't? That's strange."

He laughed. "So what do you want to do for the rest of the day, huh, lady?"

"Drink martinis. Fall asleep in a hot bath. Watch a scary movie. Have a nightmare or two. Make love to a vampire."

"I think I can make all of that happen." He gave her neck a little bite.

She looked up at the crows on their branches, some of them peering down at her, tilting their heads this way and that as though trying to read her mind. She clapped her hands once, *bang*, and they burst into the air, crying in protest.

"A murder of crows," Peter said, opening his hands as he watched them scatter. "I learned that back in school. That's what a group of them is called. A murder."

5

A WEEK AFTER PETER HAD TAKEN A NEW POSITION as a line cook at Windows on the World early in August 2001, and after they'd been living in a cramped apartment in New Rochelle for seven years, Kit put the entire amount of money she'd been left after her mother's death as a down payment on a two-bedroom co-op on West 113th Street. She and Peter wanted to start a family.

They'd gotten lucky. The previous tenants were about to begin their fourth year there when something happened and the husband abruptly returned to his native country. Kit and Peter had shown up the day the apartment was put on the market and their offer was accepted.

It was a whole new life, being in the city, one they'd planned on from the start. To raise a child there with so much to see and do—Kit herself had been taken to museums and plays when she was child every Saturday—and they wanted their son or daughter to have the same opportunities.

They moved in ten days later, and while Peter went to work at the restaurant, Kit began painting what they hoped would be a nursery. She chose a calm shade of blue, and as she worked the sun came blazing through the uncurtained window, something she never expected in a city apartment.

There was a knock at the door, and through the peephole she saw a woman looking down at her phone. The woman smiled and put her phone away when Kit opened the door.

"I'm in 4C," and she pointed down the hall. "Lisa Abrams."

"Kit Capriol."

"You look like you've been doing some serious redecorating," the woman said, taking in Kit's paint-spattered T-shirt and jeans.

"It's that obvious, is it?" Kit said, and the woman laughed.

Lisa said, "I just wanted to know if anyone had told you about what happened here last month."

Kit asked if she were speaking of the building or her apartment, and Lisa said it was the apartment, now Kit and Peter's.

Kit said, "Okay. So tell me."

"So you don't know about Lori and Raphael?"

"No. Nothing at all."

"I was told—and I don't know how accurate it is—that when they moved in everything was fine. Raphael was working at Sotheby's as an appraiser in the African art department, or whatever they call it there. Lori worked for a nonprofit here in the city. The two of them didn't talk a lot about their work. But they seemed fine. A month after they moved in, they had me and my husband over for a drink. They seemed like a nice couple. Seemed to get on really well. She was... Well, forget it, it doesn't matter."

"No. Tell me, I'm curious."

"She seemed really nervous. Little things made her jump. Like her husband putting down his glass a little too loudly. I guess things—life—got to be a little too much for her. She stopped coming out of the apartment, and the neighbor on the other side, Peggy Loring—?"

"I haven't met her yet—"

"She said she'd hear Lori crying a lot. Raphael had to go to London on business for a week, and when he came back, she was out of control. She said she kept hearing voices. Seeing things. He finally had to have her institutionalized. A week later he moved back to France."

Kit took it in. A sad story, but the apartment was now hers and Peter's.

"Would you like to come in?" Kit really just wanted to get back to painting.

"Thanks, but I've got to run. Anyway, long story short. Just thought you should hear about it." She smiled. "It's not the apartment, if that's what you're worried about."

In any event, the apartment was exactly what they'd been looking for, and just taking the time to paint and make the place their own was bringing Kit a measure of contentment— not that she needed much, being happy in her career and her marriage—that felt something like peace.

She returned to the nursery and the slant of sunlight, and for a moment thought someone was standing there, and the shock of it made her step abruptly back. But it was just a shadow.

6

WHILE PETER COMMUTED TO WORK EACH DAY, Kit resumed her rehearsals. Returning from a run one warm, cloudless September morning, she saw there had been a voicemail from Peter seven minutes earlier, a call that lasted all of forty-two seconds.

She tapped to play it through the speaker, listening to it again and again, her husband's last words to her in the moments before his death. And then she turned on the news and watched a loop of the tower collapsing over and over on this splendid New York morning without any commercial interruptions.

She looked at the time stamp on his message: 10:27 a.m.

They never found Peter's remains. He might have jumped, she thought, and childishly imagined that he'd landed on his feet and was wandering around bedazzled in Lower Manhattan. She couldn't stop thinking that he'd walk in through the door one evening or she'd wake to find him beside her in bed. Or that, eight years later when she walked Zoey home from her piano lessons with Mrs. Fischer on West End Avenue, she'd see him coming toward them, stepping out of the shadows to show his face before walking on.

Would he know her? Would Peter recognize the daughter

he'd never met? Would he have remembered anything of this life he had lost?

"If you don't see the dead, then they're really not dead," Zoey said to her one day before bed. It came unprompted, out of nowhere.

The wisdom of a seven-year-old's words struck Kit as somehow profound. It was wishful thinking, she knew. And yet how utterly reasonable, how completely ordinary it was.

"So my dad isn't dead. Not for you and not for me. And that's how it's going to be from now on."

"I'm sorry you never got to know him. I'm sorry he never got to meet you."

"But part of him is part of me, isn't it?"

Kit smiled. "Yes, that's true."

"So if I know myself, I kind of know him."

Meant to open on September 12, *The Crucible* was delayed for another week as the city and the nation mourned, then one more week, then another five days. Work seemed the only possible way for Kit to get back to living. The play ran off-Broadway for its planned six weeks. Kit never missed a performance, finding that it not so much took her mind off of what happened, but engaged her in the wild emotions of a story even more terrible than hers. And then she'd come home every night to the reality of her life: the empty bed, takeout for one, drinking alone in front of the TV.

Two days before the first performance, she discovered she was pregnant, and Zoey was born in June the following year. Kit had been a widow for nine months.

Death is all around us, she thought in the days that came after the towers fell. It's in the air, it's in the soil, it's grit under our nails, ash in our hair, dust in our lungs. She wondered if it lingered in their apartment, and if she would catch a glimpse of it in a shaft of sunlight, hanging motionless in the air.

She wondered when she'd begin to grieve. So far she hadn't been able to shed a single tear for this man she loved beyond measure.

After putting up flyers amid hundreds of others, *Have you seen this man?* with a photo of Peter taken on their wedding day, smiling in his suit, happy in his marriage, day after day on her morning run in Riverside Park she'd see the smoke and haze above Lower Manhattan, and she'd think, that's Peter: a twist of gray in the deepest blue of a New York sky.

She began to view the world as a place of portent and symbol, as though Peter might somehow be communicating with her in various obscure ways. Standing in line at a pharmacy she thought she heard his voice, certain that he'd said her name, and when she turned to look at the others behind her, to find his face among them, there was no Peter; there was no one at all. Or maybe he had only just been there, a fleeting ghostly appearance, here for a moment, gone forever.

She began to note in a pad each time she thought she saw or heard him.

October 30, 2001. No. 7 bus, corner of 56th St., Peter in the back by the window. Looked at me. Smiled. Couldn't believe what I was seeing, held my hand out, but the bus pulled away as the light changed.

December 24, 2001. Fairway Market. Stocking up for solo holiday. Not much left there. Bought a rotisserie chicken that looked more dead than cooked. Veggies. Fruit. Dozen eggs. Reach back of checkout line. Peter is leaving with two bags. I drop everything, apples rolling all over the place, eggs broken, and run after him. Outside I call for him, "Peter, Peter!" People think I'm crazy. They may be right.

The sightings trickled to an end some months later. And then, several years later, Peter returned.

September 11, 2016. At Met, trying to get my mind off the anniversary. As always, I can't be alone that day. Vermeer's "A Maid Asleep," a young woman dozing at a table. Seen it dozens of times, but it seems different now. As if it were connected to my state of mind. There's a wine bottle on the table, and a glass on its side. She's fallen asleep, the young docent suggests in her English accent. And then the woman tells her group that X-rays revealed a man standing in the doorway behind her. For some reason Vermeer painted him out. She says, "Is it the woman's lover? Or had she only been dreaming? Maybe even about him. It's a moment in time, a place between life and death, dream and oblivion."

Her words are unnerving and also comforting, because an absence implies a presence. The docent's voice and accent reminds me of Julie Christie's. What an amazing painting, I think in her voice, as though I were saying it to Donald Sutherland as together we walked through a haunted Venice.

That's when Peter with a woman and 2 children pass

through the gallery. Race down the staircase, follow out the door. He's alive, he's remarried with a new family. I catch up on the corner. Grab his arm. It's Peter. But he doesn't know me. His wife and kids are terrified.

It was as if death were no more than a magic trick, the intrigues of a cruel sorcerer.

Because it seemed so long ago that it had all taken on an air of unreality: Kit's marriage, her husband, her loss.

She switched off the light and parted the curtains. She saw the figure in the streetlight across the street, a woman in a wool coat and a headscarf, as though she'd walked out of a photo from 1950 or off the cover of a novel about loneliness, something to catch the eye on a bookshop table. She saw how the woman hesitated to cross, even though no cars were passing and nothing was stopping her. Standing there, as though trying to come to a decision.

Kit closed the curtains just as the apartment was buzzed from the lobby. She cleared her throat and pressed the button for the intercom. "Hello? Yes?"

"It's...Mrs. Malone. We spoke yesterday, if you'll remember."

Her voice was so soft that Kit had to strain to make out the words.

"I've been expecting you," she said to the woman.

Kit was dressed casually but respectably, her hair brushed and clipped in the back, her makeup subdued. There was nothing outstanding about her appearance, barely anything to remember. If you look normal, people took you to be normal, not some wild-haired sorceress promising to bring you love and riches like some of the others in the city did. She cleared her throat and pressed the button to unlock the vestibule door.

"Fourth floor, apartment D," she said.

Kit listened as the gears and cables kicked in to lift the elevator to her floor. And when Mrs. Malone stepped out of it, Kit was in the hallway to greet her. She held out both her hands and smiled. First impressions counted most, she knew.

"Of course. You must be Mrs. Malone. Brigid, isn't it? Lucy told me all about you. You're just as she described you."

The woman smiled. "That's my girl," she said. "Always the chatterbox."

They sat in a living room lined with bookcases and lit by two lamps with silk shades that cast a warm antique glow to the room, the woodwork, the bookshelves, the pictures on the wall, the framed photo of twelve-year-old Zoey at the piano. Fingers properly curved, eyes intent on the music before her. *Focus, focus,* her teacher would say.

"It's a lovely apartment you have."

"Thank you."

Brigid Malone looked around the room and paused as she noticed the photo of Zoey. "Your own daughter, is it?"

Kit smiled and nodded.

"Lovely girl."

"Thank you."

"And…she is still with us, I hope?"

"Yes. She is."

Except she wasn't. She was both with us and without us. Kit chose not to elaborate.

"And the piano," the woman said, pressing her hands together. "You play, do you?"

"My daughter does. I'm afraid I have no musical talent."

She'd bought the piano for five hundred dollars from a nearby private school that was upgrading their instrument. A Knabe baby grand probably built in the forties, it took up half the living room, its keyboard lid now closed, as it would remain until Zoey came home. It was a kind of superstition with Kit, as though it were meant to be like a rest in musical notation, a space between one note and the next. With Zoey in the hospital, it had become a neglected, untuned, useless piece of furniture taking up too much space.

"Let's chat a moment before we begin," Kit said. "May I offer you a cup of tea, perhaps...?"

The woman smiled; already she was softening to Kit. "That's very kind of you. Maybe another time? May I ask," and she unclasped her handbag and dipped her fingers in to fish out a purse, "how much will I be owing you for this?"

"For tonight? Nothing, Mrs. Malone. As I mentioned on our call, there's no charge for the first session. After that, you are free to pay whatever you feel it has been worth to you, with a one-hundred dollar minimum donation should you decide to return. If you do so, donations can be left in the basket on the table in the corner."

Thirty of those in a good month, with even larger donations coming from her regular clients, and she had something resembling an income. Between medical bills and mortgage payments, she had little money to spare.

The woman smiled. "That's grand." She snapped her bag

shut and looked at Kit. "Tell me... How does my Lucy sound? Can you actually hear her voice?"

"I can, Mrs. Malone, clear as day. Sometimes she's the age at which she passed over. Other times, she's a child. You see, there is no time there. The spirits survive in the past, present, and future."

It was a line she'd used often before. It seemed to bring comfort to people.

"Can they see what will become of us?" the woman asked.

Kit nodded. "They can see everything, in all times. And they're always with us. They stay close to their home, to the people they love. Sometimes I even think they feel the living are haunting *them*."

"That's a comfort," Mrs. Malone said, her eyes wide with something like wonder. "Knowing that they watch over us."

"Lucy told me that she left us very quickly. That she was at first confused about what had happened, but then she finally remembered that last day."

"Did she say anything about that?"

"No. I sensed that it had all been very distressing, especially for you. Part of her was unable to separate for some time. It was a struggle for her. She said that she feels guilty for what you'd had to put up with."

"Well, the doctors couldn't get to the bottom of it."

"I know. Lucy told me all about it."

7

O NE DAY SHE WAS FINE," MRS. MALONE SAID. "She was in ballet class... What's wrong, have you been taken ill?"

Kit's head had fallen back. Her body began to tremble. She sat up suddenly. "She's near..." she said quietly. "So near..."

"She's—"

"Yes...?" Kit said, tilting her head as though to listen. "Yes, I can hear you, Lucy... It's time now, Mrs. Malone."

She led the client into her consulting room, formerly a spare bedroom barely larger than a storage closet, now a warm, intimate space with a small round table covered with a silk cloth. In the center of it was a white candle, its wick neatly trimmed, the flame slender and unwavering as though painted on the air. The window was hidden behind floor-length gray drapes. The walls were bare, without distraction, save for the two women's shadows in the candlelight. A scene that could have taken place three hundred years ago or ten years from now.

They sat opposite each other at the table. Kit held out her hands, feeling the woman's dry skin against hers. "Focus on the flame. The people we love are all around us. They never leave our side. We have to remember and believe. That's what draws them to us. Faith and memory. Know that the curtain that separates us is only as fragile as the breaths we're taking right now. So let us summon Lucy."

After several seconds she said quietly, "Lucy...? Are you still here...? It's Kit. We last spoke yesterday, remember?"

She seemed to be listening to something.

"Yes, of course. What—? No, but I do have a surprise for you. I have someone here who wants to speak to you. I see her now," she said as an aside to Mrs. Malone. "It's misty, hazy— but I can see her—she's a little girl now. A pretty little girl. A happy little girl."

The woman clasped her hands together and held them to her breast. "My Lucy. She's with me now."

Kit's breathing deepened as a smile played on her lips.

"Yes..." she said, "here she is...in a pretty white dress..."

"You see, don't you!"

"No, it's not a stranger, Lucy. This is someone who misses you very much, who loves you as much today as she did when you were in our world. Now do you see?" she said, and knew that Mrs. Malone was looking around the room, hoping for a glimpse of her dead daughter.

Kit gazed at her with her distant eyes. "She can see you now, Mrs. Malone. You can sense her in the air, can't you? A kind of warmth, of something alive, someone close."

"Will she speak?"

"Through me, and only when she's ready. At this moment she's a little girl, so she's shy at that age, as you'll remember."

"Oh yes, she was," Mrs. Malone said, and the look on her face was blissful.

"Look how lovely your red hair is," Kit says. "And this beautiful garland with the ribbons."

She had let go of the woman's hand and was moving her fingers gently in the air. "What is that? No, you don't have to thank me, Lucy. I'm just so happy I could bring you two together again."

"That is certainly a blessed relief to me," the woman said, crossing herself.

"Lucy's beside us, Mrs. Malone. I can even reach out and touch her."

Mrs. Malone gazed with wonder as Kit stretched a hand out into the darkness beyond the candlelight and gently wrinkled the air with her fingers.

"I want to touch her, as well, my own dear wee girl."

"Remember that she is pure spirit. You'll only feel that and not her substance. Wait... Wait... She's asking if Delilah, is that right, Lucy—?"

"Delia," Mrs. Malone corrected, nearly shouting out the name. "My sister, her auntie—"

"Lucy wants to know if Delia minds that she's wearing the pretty dress she had sewn for her."

Mrs. Malone sat upright. "The one with the lace collar? The one we buried her in?"

Kit listened to the air. "Oh yes," Kit said. "With the lace."

Through half-closed eyes she could see Mrs. Malone was transported by her vision.

Kit said, "She looks at you with so much love. She's free now, you see. No pain. No suffering. She says she doesn't want you to worry ever again. There is no suffering where she is, no sorrow."

Kit laughed—giggled—a little, and then, in a little Irish girl's voice: "I want to dance, Mam. I want to dance all day long!"

Tears came to Mrs. Malone's eyes. "That's her—that's my little one. Stop for a while, wee girl. Stop and let me hold your hand for a bit. May I do that?"

"She's gone," Kit said finally.

"Not forever, surely?" Mrs. Malone said, nearly rising from her chair.

"Nothing in this world or the next can ever separate a mother and her daughter. Now I'm very tired, and need to rest."

"I'd very much like to come again and contact my girl."

"And so you shall."

"Is it then I'll be paying you?"

Kit smiled and handed the woman her card with only her name, address, phone number and email address on it. "Call whenever you wish, Mrs. Malone. And I'm so glad that you were able to be with Lucy once again."

She knew the woman would return, perhaps often. The entire year had been difficult for Kit; already she'd had to beg for an extension to pay her mortgage. It was only a matter of time before she might lose the apartment altogether. And then where would she go? With Zoey in the hospital she had no options: eviction would be, and the words were already there, the death of her.

She peered between the curtains as the woman crossed the street and melded with the darkness on her way to the subway. She felt both sorry for Mrs. Malone's grief and pleased she was able to alleviate it, even if only for a few minutes.

She wished someone would do the same for her.

8

IT SEEMED MORE DREAM THAN REALITY. A FILM
viewed in the twilight of hindsight. She thought of it again
as she lay in her bath after Mrs. Malone had left.

Three years earlier Kit was walking down the steps of the
Columbia University Subway Station, Zoey a few steps ahead
of her, eager to attend a concert at Carnegie Hall. Zoey had
been looking forward to it for months now, especially as the
pianist András Schiff would, among other pieces, be playing
the Mozart sonata she'd been learning. Zoey had mentioned
the concert to her piano teacher, Mrs. Fischer, who thought it
would be good for her to learn the piece before she went.

"That way you can get a sense of how a master plays
it," she told her pupil. "Personally, I was never much of a
Mozart person, save when I was younger, your age, maybe
a little older. I've grown into my tastes, though. These days
I prefer Bach, Chopin, Debussy. And I will play Bach until
I can no longer feel the keys. Music to grow old and wise
by," and she laughed. "But I think you're ready for the
Mozart. Why don't we start next week—here, let me find
the music for it." She went to her filing cabinet and sifted
through folders and binders until she found it. "You can
start feeling your way in. Then, by the time of the recital,

you may be far enough along to play it through from start to finish."

Zoey could clearly see the music in her mind's eye, on the page, and imagined following along with Schiff, moving her fingers a little on her lap: a ghost piano, just for her.

The subway platform was crowded at that time of the evening, and because the train was running late, more and more people joined them. Most wore earbuds or headphones, and nearly everyone who wasn't actually talking to another person had turned their eyes to their screens. Zoey was watching a man and a woman standing near the edge of the platform. The woman had blond hair, short and stylishly cut; the kind of hair Zoey wished she could have, instead of this mass of curls she was sometimes teased about by other kids at school. She envied people who looked like this woman; Zoey was entering her gawky stage, a little too tall, a little too thin and flat-chested, far too shy.

The woman wore skinny jeans, ankle boots, a suede jacket, and fingerless wool gloves. The man, in a leather jacket and black wool beanie, had a hand around her shoulders, while she had an arm around his waist. At one point she looked up at him, and his lips met hers before he whispered something in her ear.

People began glancing up from their screens as the air rippled ahead of an incoming train. The next thing Kit knew her daughter was on the ground gasping for air, her eyes rolling back into her head as she lost consciousness. On the platform people began screaming, others were crying, while some were saying that a woman had fallen. They kept pointing to the

tracks and looking away, while Kit kept begging people to call
for an ambulance. Having suffered a concussion and brain-stem
trauma when her head hit the platform, three years later Zoey
was still trapped within those moments, when she'd fallen into
the twilight of a coma.

Occasionally she'd seem fully alive, opening her eyes, focusing on her room, the sunlight in the window, the TV showing
reruns of some comedy series, her mother's face. And then
she'd go blank, her eyelids would flutter, and she'd vanish deep
inside herself.

Now Zoey was seventeen, and Kit often wondered if her
daughter was aware of what had happened to her, if her still-
active brain was replaying those minutes in the subway station,
or if she was living a whole other existence, a spectral afterlife
as she hovered between consciousness and oblivion.

Kit would sit by her bed in Mount Sinai Hospital, talking
about anything that came into her mind, streaming her daughter's favorite music on her iPhone, hoping for a sign that Zoey
was aware of her. Sometimes she would see the flickering of an
eyelid that ended almost as soon as it began, like a distant star
in the black of night. And sometimes Zoey would open her
eyes wide and just stare at Kit curiously, as though she were a
stranger.

It was what had drawn Kit to those who grieved for the dead
and the missing, and many of her first group of clients had lost
loved ones, suddenly and unexpectedly, in the 2001 attacks, as
she had. They all had something intimately in common, and so
she would bring the dead back to life for them. And so far she'd
failed no one. Except herself.

In the silence of the room, in the emptiness of the apartment, she could hear the water gently sloshing in the bath as she lay in it and closed her eyes. She had no idea why she felt more tired than usual after the séance with Brigid Malone. After a time, as she slid into a thin sleep, she opened them and listened.

Someone was in the apartment.

9

A FOOTSTEP; NOW ANOTHER.
The faint wheeze of someone taking a breath.

Kit pushed herself up quickly and grabbed the towel from the hook.

Missy—

Was that what she'd heard?

I—

"Who is it?" she said sharply, and there was a loud noise, as though someone had fallen, or toppled furniture over. "What do you want?"

She took a step up and out of the bath and turned the lock on the bathroom door. She was on the edge of panic, her rapid breaths starving her of logical thought.

"It's...it's Brigid again, Ms. Capriol. Brigid Malone."

"What...what do you want?"

"I was going home, then I decided I wanted to pay you for what you gave me this evening."

"How did you get into my apartment?"

"When I was coming back up to your building, a man was coming out and held the door for me. And when I knocked on your door there was no answer, and I thought, well—"

"Just tell me—how did you get into my apartment?"

"It was unlocked, Ms. Capriol. So I just let myself in, you see. I thought you'd be expecting me to return. Now I feel terrible that I did this."

It took Kit a moment to gather her thoughts. *Never turn away a client*, she thought.

"All right, wait a moment."

She put on her robe and unlocked and threw open the bathroom door. Startled once again, the woman nearly lost her balance. Kit reached out to steady her.

"You should never have done this," she said. "One day you'll do it to someone else and get yourself shot."

Mrs. Malone laughed. "Shot? Me? Don't be daft, missy."

She took some folded bills from her coat pocket and pushed them against Kit's hand. "This is for what you did for me today, to bring my daughter back into my life seeming so alive and happy."

Something struck Kit as odd about the whole situation, its structure eluding her.

"No, Mrs. Malone. As I explained to you over the phone, there is no charge for the first session. If you want to come a second time, you're free to leave a donation. Just not tonight."

"Take it."

Kit put her hands behind her back. The whole scenario seemed suddenly very odd. She'd hardly had the chance to gain the old woman's trust; that would come later. Because you never what knew your client's motives might be.

"I'll throw it at you."

"And I won't pick it up."

The woman's mouth tightened. This wasn't the meek old

woman who was so moved by her daughter's return; this was someone meaner, sterner. *Sour* was the word.

Kit opened the door and watched the old woman walk briskly back to the elevators.

Everyone's playing a role, Kit thought.

10

BRIGID MALONE GOT INTO THE BUICK PARKED around the corner.

The detective said, "What took you so long?"

"I thought I'd finish it. I'd forgotten, you see. She's a lovely young lady."

"Just tell me," he said, not looking at her.

"She wouldn't take the money. So when I came back, I thought I'd just leave it."

"Please don't tell me you did that," he said loudly.

"No, I remembered what to do. Just as you told me."

"And did she mention an amount?"

"Just that next time she'd be wanting a hundred-dollar donation in a basket she has."

"Next time," he said under his breath, and looked away. "And you understand that she actually has to take the money from your hand for me to make the arrest, right? Not something you just leave with her. We need a definite demand. This time, not the next, got it?"

She nodded. "I know. It's just—"

He looked at her. "That's how it has to be done."

He started the engine to drive her home. She could smell whiskey on his breath, whiskey and corruption.

He said, "Did you speak with a priest like I told you to do?"

She regretted that, at least. "Deceiving a man of the cloth… It made me feel dirty."

"But you told him what you were going to do, right?"

She said nothing.

"Well?"

"He seemed to think it wasn't so much of a problem."

"Because we may need him when the day comes, you understand? He may be asked to testify. This is a woman who's taking advantage of widows and widowers. Who's telling people that she can speak to their dead children."

"He's a priest. He can't betray what I said."

"Was it in the confessional?"

"No," she said after a pause. "An office. Casual, like."

"That's good. Remember his name?"

"Like you, an Italian fellow. Nice young man. I can't remember his name at all, but it may come to me at some later point in time."

Just under a half hour later he reached her apartment building off Eleventh Avenue. He looked at the stores on the ground floor. What had been Ray's Finest Pizza had been boarded up and was now up for rent. Next to it was a bodega called Two Brothers Fancy Gourmet. Standing outside it, a slender Black man in a Nike warm-up jacket grinned while a seemingly endless plume of white emerged from his lips as if he were on fire somewhere deep inside.

Before she got out, Brigid said, "You owe me something now, don't you?"

"You have the money I gave you for the Capriol woman?"

She held it out without looking at him.

"That's for you," he said. "Now go home and forget this ever happened. And never tell anyone that memorial notice was a fake. Just leave it alone. And give me the other thing."

She reached into her bag and handed him the little recorder. He looked at it and frowned. It hadn't been used.

"You've done your job." He looked away. "Just not well enough."

She took a moment. "She made me believe."

"She's fooling you, Brigid. It's all a big scam."

"It gave me faith that there truly is another place for us."

"You're done, Brigid. Go home."

She opened the door and struggled a little to get onto her unsteady feet. "I never want to do this again, understand?" she said. "Go find someone else to do your dirty business."

11

WITHIN THE FIRST FEW WEEKS OF ZOEY'S PIANO lessons, Kit had begun to hate her daughter's teacher. Famous in her native Hungary, respected throughout Europe and in the States, Mrs. Fischer had built her reputation out of what most successful creative mentors are known for—discipline bordering on brutality, what Kit despised most of all.

She would accompany Zoey to the woman's apartment on West End Avenue and sit in the waiting room, a cold tiled space with a few mismatched chairs and faded wallpaper featuring musical notation, reading a book or leafing through a well-thumbed months-old magazine picked up from a table in the corner. The single window there looked onto an air shaft. The little adjoining bathroom smelled of a cloying air freshener. She could hear everything: the words Mrs. Fischer threw at Zoey—*Lazy, Careless, Imbecile, Stupid Girl*—followed by the usual threats to cut off her lessons—everything but suggesting she'd hurl the girl out the window. And she would also hear her daughter's meek responses, *Yes. Okay. I know. I'll try.*

"No *try*, understand? No *try*, *do*. No real musician simply *tries*. Rubinstein never tried. Horowitz never tried. Do you think Glenn Gould tried? Ha! Now—do it again and again until you get it right."

Kit had known theater directors like that, mostly second-level talents yearning to become the next abusive giant of the craft, screaming at the leads one moment, screwing half the supporting cast the next. In time she learned to sift through the insults to find what was valuable there, eventually realizing that all the bluster and bullshit they spewed was mere smoke screen for what they expected the actors to discover for themselves.

It took months before she understood how valuable this woman was to her daughter, how much discipline she was instilling in her.

When the lesson was over, Mrs. Fischer—always Mrs. Fischer, never Frida—would accompany Zoey back to the waiting room. She always had a smile for Kit and a few words of praise for her pupil, as though nothing untoward had taken place in her living room studio.

"So, well, our Zoey is doing quite well, you know. You must be hearing this every evening when she practices, isn't that so, Ms. Capriol? Your daughter has a gift, one day she will shine on the stage. But only if she practices. Is it an hour at least she is at the keyboard? Because, if not, there is absolutely no point whatsoever in going on, isn't that right, my fine girl?"

"An hour," Zoey would say meekly.

After several more years of lessons every Wednesday afternoon, Mrs. Fischer finally stopped browbeating Zoey. The relationship between teacher and student had simmered into mutual respect, so that the woman would now only gently nudge and suggest instead of scream and threaten. "Yes, that is one way of playing that, and very nicely done indeed, but let's try a different fingering, shall we?"

After Zoey fell into her coma, Mrs. Fischer came to the hospital a few times to visit her. She took out her phone and quietly played a recording of her pupil playing the Mozart sonata they'd been working on. She switched it off after a few minutes.

"*That* is how good you've become, my dear. And I have a place for you when you wake up. You *will* be a musician. You *will* succeed. And we *will* get back to work on the Beethoven we were starting." And then she leaned over and kissed Zoey's cheek.

She said to Kit, "The *Moonlight* sonata. She wanted to learn it, and I felt that, well, why not, she should." She smiled. "One day, Ms. Capriol, she will play you the *Moonlight*."

"She looks good, doesn't she," the nurse said, standing beside Kit. Diane Carlson had been with Zoey ever since she'd been admitted to the hospital three years earlier. Kit visited usually twice a week, even if she were tied up with a play, even for only twenty minutes, and had come to rely on Diane for an honest assessment of Zoey's condition.

"She has color, at least," Kit said, clutching at any sign of recovery.

"And her vital signs have been reliably stable. It's funny," Diane said, looking from Kit to Zoey. "I just realized. You could be sisters. You're so much alike."

"I only wish I were half as beautiful as my daughter."

Kit knew that Zoey in this condition might even outlive her. What if she woke from her coma with no one to care for her? She'd lost her father before she was born, and now she could just as easily lose her mother. Her doctor, Phil Roman, had told Kit that Zoey's was an unusual case. There was blunt-force trauma from a very hard fall—her head hitting the platform—complicated by possible psychological trauma from having witnessed a woman falling to her death.

"Like when teenagers just want to sleep," the doctor told her. "Maybe they're just tired. Or maybe they just want to shut out reality."

Kit sat beside the bed and took her daughter's limp hand in hers. "Zoey, it's Mama." She looked at her daughter's face: her skin was as smooth as it had been when she was a little girl. Her eyes were open, seemingly looking at her mother. But there was no spark of recognition.

Kit lay the back of her fingers against her daughter's cheek and felt her warmth. *She's alive*, she'd tell herself every time, and that in itself was a consolation.

"So it's, what, a shallow kind of coma?"

"I can't say for certain," the doctor told her. "But my guess—or, rather, I'm inclined, with an unhealthy dose of salt, to say that she is somehow both in a coma and out of it." He waved his hand before his face. "In a kind of intermediate state. That's not a medical determination, of course. Just my intuition speaking."

Kit took it in. And then dismissed it. She was done with this kind of magical speculation; as if just thinking it would bring her daughter back into the world.

She looked up at Zoey's nurse. "I know I've probably asked you this a hundred times before, but do you think she can hear me?"

"We have no way of assessing that. But it's important you talk to her. Both for her and for you. I do it all the time. When I'm going through all the usual procedures, or just getting her washed, I tell her about my life, my husband, my kids, sometimes I tell her a secret. I even complain a lot. About my commute, about the weather, about my husband and my kids and my hyperactive dog," and she laughed. "In a funny way, I find it therapeutic, even though she may not be hearing me. But—listen to me, Kit—there's hope. Her condition is stable, she looks good, her brain shows activity—"

"Dreams?"

"She may be dreaming about you right now. They say that sometimes the outside world can seep into their consciousness. That they may incorporate what they hear and remember into their dreams."

"So she's dreaming all the time, really."

"Probably it goes in cycles, as it does when we're asleep. But if she dreams, I'd bet some are about you."

A whole other world for Kit. A second existence for her in a young woman's reveries.

"Tell her a story," Diane said. "Let her hear your voice. I'll leave you two alone."

"No. Please stay. I feel like you're part of our family now." The nurse took a chair on the other side of the bed.

Kit thought for a moment. "I'm going to tell you something funny about your dad, Zoey. When he was something like eleven, his aunt was visiting his mother in their house. She always parked her car in their driveway and left her keys in it. One day your dad decided to sit behind the wheel, just for fun. To act grown up. He turned the key, and the engine started. Then he backed out of the driveway and headed down a one-way street the wrong way. But he kept driving. He drove around the block, pulled the car back into the driveway, turned off the engine and just sat there, feeling as lucky as anything. That's when his aunt came out to drive home. She never knew a thing. And after that he always was a lousy driver."

Zoey seemed impassive. Diane said, "She may have heard every word you said. One day I hope you'll find out."

"Well. I guess I'll go home. I'll be back on Thursday."

The accounts manager caught up with Kit as she was about to leave the building. Having spotted her out of the corner of her eye, Kit sped up toward the exit to avoid the woman, but it was too late.

"You saved me a call. Can you just spare me ten minutes in my office? Otherwise, I can see you tomorrow afternoon if that's more convenient."

"I know what you're going to say." She'd heard it often before.

"Let's not do this where all these people are, all right, Ms. Capriol?"

She followed the woman into her office and sat across the desk from her. Kit had been in that room often before and somewhat irrationally had come to despise what the woman had done to make it her own. The photos on a bulletin board: nieces, nephews, grandchildren, friends, people drinking cocktails with little umbrellas, babies sucking on pacifiers. On the desk was a computer monitor and keyboard, a metal cup holding pens and pencils, and a bobblehead of some baseball player neither Kit nor Zoey would have recognized. A Mets banner had been tacked to the wall. As though people like Kit were supposed to feel comfortable, at home, in this sad little windowless office full of memorabilia and knickknacks that meant nothing to anyone else.

The woman glanced at her computer screen. "I'm not seeing last month's payment here, Ms. Capriol. Unless, of course," and she looked at Kit with her famous stare of death, "the check is already in the mail."

"I know I'm overdue," Kit said. "Things have been kind of tough lately. I was hoping you could give me just a little more time."

"Again."

"Yes. Please."

"This issue has been revisited a number of times over the years your daughter has been here."

"I know—"

"And you still keep falling behind."

"I just want to work this all out. And I'm not going to make a scene like last time."

That had been unpleasant, especially as Kit, as she was in the process of terrifying the woman, was also watching herself fly out of control, as though in a sequel to *The Crucible*. Afterward she felt a thousand times better and even stopped at the Bemelmans Bar at the Carlyle for a little well-earned pick-me-up of a nice dry martini, having called the woman a witless old cow before storming out.

"I know the situation is very tough for you," the woman said. "And I know that your daughter is getting the best care available here. But bills have to be paid, as you know, as pain-ful as it is for me to remind you of that." She folded her hands before her, as though to show Kit she was not about to resort to violence. "In the circumstances," she felt compelled to add. "I see from your account file that you're still unemployed. Unless something, some opportunity, is impending that we should know of...?"

"You know I'm an actor. I can go for a year or more without a job, lose insurance through the two actors unions I belong to because I haven't had any gigs for a while, and then I could suddenly land a Broadway play or a role in a TV series."

Her most promising recent opportunity had come when, a month earlier, she read for the lead role of the blind woman, Susy Hendrix, in a revival of *Wait Until Dark*, to be staged at the Belasco Theatre. She wasn't surprised to see at least thirty other women vying for the same role, four of them Broadway veterans.

For a week she'd worked on preparing the chosen scene and felt she could convincingly portray a blind person. After all, she did something like it when holding sessions, the light in her eyes visibly fading, as though she were gazing into some forbidden dimension.

Once the first five women were dismissed with the usual polite and disingenuous compliments, the director suddenly decided on someone who hadn't even read that day. Of course it was a woman with extensive theater and TV experience, a name that would easily draw in audiences.

Another day wasted, and Kit took the subway home, getting out at the same station where Zoey had collapsed. Sometimes Kit would stand where she'd been that evening, trying to understand what her daughter had witnessed, how much she'd understood of what was taking place. All Kit knew was that

a woman had lost her balance and fallen onto the tracks. Yet
Zoey had seen it all, while her mother seemed to have missed it
completely; avert your eyes, be distracted, and a person vanishes
forever.

The money was starting to dry up. After a busy two months
with consultations sometimes three times a week, it had been
quiet lately. When she'd first started, just after Zoey had fallen
into her coma, Kit was making upward of a few thousand a
month. Most of her clients were family of 9/11 victims; others
had lost loved ones in the war in Afghanistan. Not seeing a
body, not even a trace of DNA, might mean the person was still
alive. But, like Kit, they knew better. *Death is not final*, she'd say
to clients, and they would nod in agreement, because always,
always, they wanted to believe.

Even with only a simple outline of the deceased's life she
could flesh it out, fill in the spaces, use the power of suggestion.
She knew she'd gotten it right when she heard the wonder and
delight in the sitter's voice as she brought the dead back to life:
voice, facial expressions, sometimes even gestures.

She understood it all too well. Grief had been her compan-
ion for a long time. She and it ate together, jogged together,
even slept and dreamed together. While all she was doing was
helping people believe their loved ones weren't gone forever.

"So what do you suggest?" she asked the accounts manager.
"Should I just let my daughter die?"

"Of course not, Ms. Capriol. Now let me just review once more
your history with us here. You're currently a month in arrears.
One more month and—my hands are tied, you understand—this
may have to be passed on to a collection agency."

"And my daughter...?" She imagined having to wheel her comatose daughter onto Madison Avenue and somehow get her home from there.

"Just a moment," the woman said, scrolling up the screen. "Ah. This is something I must have missed. I see that your husband died on September 11th." Her tone considerably softened. "Let me take a moment to apologize to you for being so abrupt just now. I wasn't entirely aware of your circumstances." Her voice softened. "Was there perhaps a legacy involved? Or some reimbursement from the government?"

"Very little. And he had no life insurance. He'd only just started as a line cook at Windows on the World. Before then he worked at a restaurant in Westchester. A regular customer with connections recommended him to Windows, and he eventually was given a job there. He was excited, and the pay was much better, and we moved to the city. On that day he had the early morning shift." There was no point in saying more.

"I am so very, very sorry, Ms. Capriol."

"There was no body. There was just...nothing."

The woman put down her pen and sat back. "I know that whatever medical insurance you've been able to pick up doesn't pay all the costs, and that can be a genuine hardship. Can I get you to promise that at least a partial payment will be coming in very soon? If so, I think I can make this work for you." And now she smiled. "In fact, I *will* make it work."

"Thank you so much. I'll do my best," Kit said, getting up from her chair, carrying her empty promise all the way back home.

12

H ER PHONE CHIMED JUST AS SHE WAS WALKING into her apartment.

She put down her bag. "Kit Capriol."

She listened. *Here comes luck*, she thought. "Let me get a pen."

She walked into the little kitchen and grabbed a pad. She wrote: *Tony DeLuca.*

"I've got that..."

Below his name she added *Angela*. Then: *Wife. 9/11 Cantor Fitzgerald, Flr. 102, N. Tower.*

Not many floors below Peter, she thought.

"I'm actually on another call," and she checked the name she had written, "Mr. DeLuca. May I get right back to you—?"

She wrote down his number. One of the fluorescent tubes in the ceiling fixture began to stutter. She looked up at it, then when the bulb flickered one more time and died, she switched it off altogether.

She sat at the little table holding her computer and reference materials, and turned on the desk lamp. The *New York Times* book of 9/11 profiles, as always, fell open to the page with Peter's photo and the piece she helped write about him. At first she'd found it too painful even to look at. But over time she'd come to look forward to coming across it, as though she'd somehow, impossibly, become accustomed to his absence.

> Life of the party, they called him. Best friend to everyone who knew him. Class clown when he was growing up in the Bronx. "Then he settled down. Though not too much," his widow, the actress Kit Capriol says. He attended Vassar, helped pay his tuition by working in the school kitchen, and excelled in the drama program, where he met his future wife. Finding more satisfaction in cooking than in being onstage, he was accepted by the Culinary Institute of America in Hyde Park, where he learned the skills he brought first to a Westchester restaurant for six years and afterward to Windows on the World. It was his dream job, he said, to work where all of New York City would be at his feet. He leaves his wife, Kit.

And there was Peter, all grin and happy eyes. She remembered when the picture was taken, at a friend's wedding. She remembered because a few minutes later Peter led her outside and asked her to marry him. It seemed to her the corniest thing anyone could ever do—after all, she had specialized in experimental drama at college—but coming from Peter it was touching and heartfelt, and of course there was only one answer.

He was like electricity, the most alive person she had ever met.

Zoey was in a coma. Peter was particles of dust in a Staten

Island landfill called Fresh Kills. Kit was alone in the world. And death was just a number.

She touched the photo. "Oh, Peter. How I miss you."

And how I miss you, she could almost hear him say.

13

IT WAS FROM AN OLD SNAPSHOT, PREDIGITAL, ITS colors slightly faded, cracks in a corner of the photo like the beginnings of a spiderweb. Angela DeLuca is blond and pretty and maybe all of twenty-five, with a heart-shaped face and blue eyes. She seems to be sitting by a pool or on the beach, and wears a blue bathing suit.

Kit went quickly through the details, then read them again before making a few notes on her pad: *Admin asst. Nephs & nieces. Fav. Vacation—Aruba.*

Angela, she thought. *Angie. Angel of happiness.*

She read it through a second time. Nieces and nephews, but no information on nearer relations. Nowhere was there mention of a husband.

She Googled *Angela DeLuca obit. Cantor Fitz*—

And found one. An obit posted by a Westchester funeral home with a more formal photo from the *Times* piece, a headshot undoubtedly for her company's website taken a few years later, but an obit that was listed as private. She had no further way into this woman's life.

"Mr. DeLuca? This is Kit Capriol returning your call."

"So do you think you can help me? It's been almost twenty years and—"

"Please tell me a little about Angela. So I can seek a lifeline to her. Something the two of you treasured together. Again, I make no promises that I'll succeed. And there's no charge for our first meeting. After that donations will be appreciated. Fair enough?"

There was a slight pause. She was used to that; she knew it probably sounded to him like a backdoor deal. Which, of course, it was.

"Yes, okay."

"And may I ask how you found my name and number?"

"A woman who used to be a neighbor of mine," he said. "Brigid Malone? She was really impressed with what you did for her. So when can I come up to see you?"

Now it was Kit's moment to pause, as it came to her yet again: Brigid Malone wasn't what she seemed to be.

14

Tony DeLuca looked out her window onto 113th Street.

He watched a delivery man on a bike pull up to the building across from hers and run through the rain into the lighted vestibule to be buzzed in. He saw a light come on in a third-floor apartment: a silhouette looking down on the street, and then over at him. He saw the delivery guy push open the door. After a few moments the man in the window lifted a wineglass to his lips and, still looking across at Tony standing in Kit's window, sipped from it. The whole meaning eluded him.

Kit's reflection joined his as she stepped up alongside him.

"Sorry to keep you waiting." She'd had to review her notes on Angela one more time.

"Nosy neighbors you got there," he said, nodding to the person in the window.

She shrugged. "It's New York," she said, closing the curtains. "Let me take your coat."

"Sorry it's so wet."

"It's spring," she said. "It's supposed to rain."

DeLuca appeared to be in his late forties, a short, slightly stocky man with the face of someone from an old black-and-white movie, the weary guy from Brooklyn in a platoon in

Anzio, or a palooka who worked in a dead-end bar on Ninth
Avenue, loaded with small talk that went in circles, like the kind
of man you'd see in a gangster picture, a guy with something
to hide and things to do, drifting toward a bad end. His hands
were small and pale. No wedding ring. Casio watch. The basics.

It's easy to know a lot about someone just from how they
dress, what gestures they use, how they look at you. Having
become adept at it over the years, Kit found the skill also helped
her as an actor. She knew too many of her colleagues who
became inert when delivering lines, as though they depended
on the words alone to convey meaning. The ones that knew
how to use the air around them, how to get into someone else's
space, were the ones who usually got the roles. They weren't
just inhabiting a character; they were living it.

But this one was just a little too blank.

"Nice place you have here," Tony said, looking around the
living room, pausing to take in the piano, finally focusing on
the photo of Zoey at the piano. "Apartments like this are hard
to find, I guess."

"My husband and I got lucky. Being in the right place at
the right time."

"You said 'husband.'" He looked around for the hidden
threat.

All she needed was to convince him that Angela hadn't been
lost. She was right here beside him. See?

"My husband is no longer with us."

It could have meant anything: divorce, death, or life behind
bars, his mind traveling to dire places.

"So how do we begin this thing?" he said.

"Let's just chat for a minute. Tell me about Angela. How you came to meet, what you remember best about her."

She waited. He said, "We married ten months before, you know, the thing happened."

"I'm sorry. Losing her so young—"

"Yes—"

"Still so painful," she said.

"She was smart, you know? Had a good job at Cantor Fitzgerald. A step up from secretary, she used to say. But a step lower than the cleaning crew," and he laughed a little too loudly.

"She sounds like she was a lot of fun. How'd you meet?"

"At my buddy Joey Russo's cookout. I've known him since first grade. Angie and me, we just hit it off. Like we'd been friends forever. After everyone else left, we walked, I dunno, for like two hours? You know, just talking?"

"You and Angela always had a lot in common."

He offered her a smile full of wonder. "You knew that, huh?"

"You honeymooned in"—she closed her eyes, tilting her head as if to listen—"Aruba." She opened them. "Is that right?"

"Whoa, you are good."

She smiled. "I have my good days. And sometimes my not-so-good days. You see, I also lost my husband on that day."

"I didn't know… I'm sorry," he said, his smile shifting into reverse.

"But that's when I got my gift. My ability to converse with the departed."

She adjusted her posture, signaling a change in tone and subject. "Remind me of what you do for a living."

He said, "Guess you can't see that on your own," and his eyes sparkled.

"No. With those still with us it's a whole different story. I rely on others to tell me about themselves."

She glanced discreetly at her watch. She was tired from the hospital visit, tired of all the weeks and months and years she'd been going, tired of being always broke.

He shrugged. "Pipefitter."

But when she shook hands with him, his skin was as smooth and soft as her own.

She lit the candle and closed the curtains in the little consulting room. The flame sputtered and narrowed.

"Shall we begin?"

She looked at his face in the candlelight. He was examining her, she thought, trying to read her, and she would bring that to an end quickly enough. She held out her hands and nodded. "Put yours in mine."

She shut her eyes and began to speak quietly, reassuringly. "The people we love are all around us. They never leave our side. We have to remember and believe. That's what draws them to us. Faith and memory. Know that the curtain that separates us is only as fragile as the breaths we're taking right now."

It had taken her several attempts to get the lines just right before she started reciting them at her consultations. The trick was to touch on key words such as *love* and *believe*, *memory* and *faith*. Words that convinced most that she was on the side of the angels.

She opened her eyes slightly to see him staring at her. As if watching from afar.

"Close your eyes," she said quietly, "and let Angela fill your mind. Angie, you used to call her, didn't you?"

"I did," he whispered.

"The strength of your memory will help draw her to you. Show that you're willing to let her in. Believe and remember."

There was a tightening of the air, along with it a ringing in her ears, a high-pitched sound that was becoming painful, dissipating as quickly as it had come on. Something was imminent. Something over which she seemed to have no control.

She was no longer in the apartment, in the room with the candle flame. She was in a zone of uncertainty, some dark unspecified area that seemed to be outside the apartment, in another dimension.

The pressure in the room grew tighter, her breathing became more labored, and the more she tried to grab onto reality, the more she felt drawn away from it.

This was death, she thought, the fading of the light, the absence of sound, the withering of the soul. She had the fleeting sense—as though some kind of weight had lifted from her—that she had quietly passed out of this existence, that in those few seconds she'd become an unwanted guest in someone else's haunted life.

She lifted her hand to find something to hold onto, something real that would bring her back, and the more she stretched out her arm, the quicker she rose to her feet, the greater the pull downward, and now she was in a tunnel. Walking along it. A long strand of dim lights hung from its roof. There was the smell of decay, of bodies that had once been alive, human or animal. She could feel the ground starting to vibrate; in the back of her mind she could sense the noise.

Now it was coming. Getting closer. She had to run. She had to stay ahead of it. Now there was no way out. Death was an engine, inexorable, noisy, smoky, on the verge of catching up with her and running her down. She felt herself losing her balance, as though she were being pushed off an edge, when she opened her eyes and slammed her hands down on the table—

15

"STOP IT!"

Silence and stillness. The rain against the windowpanes. The client was looking straight at her. He obviously hadn't heard or seen a thing.

"You okay?" DeLuca said, looking alarmed.

Her clothes were damp from sweat. She felt as if she'd just survived a physical ordeal, a struggle, a steep climb.

"I'm all right. I'm sorry." She switched on the light and snuffed the candle with her fingers. "I guess I'm emotionally not in the right state. It's been a long day."

She walked him to the door. Her hands were shaking and she felt suddenly unwell.

"Well... Thanks anyway," he said, and she locked the door behind him.

The lights still off, she opened the curtains in the consulting room. It had begun to rain even harder, a wind-driven storm that had been threatening all day.

She walked out of the room and shut the door. The quiet was more benign now, the pressure had abated. Every sitting before this was a choreography of the uncanny, from the lighting of the candle to the end, when the spirit faded into nothing: a matter of atmosphere and mood, pace, tone and suggestion.

Most of all, it was a performance. But this time something had taken control of her, as though she were receiving a message, something significant that she couldn't interpret.

Without taking the time to brush her teeth or wash her face, she stripped off her clothes and got into bed, instantly falling into a heavy dreamless sleep.

The phone rang at just past seven the next morning. Something had happened to Zoey.

16

'M GOING TO BE HONEST WITH YOU, KIT," DR.
Roman said when she arrived at his office. "We had a bit of
a scare last night."

"What do you mean?"

"We had a code blue. Zoey flatlined for a very brief time—
seconds, really—before we brought her back."

"And you waited until seven to call me?"

"We wanted to make sure that she was once again stable.
That can take time. And she is. I promise you that. We performed all the tests, and nothing has changed."

"Are you saying that Zoey *died*?"

"More like a momentary interruption. A hiccup."

"What time was this?"

"I can tell you exactly." He checked his computer screen.
"8:57 p.m."

Just when Kit had been in the room with Tony DeLuca.
When she felt as if she, too, were dying.

"Look—let's go to the cafeteria and get coffee, okay? I think
we can both use a break."

Dr. Roman had been Zoey's physician ever since she'd been
admitted to the hospital three years earlier. Were things more
dire, he would have kept her in his office to say it.

It was busy in the cafeteria, with doctors, nurses, and visitors taking up several of the tables. Some typed on their laptops or scrolled through their tablets or phone screens. A woman a few tables over from theirs said into her phone, "We buried her last Thursday."

"You know what?" the doctor said. "I'm hungry. You want a bagel or a Danish or whatever?"

"I never had breakfast."

He stood. "Perfect. My treat."

While he went off to get coffee and bagels, Kit checked her phone. She had three messages, one from her pharmacy saying her prescription was ready, another from a past client who wanted to schedule another visit, and a voicemail, from Brigid Malone, asking to see her again.

The doctor put a plate in front of her. "Have you been taking care of yourself, Kit?"

"You mean eating? No, I try to make sure you doctors feed me on a regular basis. Otherwise, I subsist on a diet of vodka and pinot noir."

He looked momentarily concerned. "Seriously?"

"Only half," she said, tilting her hand this way and that.

It reminded her that she had another meeting that week with the widows and widowers group that met at the 92nd Street Y and which required several drinks afterward to shake her loose from all the desperation that filled the room for nearly ninety minutes.

Every grief, as she'd come to learn, was a private one; intimate, a thread connecting two people, one alive, the other dead. Yet the words were common to all of the attendees:

alone, *depressed, missing, hopeless.* It was what lay behind them that mattered. And that made her the medium she pretended to be, treating every client with respect for their individual narrative.

In her first attempts at forming a story of her own for the group, she spoke of how she and Peter met, and of the day she'd lost him, and what Zoey had said about how just by being herself she kept something of her father alive. When she was done, the moderator said, "But Kit. You still haven't told us how you're doing these days, a year after you lost Peter."

"Fine," she said, and looking around the room she saw one skeptical face after another.

"Okay," she said. "Not fine. No, not really, not at all. I can't stop missing him each day. I still can't believe he's dead. I still think I'll come home from an audition or my shrink one day and find him waiting. It's like..." And she seemed to drift off as the others waited. "It's like..."

She didn't know what it was like. Looking around, she saw more than a few heads nod in agreement.

"It's fine," she said, as if to end the conversation.

"What makes it fine?" the moderator said, and Kit was going to answer: *booze, men, sleep.* In that order.

Instead she said, "Nothing. It never gets better."

And yet she returned every month or so, just to see who had left and who had come to replace them. Because she learned that living alone—being alone—was almost as bad as losing Peter. The long goodbye, she thought, that never seems to end.

Sitting alone at a table by the cafeteria wall was a man wearing tinted eyeglasses that reflected the overhead light and blanked out his eyes. He seemed to be staring at Kit, as if he recognized her from somewhere. Dr. Roman turned to look.

"That's Albert Eakins. Prince of the underworld." He laughed. "Morgue attendant. Been here a long time."

When she looked again, the man in the glasses was no longer there. As if he'd never been. *In the midst of life I am in death*, she thought, plucking the line from her memory. No, that wasn't it. *In the midst of life* we *are in death*.

"I'm going to ask you what you might think is an insensitive question, for which I apologize in advance. Zoey's now, what, sixteen—?"

"She turned seventeen a few weeks ago."

"So let's say she'd never fallen into a coma and was maybe about to become a freshman in college. You're an actor. How would you be living your life now?" He sat forward and held up a finger. "Right now at this moment."

She said, "I might be based in LA. Maybe working on a series, probably studying with a coach, showing up for auditions. Sitting in traffic. Long walks on the beach, nothing for lunch, prosecco at three. Bed by nine."

"Really?"

"No, I'd probably be living in a studio apartment in the Valley and waiting by my phone. Just like every other unknown actor."

"Do you see yourself being a success?"

Kit laughed. "I'd be in the wrong business if I didn't."

"So it's a career built on dreams." He gathered their empty plates and cups and dropped them in the bin. "Let's go up and pay a visit to Zoey."

On the way up in the elevator to Zoey's floor, Kit received a text message. It was from Tony DeLuca. He wanted to see her again, and soon.

17

ZOEY'S ROOM WAS AS SHE'D LEFT IT THE NIGHT she'd fallen unconscious on the subway platform. There were her schoolbooks and notebooks and a shelf of CDs. A stack of music books. The posters and pictures she'd hung on the walls, classical pianists—Michelangeli, Gould, Yuja Wang—intermingled with a few rock stars. There was a photo of her piano teacher, taken during a concert in Mrs. Fischer's native Budapest when she was in her twenties.

The inexpensive makeup Zoey had bought at Duane Reade, by now stale and useless. And her sneakers on the floor, one lying on its side, just as they were every day since she'd last been in her room. A snapshot of a life interrupted.

Kit switched off the lamp when she heard the buzzer sound.

"I'm a little early," Tony DeLuca said.

"Mr. DeLuca. I have to be honest. After our last session, I'm not sure I can guarantee success tonight."

As an actor she'd never lost control of a part. But this time something had begun to weave its way into it.

He seemed surprised. "I thought it was a good start."

She looked at him as if through a thick haze.

"Please?" he said. "It would mean a lot to me if we could contact Angie."

As before, they took their seats at the table, the lighted candle between them.

"So let's take a deep breath, relax, and open our minds. I want you to think of Angie, focus on her, on your memories of her, your happiest times together. This may open the door for her."

"So no guarantees?"

She smiled. "I don't sell cars, Mr. DeLuca," she said. "But I always try my best to help others. So let's begin now."

Palms up, Kit's hands slid across the smooth silk cloth. He placed his hands in hers as she closed her eyes. *Angie*, she thought, bringing to mind the photo of the woman she'd already seen. She thought of the woman's heart-shaped face. She thought of the eyes, slightly unfocused, as though she usually wore glasses.

Otherwise she had nothing to build on. This woman was a complete cipher to her. And so far, Tony DeLuca had told her almost nothing about his wife.

Kit's breathing became shallow, regular, calm. "Angela... So far away... Tony's here, Angie... Waiting for you..." Now the breaths came deeper and more quickly. "She's... Wait...wait... She wants to tell you—"

He sat forward. "Tell me what?"

"She wants to say that she will always love you. That she's always with you. She has a message for you... It's...it's about that time in Aruba... There was a night there on your first trip—"

"Yes?"

"I don't... I can't make it out. Angela, please speak to me...

Oh, I see. Yes, I understand." Kit smiled. "You don't have to be shy with me, Ange," and she laughed. "Really? It's that personal?"

"What's she saying?" Tony asked.

Kit laughed again. "Well, that *is* personal. I'm not sure I'm the right one to tell him. Wait… What's that? You're going to save it up? Tell him yourself? But how, Angie?"

Tony sat forward, eager to hear.

"Wait, Angie. Don't change the subject, okay? Tony's right here, sitting across from me…"

"Can you see her?" he said.

"She can see you now. She says you look as good as the day you were married."

"Did she really say that?"

"She says that the morning…it happened…the last thing she remembers you doing is kissing her goodbye, wishing her a good day."

And now she heard something, a woman's whisper. *Help me… Please save me… Please…*

She glanced around the room. There was no one beyond the two of them. The air seemed to carry the scent of decay and the astringent memory of suffering.

"Who are you…?" she whispered. "How can I help you…?"

"You okay?" Tony said, and his voice sounded muffled, faraway, insignificant.

Then came the sound of weeping, the sad despair of a woman lost in a tragedy.

"Tell me who you are…"

Tony stared at her. "Are you trying to say something to me?" he said, and the voice that had come to her fell silent.

Kit opened her eyes. "I think we're done here, Mr. DeLuca. I'm suddenly not feeling well. I need to lie down and rest."

Whatever had just happened had left her bereft and as despondent as the woman she had heard.

"Did Angie say anything more to you?"

She stood and blew out the candle. "We're finished."

18

LIKE A SET FOR A MOVIE OR TV SHOW: COMPUTER monitors, keyboards, the dying remains of a honey-glazed doughnut, a half-empty Starbucks cup, a bent paper clip, a scattering of notes. A look of boredom on the two detectives sitting across from each other.

Dave Brier had already done his due diligence, searching the web for whatever he could find on Kit Capriol, ending up with nothing more than mentions in theater reviews and IMDb cast listings for her film and TV work:

- Woman in bar.
- Waitress #3.
- Hysterical witness to an accident.
- Detective Claire Bigelow (Episode 1).

"An actor." Dave sat back and smiled. "Cute, right? Goes hand in hand with her shtick. Plus"—he pulled out a stack of web pages he'd printed out—"she's earned herself a shitload of good word-of-mouth. Bloggers. People on Facebook and Twitter, people who were satisfied with what she'd provided for them. She doesn't even work under another name like most of the people we investigate."

"Could mean she's the genuine article," Tony said.

"Or it's the perfect cover."

Over the past three years, Kit had earned an online reputation in the grayer stretches of the internet, known to its devotees as the Dead Zone: Spiritualism Hub, The Afterlife Chronicles. People who'd lost family members on 9/11 and in the war in Afghanistan had posted how happy they were with her services. They used words like *kind, caring, friendly, genuine*.

Very few expressed doubts as to her authenticity as a medium, but nearly all felt that she'd helped them find that elusive closure they'd been seeking. From what Dave could see, she never engaged with people online, never responded to questions or suggestions, and was absent from the usual social media platforms: Facebook, Twitter, Instagram.

"Everyone leaves a trace," Tony said. "Like an animal— either there's a paw print or a pile of shit."

Dave laughed. "Not in her case. I mean, she gave you her card, so we already have her phone number and address. As far as we know, she's not peddling drugs or anything like that. She's a widow. Lives alone in a Morningside Heights co-op. Spotless record—"

"You mean no one has been onto her game before?"

Brier shook his head. "People like her. Think she's the real thing. Nobody's come to us with any kind of complaint. There's not a lot to throw at her, Tony."

"Apart from the shell game she's playing. C'mon, Dave, you know we're really trying to crack down on these people."

"She's obviously a pro at this, Tony. All we have to prove

she's a phony is the Irish lady's testimony, and you said she's backing off."

"Brigid bought the whole act, top to bottom. Says she wants Capriol to put her in touch with her dead daughter. The real one, not the one we made up. I mean, what can you do? Mother Machree will probably hobble back a hundred more times, part with her social security payments, and walk away thinking she's been talking to a dead kid. But there was something else. When I was there with Capriol—the second time—things got a little weird. Weirder than the first, anyway. She seemed to be hearing or seeing something, and it was like she wasn't there anymore. Like she stepped into another world."

Dave said, "And this is after how many drinks before you got there?"

"I was sober as a baby, Dave."

"Sounds like a nice bit of theater," David said. "Something out of a horror movie, maybe. Works every time, right? And it pulled you right in, didn't it?"

"I just don't know where it came from. And I didn't hear a damned thing. Except..."

Brier looked at him.

"Except she also started talking to someone else. And there was no one there but the two of us."

"She's good, isn't she."

"I've never seen anything like it," Tony said. "She has all the right moves. More than most."

"Any luck in her getting in contact with your make-believe wife?"

"She was obviously trying to wing it, but it didn't pan out."

"You never knew this Angela DeLuca, anyway. Unless Tony Cabrini has someone dead he wants to talk to."

Tony laughed. "Yeah. My brother-in-law. He died owing me fifty bucks. Never saw a penny of it."

"Always a good way of getting out of your debts."

Dave tossed the pencil he'd been jiggling onto the desk. "All right, tell you what. Let me take over the case."

"I really want to pursue this one," Tony said.

But Kit had already seen too much of him. "A fresh face is important here," Brier said. "I did a little more searching. Her husband worked as a cook at Windows on the World. Died on 9/11." He looked at his notebook. "Peter Capriol. Like everyone else described in the *Times*, he was the life of the party, a great husband, great friend, loved cooking."

Tony said, "Funny, isn't it. Everybody's perfect when they're dead. Until then they could have been the biggest assholes in the world. Guess when you die everyone all of a sudden remembers you were fun to be around, lots of laughs. Wonder what my wife's going to write about me."

"The irony is that she's taking advantage of people just like herself, who've lost husbands and wives to the attack or in the war. Easy money, I guess, for tugging at the heartstrings." He sat up and rearranged a few things on his desk. "It's my case now, Tony. I think I know just how to deal with her."

"You know I need the promotion, Dave. I need to be in a better pay grade. Our rent keeps going up, we've got a kid to support, so, c'mon, give me this one, at least. You're always the lead on these things. I need a boost for a change, you know?"

Dave looked at him. "Let me see what I can find out on my own."

Tony stood and took his jacket off the back of his chair. "Why do I see all of this going completely wrong?"

19

I T CAME TO HER: THAT TIME SHE'D FIRST SEEN HIM, the winter before, when one night after a few drinks she had walked out into an unexpected ice storm and slipped and fallen halfway across Broadway. A hand had reached down to pull her up just as the lights changed.

"Are you okay?" he said, and she realized how shaken it had left her, falling in the street like that. She could have been killed.

"I'm okay, yeah, thanks." And she finished crossing and walked back to her building.

"Sure of that?" he called, and she glanced back when she reached the sidewalk. But by then he was gone.

It was the same man now sitting at the bar with her.

The bar at the restaurant Kit regularly went to was a block from her building on Broadway, on most nights filled with Columbia and Barnard students as well as a few neighborhood locals like herself and the occasional professor or two. She went there to remind herself what real life could feel like: the sounds of voices, the laughter of others. Young people nearer to Zoey's age.

The place served mostly Mexican food, the decor being more Día de los Muertos than the stereotypical sombreros and vihuelas, its shelves covered with merry little figures of skeletons, all dressed up with nowhere to go.

Kit had started going there often after Zoey was hospitalized, especially if she didn't have a rehearsal or an audition the next day. After a few drinks she'd end up chatting to some man at the bar, and more often than not taking him home for an hour or two of what passed for pleasure. She sometimes tried in vain to recall the names, their faces a drunken blur. The forgettable ones, she thought, long forgotten.

There were three stools open at the end of the bar and she took her preferred one at the end. The bartender greeted her with his usual welcome familiarity. A friendly face, she always thought, a willing listener.

"All alone tonight, Kit?"

She laughed. "Nothing new there, right?"

He picked up a clean glass. "The usual?"

Double vodka rocks, same as always.

"Anything from the kitchen? Nachos or a couple of tacos?"

"Not tonight. But thanks, Louis."

Dinner at home had consisted of toast and scrambled eggs. Easy to make, easy to eat, a snap to forget. What had happened during the consultation with Tony DeLuca had left Kit with a knot behind her eyes and a headache that wouldn't go away. Though she had stuck to the usual script, this time she'd felt as if for a few moments she truly was communicating with the dead. This sense of being drawn to some other place was both foreboding and perversely comforting. You can't really talk to the dead, can you?

Maybe staging too many séances was to be blamed, like

spending too long over a Ouija board, as she used to do with her friend Amy when they were twelve. There was one spirit they communicated with, someone named Lil Penny—the entity spelled it out for them, a name that was hardly spooky.

They asked Lil Penny silly things, like should Amy buy the jeans she'd been dying to have, or whether Kit would ever have a boyfriend.

And now, as Louis set her drink in front of her, she remembered how she'd asked Lil Penny if she could tell Kit her future. And the planchette sped around the board, spelling out *U DED*.

She and Amy put the board away and never looked at it again. "It's just silly stuff," Amy said. "Don't even believe it."

"Rough day?" The voice came from the man who'd taken the stool two down from hers, and when she turned to look, she remembered him reaching down to help her off the street. Something about the warm way he smiled had remained with her since then.

Forties, anyway, somewhere around her age. Good hair. Sad, thoughtful brown eyes. Slow, deliberate movements. No wedding ring. *There is a weight on this man*, she thought, reading him entirely.

She betrayed her mood with a little smile. "My day...? It was just...full of surprises," she said.

"Good ones, I hope."

She sipped her drink. "Nah. Not really."

"Don't you hate that?"

Now she offered a much bigger smile. "You think?"

It was the kind of give-and-take, like jazz musicians trading fours, that she and Peter could get into at a moment's notice.

It was both a little too familiar and oddly discordant doing this with a total stranger.

"You come here a lot," he said as the bartender set down his Corona, a wedge of lime perched on top.

"So, what, you know me?" she asked.

The man laughed. "I've seen you here before."

"You once saved my life," she said, and he said he'd remembered it, too.

"Gotta be careful out there," he said.

"So you live in the area," she said.

"Not too far from here. But let's have a contest. I also had a pretty lousy day. How bad was yours, really? On a scale of, say, one to a billion?"

She thought she'd heard every come-on available to mankind, and now she added a new one: someone who could recognize another's disastrous day.

"Let's just say mine was a killer," and she began to laugh.

"Oh good, I like dark comedies," he said.

He introduced himself as David Brier.

"Kit Capriol," she said, shaking his hand.

"Really?"

"What?"

"'Kit'? That's a new one."

For once the sound of it embarrassed her, and she found herself uncharacteristically blushing. "Yeah, well, my parents were cat lovers."

"I don't know when you're being serious," he said.

"You don't know me at all."

He laughed. "So, Katherine, right?"

"With a C, not a K."

That took him a moment. "How could you tell?" he said, and she smiled and tapped the side of her head.

Divorced, she thought, assessing him. *Maybe a year ago, maybe less.* She could see that, too, in his eyes. Like a barely healed wound.

No. The wife is dead.

"Around the time I was thirteen and not very cool I decided I wanted to be called Kit." She shrugged. "It's easy to remember, easy to spell, and no one can figure out who or what you are. I guess eventually you have to graduate into who you'll really become. Probably took you a few years before you went from Davey to Dave to David, didn't it."

He laughed. "Bingo," he said and clicked his bottle against her glass.

It was as if the anxiety of the day was beginning to lift. This wasn't like her usual encounters. This man seemed somehow invested in the moment. And because she had been so long out of practice in these things, she felt herself backing away, as if wary of sharing too much about herself. You had to read people carefully; you had to know just how to engage with them. After all, she needed the money, and soon.

"So what's your story?" she asked.

He tilted his head. "Meaning...?"

"What's making you so unhappy?"

He took a breath. "It's been tough... My wife... Her name was Caroline—I always called her Caro—she died last year, and, well, you know how it is, you have good days and bad ones. This one wasn't especially stellar. I don't hold out much hope for tomorrow, either."

Kit put down her drink. "Jesus, I apologize for being an ass. It's hard. I know. And I'm so sorry."

"I am, too. Every day I'm alive."

"Everyone loses someone eventually," she said.

"Who have you lost?"

"Who said I lost someone?"

"Your eyes," he said, and she wondered what else she was revealing.

"My husband. Eighteen years ago this September. North Tower."

He looked away, as if fearful he might see too much. "That's brutal. I'm sorry."

"It doesn't get much easier," she said.

"He worked there?"

She nodded. "Windows on the World."

"I'd eaten there."

"So had I. The day before it happened." She smiled, and her smile turned into a fit of laughter. Her manager had flown in from LA for meetings and wanted not just to catch up with her client, but to see the view from the restaurant windows. "I hated the food and never told my husband."

"Really ordinary, right?"

"And here's the kicker… He cooked some of it."

"Chef?"

"Worked the line."

"Hope you forgave him."

Her smile went into neutral. "It was too late."

"So can I buy you another?" he said.

She'd gone through her first drink like lightning.

She wondered where this was all going; she wondered if she could finally break her pattern of one-night stands. "That'd be nice. Thanks."

He said, "When Caro went, it was so…sudden, you know? Just completely unexpected. You get married, you figure you'll both have a long life together, and then…"

She thought: *pancreatic cancer.*

"Well, she had pancreatic cancer. Came on kind of suddenly, as I guess it does. She died three weeks after she was diagnosed. Good days and bad ones in between." He waited until the bartender served them. "It happens so quickly, and then you think there was so much you wanted to say, so much you needed to do for her."

By now they were facing each other. She could see the story in his face, the way the light in his eyes changed when he told her. She tried to form a picture of the woman. Girl-next-door type, probably four or five inches shorter than her husband. A few years younger, too. She saw a dying woman in her hospital bed, gamely trying to seem optimistic.

"How old was Caroline?"

"She'd turned thirty-five a month earlier."

Light-brown hair. Slim. Kit could see her before her mirror, putting on her makeup. She could see her stepping into the bedroom to dress. Caro was coming to life for her, like invisible writing over a candle flame. And even if she were wrong, even if she'd pictured someone not remotely like this woman, she could at least sense a presence, something more than a name. A woman just off to the side, watching. Listening.

"I was on my way to the hospital," he said and waved the

air away. "I don't even know why I'm telling you this. I mean, you don't even know me."

"But I'm willing to listen."

"So it's the hospital up on 168th, New York-Presbyterian. She loved these cookies from Magnolia Bakery, the one on Columbus Avenue. She called them her guilty pleasure, and I'd bought her a box of them, and when I got to the hospital, she was gone. Her bed was empty, the light was off. That's what they said to me—'She's gone.' Like an idiot, I thought she'd gotten up and left without telling me and that I'd see her when I got home. I even pulled out my phone to call her, but I could tell from their faces I'd gotten it all wrong. Guess it happens a lot. Hospitals really suck sometimes."

Kit put a hand on his arm. "Something like this just stays with us, doesn't it."

"And then on my way home, I was in a kind of shock, and I realized I'd left the box there, and then all I could think about were those damned overpriced cookies."

It's the most human thing in the world, she thought. She pictured the nurses on duty passing around the box, polishing them off, licking their fingers, another day done.

"And what's life like for you these days…?" she asked.

He considered it. "Well. I'm still alone." He laughed. "Even though sometimes I'll walk into a room and think she's there. As if nothing had ever happened."

She smiled and gently rested her hand on his arm again. "I know what that's like."

"Happens to you?"

She sipped her drink. "Like maybe ten times a day?" and

they laughed. "I walk around my apartment and keep bumping into Peter. Sometimes I walk right through him. Sometimes I think he walks right through me. The thing is, David, Peter *is* there. And so is Caroline."

"What do you mean?"

"Just that. She may have left this world, but she hasn't left you. She's always with you."

"I wish I could believe that."

"I know that it's true. Just sensing that Peter hasn't completely left makes me feel so much less alone."

Of course it was a lie. When Peter died, all that remained were some photos and videos and memories. What she kept walking into and through was this gap in her life, this canyon of loss.

"I wonder..." She took her card from her bag and handed it to him.

20

I PROVIDE A SERVICE TO THOSE WHO WANT TO REACH those they've lost," she said.

"You're serious?"

"It continues to bring comfort to my clients."

"You mean like, what, Ouija boards—?"

"I know what you're thinking…crystal balls and ectoplasm. It's nothing like that. I do individual consultations. It's a way for people to step outside their lives, to open themselves up to possibilities they could never have imagined. You see, the voices of those we were closest to are still alive, still within us. As long as we remember them, they never completely fade away. But it's as if they're trapped in a scene in a movie, playing it over and over again, never getting it right, because they can't grasp it—"

"Their own death—"

"Exactly. They can't be free until they've reconciled themselves to what has left them as bereft as we are. You see, it's not only the living that mourn. The dead mourn *us*."

He shook his head in disbelief. "Well. That's a new one."

"Unless, of course, you've heard differently."

"I don't know if you're absolutely bonkers or you know something others don't."

"It's a gift" was all she said.

Pitching this was like rehearsing: the endless afternoons saying the same lines twenty different ways, and finally, over time, your character comes to life, and you can sell anybody pretty much anything you want.

"Once they realize they're truly no longer with us, they learn to accept it and go in peace," she went on. "Until then they're confused. Think of all the houses people say are haunted. It sounds like just another scary movie, something you stream late at night when you have a bag of popcorn and a bottle of wine handy and nothing else to do. But that's what remains of people after something sudden has happened."

"You mean they're trapped."

"Right. They can't get free of their own present. Which is now our past. But the living can liberate them just by reaching across to their world and assuring them that all is well. You hear those words in your head, the ones they said to you, the ones you remember. But memories always remain. And once memories are gone, then the person we've lost begins to fade. That's why we always work hard to remember everything about them. It's what keeps them near us. And, if we're lucky, in the end we feel joy that we're reunited with them."

He shook his head. "Funny you put it that way. I mean, I keep going over those last days in the hospital. I remember the smell of the room, the view out the window, the names of her nurses, the way Caro looked at me with that sad smile of hers. Like she knew what was coming."

"It's because you haven't let go of Caroline. In your mind you can see her, you can hear her. You just can't reach out and touch her. But she's there, David, she's still part of you. If it's any consolation, she's no longer suffering. Like I said, you walked in here—and see...? She's right beside you."

She shifted her eyes slightly off to his left, and she could see the effect it had. How his pupils dilated and his smile faded as he turned to look.

21

"D O YOU ACTUALLY *SEE* THE DEAD?" HE ASKED.

She could tell him anything she liked, but most of all she'd tell him what he wanted to hear. "Sometimes."

"Are they—?"

"Just as they looked when they died? No. Often they're much younger. Sometimes they're the same age. But they always look healthy and happy."

"Because they are?"

"Once they've made contact with us, they're liberated, David. They've been released from pain and suffering."

Again she rested her hand on his arm. Break the intimate space. Move into their lives. Make them see how *necessary* you are, how much they have to depend on you.

He took a long pull on his beer. "Have you been able to make contact with your husband?"

"That's the thing. I can do this for others, but not for myself. And meeting someone like me has its risks. You must be thinking this is a total rip-off, right?"

He laughed. "Well…"

"I get a lot of that. But only if an actual transaction is involved. I know about these sidewalk psychics who tell people they look unhappy or lonely or whatever—because sometimes people just look that way—and then promise to make their lives better. They'll help them find a new husband, or get a better job, or destroy their enemies, or make a lot of money, and after the person has handed over thousands of dollars and bought a bunch of useless trinkets and candles, nothing is different."

"Except they'd been fleeced. But isn't that what you're doing, kind of?"

"I guarantee nothing," she said. "I work under my own name, and the first session is always free. Does that sound like a scam? If you're satisfied and want to return, a donation is appreciated for each visit afterward. As my sessions can run as long as forty minutes to an hour, I suggest a minimum of a hundred dollars. Not asking, just suggesting."

"What do people usually offer?"

"I've had clients who've left me two or three hundred dollars per session. Once, a widower gave me five hundred dollars every time he had a consultation. And that was once a week for the first month. After that, because I was successfully able to channel his wife, he was giving me double."

"In cash."

Now she laughed. "Always."

The man was a well-known film producer whose young wife had committed suicide. He wanted to know if he had been the cause of it. It took eight sessions to convince him that her death had been accidental. It involved far too much research on Kit's part; the wife was an up-and-coming actor originally from Georgia, and as video was available online, Kit was able to mimic how she'd sounded. By including a few personal details—also easy enough to find on the internet—she'd lent the man's wife the reality denied her in death. But it had been a journey for Kit. For the wife to go from thirty Nembutals and a bottle of Jack Daniel's found next to her body to an accident was a long and difficult journey. But in the end he'd bought the narrative.

And then he kept coming back, begging to spend time with Karen, because, as far as he was concerned, Kit had taken her place in his life. After mastering the voice, she'd even worked up a suite of gestures for the dead woman. And though he might have just been enjoying the nostalgia of her performance, he seemed entranced by Kit's talent. To the point where he began to believe she had somehow become Karen, in his mind even beginning to resemble her. He became obsessed with Kit, buying her clothes and jewelry that his wife would have liked, giving her money, eventually asking her to marry him, as if he could live a part of his life all over again, this time with a better outcome. It was like a movie, Kit thought back then: you take a tragedy and give it the happy ending that might have been, before it all reverts back to tragedy.

Though the money was good enough for her to cover medical copays and hospital fees, after several more sessions it became impossible for her to go on. The producer wanted her to accompany him to the Golden Globes in LA, where one of his movies was up for a number of awards. "Everyone will be staring, because I'm with my Karen again," he said. "And you'll get to meet some big stars. I know them all."

That was the danger: he'd come too close to her reality. During their next session she said that Karen was no longer reaching out to her.

"She's gone, and I'm sorry."

"Try. Please try again. I'm so damn lonely."

"I want to help you. But she's just...gone. She's no longer within me."

The next thing she'd heard was that he'd flown to Hollywood for the ceremony at the Beverly Hilton, and after his movie had lost out to another picture, he raped a young up-and-coming actress in his hotel suite. Which was when twenty-six other women came forward to tell the exact same story from over the years. One of them said, "He kept talking about his dead wife. As if I was supposed to feel sorry for the fat slob."

"Guess you're pretty good at this," Dave said.

She smiled. "Try me sometime."

He looked again at her card, turned it over, then back to the front, and slipped it in his pocket.

"You're either the best rip-off artist I've ever seen, or the real thing," he said.

She smiled. "Which do you think it is?"

He slid off his stool. "Maybe one day I'll find out for myself. I enjoyed meeting you."

He shook her hand and before leaving held it for a moment too long, as though secretly passing something to her.

"Fast worker," the bartender said as he came over to clear the glasses and bottles.

She looked at the door. "Any idea who he is?"

"Cop."

"What?"

"He's a detective. One of the waiters recognized him from another restaurant he used to work at."

"You're serious?"

He nodded. "Bartenders only lie to drunks, Kit."

And now she wondered: Who, exactly, was playing whom?

22

DAVID BRIER

Three of them: in Manhattan, in Brooklyn, in Sag Harbor.

There were two on Facebook: an African-American in Los Angeles; a Vietnam vet in Morgantown, West Virginia. Nothing connecting the name to the police.

CAROLINE BRIER

A junior studying nursing at North Dakota State University.

CAROLINE BRIER OBIT

Caroline Brier was born in Sacramento, California in 1916 and died in Oakland, California in 1964.

But his Caroline Brier, it seemed, still hadn't died. Or at least there was no public record of it. Which probably meant that she had kept her maiden name.

All Kit knew was how his wife had died, and that she liked certain cookies sold at Magnolia Bakery. It was an anecdote she could hang on to. But for a séance she hadn't a wisp of ectoplasm to work with.

23

KIT SENSED IT BEFORE SHE'D EVEN SHUT THE
apartment door behind her. The way the air felt, heavy
with the presence of another.

She said, "Is someone here?"

She walked into the kitchen, then the bedroom and the
bathroom. No one.

Two apartments in the building had been broken into over
the past few years, on the second and fifth floors, and the other
tenants worried that their place might be next. Now Kit wondered if hers had become the third.

The door to Zoey's bedroom was closed, as it always was.
She opened the door and peered cautiously into the twilight of
the room. Nothing seemed different, except the air was cooler
here, nearly chilly.

But she knew someone was in the room.

"You can speak to me," she said, and her skin prickled as
she said it. She imagined someone had gotten into the place
and she had stumbled into the scene before they were able to
leave.

"I have nothing in the apartment that's of any value," she
said loudly. "If you want something, please just take it and go.
There's no need to be afraid. I'll go into another room so I

won't see you. Just let yourself out, and there'll be no trouble, I promise. I won't call the police."

She listened, and heard nothing. *My imagination*, she thought, and she felt a wave of relief. She looked around the room she had come to know so intimately over the years. It was where Zoey had been a baby, a toddler, then an adolescent. It held her scent and her memories.

Kit switched on the overhead light. The closet that she always kept closed was now open, full of Zoey's too small and out-of-date clothes for her seventeen-year-old daughter. She ran the back of her hand along them, the shirts, the jeans, the more formal things she had worn when she performed at recitals. She took one of the blouses and held it to her face before shutting the closet door.

But something was different. The sneaker that had lain on its side all these years was now sitting flat on the floor, neatly lined up alongside its partner.

I am going mad, she thought.

The drawer of the nightstand had been left open a few inches, even though she always made sure all the drawers in the house were shut, a quirk she'd had ever since Zoey as a toddler had run into an open one and badly cut her forehead.

She slid the drawer out. Everything seemed the same as when Zoey had last used it; all was where it should be: a crumpled tissue, earbuds, half a pack of Orbit chewing gum. The tickets to the András Schiff recital, never redeemed. And then she stopped, took a breath, and picked up the snapshot that hadn't been there before.

It was of Peter and Kit at the sculpture park at Storm King, up on the Hudson. Kit hadn't seen the photo in twenty years. It had been stored in the back of her closet in a cardboard box filled with other photographs and memorabilia.

To the right of them in the photo was a picnic table, on it a bottle of prosecco, a few plastic wineglasses, one of them tipped over. An open cooler. The other half of a sandwich, yet to be eaten. The two of them standing in front of a tree with their arms around each other: blue skies and bright sunshine and, beyond the monumental creations that dotted the landscape in the bright midday sun, a glimpse of the Hudson River, suggested by a subtle shift of light. She brought the photo closer and looked at Peter's face. His right eye seemed blurred, and when she tried to scrape at it with her finger, she realized it was in the photo itself, a flaw in the image.

She couldn't remember having their photo taken that day. She wondered where Zoey had found it.

She looked at Peter's smiling face, his blurred right eye. At herself, as she stood close to Peter. And then at the ground behind him.

A crow was standing there, its beak wide open as it looked directly into the lens. She stared at it for a long moment before putting the photo back in the drawer.

The world was full of signs and symbols, the universe a murder of portents.

24

WIDOW. MOTHER. ACTOR. ALONE.

It was how Kit described herself the first time she met with Jackie Barnes, a therapist who was known for her work with widows and widowers, two months after Peter's disappearance. *Death* was not how Kit defined it, because no one had actually seen him dead on the ground, in the morgue, a body in a box. He seemed to exist in some obscure middle region, suspended in a hazy no-man's-land between the living and the dead.

She'd been reluctant to see Jackie, or any other shrink. Her mother had been in analysis for years, and all it earned her was an elegantly staged suicide, like a scene from a movie whose name no one could recall but would always remember it was in Technicolor, with music by Max Steiner. But Kit's friends and fellow cast members from *The Crucible* had convinced her to seek help to deal with her despair.

There'd been no funeral for Peter, no memorial service, no condolence cards, no casseroles delivered to her door. People didn't know what to say to her, and told her so in just those words, *I don't know what to say, Kit.* But then, again, neither did she. That's when she knew she needed to seek help.

Jackie explained during their initial session that it was the first question she asked of all her new clients: *Define yourself in four or five words*.

"That doesn't sound like it has much of a future, Kit," she said when she'd heard Kit's response.

At first Kit saw her on a weekly basis. Over the years the spaces between visits had begun to stretch. Monthly; then every six weeks; sometimes for long periods not at all. The issue was usually money. Now it was always money. It had been that way, money in, money out, for three years, as she waited for auditions and job offers. Now *money in* was only a rare occurrence. It was a wishbone existence, she knew, reliant on childish expectations. Yet hoping things might change for the better kept her alive.

But now something had happened. Now, she thought, she was beginning to go mad, just like the previous occupant of her apartment apparently had. And just like her mother. She called Jackie the next morning and briefly explained what the issue was.

The last time Kit had seen her was a few months after Zoey had been hospitalized. Now when Jackie opened the door, three years since her last appointment, Kit barely recognized her. Her long brown hair had gone completely gray and had been cut short. She told Kit that since their last meeting she'd undergone treatment for breast cancer that had metastasized, was given a year to live, and thanks to chemo and radiation treatments was now in remission. She looked thin and a little wasted, like a refugee from the land of the dead, and yet her smile was as it always had been, wide and welcoming, a little big for her face.

She took Kit in her spindly arms and held her for a moment.

"Let me look at you... Well, I'm jealous. You don't look a day older than when I last saw you. I look like I've been in the trenches."

Jackie led her into the living room. That had changed, as well, with new bookshelves in place and several photos of grandchildren, new additions since Kit had last seen her.

"How have things been for you since we last met?" her therapist asked.

Kit took a moment to gather her thoughts. "Interesting. Like I told you when I called."

"All you said was that you thought you were going crazy. Your words, not mine."

"Well, yeah, actually I am kind of concerned about the state of my mind. My sanity, I mean."

"Tell me first about the state of your life. It's been a while, so I need to catch up. How is Zoey?"

"No change."

Jackie nodded. "Are you still single?"

"Very," Kit said, her mind returning to that evening with David Brier. For some reason she'd found it hard to shake him from her mind. There was something about him that seemed to her genuine: his gentle, amusing manner, how he grieved for his late wife.

How he was a cop. And the thought of it passed like a cloud over her memory.

"Okay, so have you allowed yourself a social life at all? I mean, losing Peter was a trauma for you. It's tough to recover from something like that. In your case it's been, what, nearly twenty years?"

She said it with a tone almost of disbelief. Was all that time really too long? Maybe it wasn't long enough. And maybe Kit was holding on to it for all the wrong reasons. In earlier sessions Jackie spoke of guilt, and Kit had to admit that, yes, she did feel guilty about Peter's death.

"But you couldn't have prevented it, Kit. No one knew what was going to happen that morning. Your guilt comes from some other place. Some deeper place within yourself, maybe."

And when the guilt disappears, does the memory of him also fade?

Kit told her of the man she'd had a relationship with a few years earlier. "He struck me as being perfect for me. He was older—"

"By how much?"

"Eleven years. He was a teacher at an all-girls private school on the Upper East Side." She mentioned the name of it.

Jackie said, "I graduated from there. Too long ago for it to make any difference today. Tell me how you met him."

"At a bar."

Jackie smiled. "You always pick up men in bars these days?"

Again Kit thought of David. It hadn't been a pickup, not in the usual sense, and though a part of her was wary of him, another part was intrigued, perhaps drawn to the man just because of the risk of the thing. Cop. Widower. There seemed to be a space between the two identities that eluded her. From now on she'd be careful if she ever ran into him again.

Give nothing away. Take nothing in return.

Kit laughed. "It had become a habit with me, I guess. Not that much anymore."

"Tell me about this teacher."

"Ian—? He was brilliant," Kit said, spreading her fingers in the air. "Well read, thoughtful, cultured. Loved going to the theater, loved the movies. Fluent in a few foreign languages. Fun to be with. At first."

"And sexually?"

"It was…fine," Kit said after a pause. "There were things he liked to do that were kind of new to me."

"And you did them—?"

"It took a little getting used to. And some patience on his part. But," and she blushed a little, "you know how it is."

"You wanted to please him," Jackie said, and Kit nodded. "Were you afraid of him?" and now Kit looked at her.

"How did you know?"

Jackie let the moment linger.

"It took time," Kit said. "He taught me well. Preparing me for a life with him. But something kept nagging at me, some…sense, I guess, that I wasn't seeing Ian as clearly as I should have. That I'd bought the package without completely unwrapping it."

Jackie smiled and wrote something in the Moleskine notebook she always had with her at these sessions. "Nicely put." She looked up at Kit. "And then what happened?"

It unfolded gradually, as though he needed to draw her in closer, make her feel as if she were somehow indebted to him. Make her feel as if without him she'd be lost. He learned her vulnerabilities, understood how to prey upon them.

Little things at first. Verbal slights. Insults across a restaurant table when they went out with friends, mostly his. He never physically hurt her; everything was on an intellectual level, the pain of knowing less. Or being convinced she did.

"And you did what...?" Jackie asked.

"I left him," Kit said. "It just came to me in a flash. I ended it cleanly after three months."

"And...?"

"I missed him at first. It was painful... But I'd keep thinking back to how he'd treated me, as if I were an accessory. Like a necktie or an expensive wristwatch, something for others to admire. He introduced me to his friends as 'The Actress,' and they'd expect me to perform for them like an organ-grinder's monkey."

"And did you?"

"C'mon, Jackie. You know me better. I only act for money."

For a while afterward, Kit had kept a wary eye out for him whenever she left her building, and at a performance she'd always scan the audience at the curtain call, wondering which row he was in.

He began standing outside across from her building at night, staring up at her window. Leaving voice messages every few days. Sending pathetic emails threatening suicide. At first she answered them, telling him that she had moved on in her life, and wishing him the best for his own future. Then came the begging texts, *Please come back to me,* and the apologies with all the usual excuses, *I don't know what came over me, I'm under so much stress, can we please give it another try?*

A few years later, long after the texts and emails had stopped, she looked him up. He was still on the staff at the school. Other than that, there was nothing in social media, not even a hint of how he was living. She imagined him with another woman, forcing her to go through the same stages she had endured, this obstacle course of a relationship, wasting a year on a man not worth anything more than a well-stocked library, the ability to order dinner in French, and a taste for expensive burgundy.

Kit smiled. "That's where the story ends. He's out there somewhere, here in the city."

"Are you still afraid of him?"

"I'm the one that got away. And he always hated to lose. So, yeah, I keep an eye out when I think of it."

"But that's not why you're here, is it. Because that was some time ago."

She briefly told Jackie about her work as a medium. "It's all acting," she said.

"Well... This raises some moral and ethical issues, of course."

"I'm aware of that. But more often than not my clients seem comforted by these sessions. In a way, I provide a service for them."

Jackie laughed. "Hey, that's my job, you know."

"It's the easiest way for me to cover some of my expenses for Zoey's hospital care and the mortgage payments. It's been really hard. I wake up every day and hope that someone calls, that a client will want to return. The problem is that the other night I was holding a séance for this guy who'd lost his wife on 9/11. And—I know it's going to sound crazy—but I heard something. A woman's voice."

Jackie cocked an eyebrow. "The man's wife?"

Kit thought for a moment. "Maybe. I don't know. But it was the first time I lost control of the thing. I always provide the voices, I'm always the one to summon the spirits."

"Where did the voice come from?"

"Just…in the air, maybe?"

"Or within yourself…?"

Then that would truly be madness.

25

D ID THIS MAN HEAR IT, AS WELL?" JACKIE ASKED.
Kit shook her head. "Tony didn't react at all when I was hearing it."

Jackie made a note of the name. "And you're afraid of, what, that you're starting to suffer from delusions?"

"And then I thought, well, maybe this woman is trying to reach someone else. As if the phone lines had somehow crossed."

"Maybe you really are psychic," Jackie said.

Kit laughed. "Would that make it any better? Like I said, it's all an act."

"Sometimes an act repeated over and over again can achieve its own reality. You may have"—she sought the word—"engendered some other entity. Whether within your own mind or, I suppose, from outside it." She smiled. "But as you know, we psychologists tend not to rely on the spirit world for our conclusions."

"You're thinking I'm going insane, aren't you?"

Jackie moved from her chair to sit on the other side of the sofa, closing the space between them. She said, "So now you're diagnosing yourself? Or just predicting the future?"

Kit laughed. "I know, I know. But I'm just trying to make sense of things."

"And this has never happened before?"

Kit shook her head. "Like I said, all the voices are my own."

"Because you're an actor."

"Right. I can do most of them, down to the accents. Children, old people... I research the life of the deceased as much as I can from public records."

Jackie smiled. "Well, that's kind of creepy."

"No different from working up a character I'm playing."

Jackie made a tent of her fingers and just looked at her.

"I am crazy, aren't I," Kit said.

"We don't use that term, Kit."

"But you're thinking it."

Jackie smiled. "So now you're also a mind reader?"

Kit laughed. "Only on a part-time basis. But that wasn't the only strange thing. In our first session—"

"With this whoever, this Tony—?"

"I had this sensation that I was about to fall from a height. Like a cliff. I could feel myself being pulled down, and I couldn't get out of it. It was a physical sensation, something I'd never experienced before."

"A vision, you're saying?"

"No—a feeling. But it was real, it was intense and terrifying. I felt completely helpless. I thought I was going to fall to my death."

Jackie made a note in her pad. "Have you been on any new medications recently?"

"Absolutely not."

"And the drinking...?"

"Well, yeah. I mean I don't binge or anything like that. But a few drinks at the end of the day seems to do the trick."

"Sometimes more than a few?"

"Depends on how bad the day was. I try to visit Zoey three days a week. That takes a lot out of me. I mean, it's emotional, it's difficult, seeing my daughter like that. She and I have lost three years of our life together. Important years for a young woman, when she'd start dating, when she'd be thinking about college. Then I have my clients, and sometimes I have an audition. I've already got one lined up for later today."

"Good luck with that," Jackie said brightly. "Have you had any other hallucinations or—"

"This wasn't a hallucination. This was *real*. I was going to fall. Like in a dream when you miss a step and your leg jumps and you wake up. Except I wasn't asleep. There was nothing to wake from. It was real. It was happening."

Jackie considered it. "Are you afraid of heights?"

"I'm afraid of falling. That's different."

"Of being out of control, is that what you're really saying?"

"Falling," Kit said.

Kit hated it when Jackie quickly got to the heart of things.

"Are you afraid of dying?" Jackie said.

Kit had never been asked that. But she didn't have to think about it. "Isn't everyone?"

"Maybe it takes getting close to death to cure us of that fear," Jackie said. "What I'm really concerned about is if you're experiencing what you'd told me happened to you after Peter's death."

"That was my own choice, Jackie. I was depressed, I felt things going out of control, and the clinic helped me."

"Electroconvulsive therapy, you said."

Kit paused. "Yes."

"How many sessions?"

Kit thought for a moment. "I don't remember."

"And you told me your mother committed suicide."

"That had nothing to do with me," Kit said. "I wasn't even living at home then." She looked away. "She had...issues. She'd been diagnosed with schizophrenia."

She remembered her mother hearing voices in an empty room, answering questions that no one had asked. She looked back at her therapist. "Don't even go there with me, Jackie."

Their time just about up, Jackie excused herself and left the room. Kit heard the bathroom door close. She took the moment to stand at the window. It was one of those perfect spring days, so warm and clear beneath a cloudless sky that it seemed as if time had come to a stop, that the world outside the window was a kind of portal that would lead her to some profound epiphany. It seemed to be waiting there, a moment of clarity that would pull everything together for her.

Kit heard the toilet flush before Jackie returned to the room, joining her by the window.

"I'm not capable of judging exactly what's happening to you right now. This is pretty much beyond my duties as a therapist. I know you've been through a lot. Your husband. Your daughter. Your precarious financial state. And things like that can throw your emotional balance off."

They walked together to the door.

"I can't diagnose it," Jackie said. "I can only help you try to make sense of it. There may truthfully be some supernatural reason for what you've experienced. Or maybe not. I'm not an expert in the occult. My suggestion is to take notes when these things occur. And if you can swing it, come see me in another few weeks. Sooner, if you feel things are going out of control. Okay? I'll always be able to slot you in."

Kit gave her a hug. "You'll send me a bill?"

"I'll do no such thing," Jackie said. "Not until our next session."

26

"SORRY I'M LATE. SUBWAY."

The usual lame excuse of the out-of-work New York actor. She was so late that the last small group of actors was heading out the door.

One of the producers, Blake something, must have just flown in from Southern California. Tanned, fit, a man for whom bread never passed his lips.

He said, "And you are...?"

She handed him her résumé. "Kit Capriol."

He glanced at the page. "Right, right, your manager emailed it to us sometime last week."

"Again, apologies for being late. I'll get out of your way."

"Hang on a sec. We still haven't found the right fit."

She looked at him. "Really."

He glanced at a woman sitting on a folding chair off to the side, her legs stretched out in front of her as she casually assessed Kit. "Rita Daly. Our casting director."

Rita smiled at Kit. "I'm just going to watch for now, okay?"

"Let me be frank," Blake said. "We originally had a more or less firm commitment from an actor who'd starred in a long-running Showtime series." He mentioned her name. Kit knew her work and had met her once a few years earlier.

"But she was offered a Broadway play and decided to step away from our project. So we're still looking for the right actor. The thing that really jumps out for me on your résumé is your gutsiness. You take on roles in more radical productions—and I don't mean politically radical. Just...different. You don't seem to like playing it safe. And I can see you got singled out in a number of reviews."

"For better or worse," she said.

For some reason she felt relaxed, a new sensation when it came to auditions. Especially as he laughed at what she'd said.

"So as we emailed you a few days ago, this is a script called *Chasing Daylight*. Set in 2003, just after the Baghdad museum was looted. Right now we're looking at a limited cable series, mainly shot here in New York, with additional filming in Morocco. Maybe ten episodes, with the potential for a second season and a new story line. So far we have a pilot, which is what you'll be reading from. The main character is an award-winning photojournalist who's addicted to war. He'll go anywhere where there's conflict. He returns from the war—this is set some years ago, of course—not realizing that he'd accidentally taken a series of photos of a crime in progress implicating a high-ranking U.S. military officer. He comes home and, well, the shit hits the fan. Lots of people want to get hold of those photos, and his family's at risk. Just as he is. Long story moderately short."

"So what role am I reading for—the wife, the girlfriend...?"

"Neither. We want to make the lead character a woman. There are lots of famous women war photographers, and the dynamic could be very interesting. She's largely in a man's world and has to compete just that much more fiercely. She's restless, always wants to be in on the action."

Rita said, "We know how risky it is hiring someone without a recognizable name for this kind of lead role. Especially as a big name attracts financing and other commitments. But so far no one has worked out for us. So we're looking for a voice. Someone who doesn't just look the part but can inhabit the character from the inside out."

If she landed this role, then her work as a medium was over. Bills could be paid, her mind put to rest. But she also knew that in the end she would never land the part. She wondered why they would even bother to go ahead with the audition.

"I'll be honest with you," Kit said. "I need this job. I need the money. I'm a widow with a daughter who's been in a coma for three years, and I'm really just kind of broke."

Blake had obviously heard hardship stories before, and his expression registered both disappointment and a slight distaste.

"I'm sorry," she said. "I shouldn't have said that."

"It's okay." He looked at her résumé. "Ms. Capriol."

"Kit's good."

"Kit. Listen, I know—people have lives, people have worries, people get sick. But right now let's just see how you handle a few scenes."

Rita said, "We're going to shoot video of this"—she stood to switch on a small camcorder mounted on a tripod—"so we're able to share it with the others back in California. I know you've done this before. Can you put your hair up, please? Just casually, okay? I have a clip if you—"

"No, I've got one." Kit took a clip from her bag and carelessly put her hair up, something she often did, anyway.

"Good," the woman said.

Blake handed Kit a few pages of a script. "The opening scene takes place while the photographer—called Nick here, but to make things easier we'll call her Kit—is embedded with a platoon in Iraq while they return fire with an active sniper. Kit bobs and weaves her way around the action, snapping photos. She gets right into the heart of it, dodging bullets, keeping out of the soldiers' way. She has no dialogue in the scene. Just action. Because you'll be wearing a helmet, the audience assumes you're a guy. At the end of the scene, when the skirmish is over and the sniper's killed, you take off the helmet, shake out your hair, and people will see you're a woman. You'll be reading the scene after it. Kit's arrived back at JFK after months oversees, away from her husband and thirteen-year-old daughter. Go to page three, please."

Airport terminal. Moving walkway. War-weary photographer with camera bag slung from her shoulder, beaten-up duffel bag by her side. Still wearing the dust of battle on her clothes, her Kevlar vest, in her hair.

Got it.

"Let's see how you handle the tone here. Just wing it. She'll be addressing the camera as she makes her way through the terminal. She's almost asleep on her feet. She can barely keep her eyes open. She looks as if she'd just stepped away from a pitched battle and could use a solid twenty-four hours of sleep. But she's already missing the excitement of her work."

Kit quickly reviewed the opening lines and cleared her

throat. She turned her back on them, took a few deep breaths, then turned back. Her shoulders slouched. She settled on a Bronx accent.

"Some people like the scent of roses. Some get off on the aroma of coffee. Me...?" And she shrugged and offered a wry smile. *"I love the smell of jet fuel. Even when I'm asleep on my feet and all I want to do is crawl in a hole and die. It's like the smell of glue to a kid building model planes. Or"*—and she threw in a little laugh—*"the bittersweet bloom of a single malt to a Budweiser drunk..."*

"Okay, that continues now that you're in your car, driving home to see your family. And..."

"It's the smell of risk, and, man oh man, do I get high on that. Kinshasa. Kabul. Baghdad. Pick a city. Any city. Put me in it...call it home."

"And the last word lands when her car pulls up to her house. I enjoyed that, Kit. You added some nice edge to that. I like the tone you chose."

"Streetwise," Rita said. "Ballsy. A touch of Pacino in the voice. Nice one, Kit." She seemed genuinely pleased.

Kit was asked to run through another scene, some five pages long, with Blake taking the part of her character's husband: the give-and-take of a marriage that was all too familiar to her.

Blake set aside the pages. "That was very, very nice. Thank you very much."

Rita said, "I just want to take a few still shots, okay, Kit?"

She took some headshots with her iPhone. Rita was a little shorter than Kit, no more than five feet, slim and fit in her skinny black jeans, black T-shirt, and a splash of color in the scarf knotted around her neck. She wore her sunglasses on top of her spiky blond hair. Kit knew the look well: all California, all the time.

Rita said, "So we'll be in touch. If interest continues, we'll be calling you in for a second reading." She walked Kit to the door of the rehearsal room. Quietly she said, "Don't feel bad you lost it a little with that thing about your daughter being in a coma. It happens, believe me."

"It's true."

"I could see it in your eyes."

Kit couldn't resist. "You've lost someone recently, haven't you?"

The woman's expression dropped. "How did you know that? My mother died a few weeks ago."

"Actor's intuition, I guess. I'm so sorry I mentioned it. And my condolences."

She was tempted to hand the woman her card but decided to let it go. Not every poignant moment called for a séance.

27

K IT MUST HAVE FALLEN ASLEEP ON THE SOFA AFTER she'd returned, because when the buzzer rang, it took her a moment to realize where she was in the dark, unlit room. She rubbed her face as she somehow found her way to the intercom by the door.

"What time is it?" she said.

A familiar Irish voice said, "It's just gone eight. It's Brigid Malone, Ms. Capriol. I hate to be disturbing you like this, but—"

Shit, Kit thought. "I'm sorry, Mrs. Malone, but you really need to make an appointment in advance and—"

"It's important, missy. It's important I speak with you. Something's been weighing on me."

Fuck, Kit mouthed, and calmly said, "All right."

She buzzed her into the building and waited for the woman to knock. She looked through the peephole to see Brigid in the dim hall light, wearing the same wool coat and headscarf as before, carrying the same worn leather handbag. How diminished she seemed.

She opened the door. "Mrs. Malone." She hoped the woman wouldn't pick up on her tone of disapproval.

"I'm so glad you're here," the woman said, touching Kit's hand with her papery fingers.

"Like I said, you really should have called and made an appointment."

"I know. And I apologize. But it couldn't wait."

"All right. If you insist."

The woman quietly said, "Here it is, then. There's a policeman out there. He's been watching you."

Kit looked at her with alarm. "Now? This minute?" She was about to go to the window to see for herself. "Where?"

Had David Brier been stalking her the entire time? How long had it been going on? And again she remembered when he'd reached down to help her off the street nearly a year earlier and wondered if that was where it had begun.

"Just...there. Away from here. I knew him from when I was his neighbor, you see. That's why I came that first time you called me. The whole thing was arranged to happen that way."

"So you didn't have a daughter named Lucy?"

"No. But in truth I did lose my little girl so long ago. And I was wondering if, maybe, if I paid you enough, I could ask you to bring us together. Even for a little moment." She pulled a slim bank envelope from her bag filled with several crisp ten-dollar bills.

Kit sighed. "I'm not sure this is the right time, Mrs. Malone. You see—" Out of pity she was about to tell the woman the truth. There was no need in drawing Brigid Malone into any sort of false hope.

"If you could just try," the woman said, stepping into the apartment and letting the door shut behind her. "Just this once. Please, missy. It would mean the world to me."

"All right. Just this one time, though. And I won't take your money now, is that understood?"

She led Mrs. Malone into the consultation room. "First tell me about the detective," she said.

"He's the one who calls himself DeLuca... That's not his real name. It's Cabrini, Tony Cabrini. He's been using me, you see. He's been paying me to pretend I'm the mother of this girl Lucy. But I haven't anyone by that name in my family. It's all make-believe. He put me up to it. Paid me money."

At least it wasn't David Brier.

"Are you saying that the memorial notice was planted in the newspaper?"

"That's what I'm saying to you. That man Tony wanted me to make you take my money. And then I was supposed to go to a courtroom somewhere and tell the judge about you."

Kit had always suspected this would happen one day. She knew the police had been making a serious effort to clamp down on psychics and mediums. But she was unlike most of the others. She didn't work out of a storefront with a garish neon sign in the window, or pull people off the street and convince them she had all the answers. She didn't channel five-thousand-year-old Incan princesses or long-dead Cherokee warriors. She approached potential clients as someone with a comforting message, offering them a chance of reconciling themselves to their loss. She never made any promises or directly asked to be paid. And now she had two cops in her life.

Now she could lose everything.

Kit sat back and looked at her. "Did he ask you to record anything?"

"Funny you say that. He gave me a little device to tuck away in my bag." She smiled. "I guess I forgot to turn it on."

Kit took a deep breath. "Is it with you now?"

"No, missy, of course not. I gave it back to the man. I want nothing more to do with him."

"Is he waiting for you outside?"

"No. He doesn't know, you see. He doesn't know that I wanted to come back on my own, because I wanted to talk to my Deirdre. The little one drowned when she was only six, in a pond when we were visiting in Wicklow. A terrible, terrible thing to live through. I was having tea with my sister Siobhan and realized that Deirdre had gone out to play with this neighbor girl she liked, Fiona Byrne, and it had been nearly an hour, and when I went out to call her..."

Kit could just about see it for herself: a girl floating facedown in the pond, her arms away from her sides, her blond hair spread out on the surface. A scene from a haunted movie viewed long ago.

Mrs. Malone paused to gather her words. "When I called her and heard nothing back I started walking down the hill behind the house. It was called Shone's Hill, you see, and I kept calling and calling and running as fast as I could, down the hill, and there was just this silence, birds singing and such, and when I reached the pond I saw my poor little one in it, just floating like that, you know, with her face in the water. Her arms were out like this, just stretched out so natural-like... I never had another child, never married again after my Brendan died. It broke me badly, it did."

Kit said, "You've lost so much."

Deirdre, she thought, and in her mind she could almost too clearly see the little girl running down the hill with her friend.

"And what happened to the other girl…?"

"Fiona? I hear these days she walks the streets of Galway and talks to men." Brigid's eyes grew wide and happy. "I just want you to give me back my daughter. It would be a blessing."

28

THE STRIKING OF THE MATCH, THE LIGHTING OF THE wick, the hush that held the room in suspense: a ritual demanding silence and reverence, restraint and, most of all, belief. The candle lit up Mrs. Malone's face, and Kit could see the smile of anticipation, the bright sadness in the woman's eyes.

"Mrs. Malone. I just want to explain that I understand your genuine grief over Deirdre. But I can't guarantee that I'll be able to speak for your daughter tonight." She spoke as comfortingly as she could. "But I promise you that I will try."

She wondered how much she could believe the woman. There was always the chance that one of the cops was behind this visit.

"Just this once more—?" Brigid gripped Kit's hands for emphasis. "Please?"

She knew she would fail. With no time to prepare, she'd be inventing a dead child out of nothing.

"Give me something to help me summon her, Mrs. Malone. A nickname, or a favorite pet, or an item of clothing. A song, even."

"I have something that's hers with me. It's always with me." The woman reached into her bag and brought out a silver locket in the shape of a claddagh: two hands holding a heart. "Open it," she said. "And mind you're careful."

In the locket was a twist of blond hair behind a glass screen. Inside the lid was an image of Jesus with a glowing heart.

"She had the most beautiful blond hair you'll ever live to see. My brother Liam had that made for me after my girl had gone over."

It struck Kit as heartbreaking. It was all the woman had left of her daughter: her fading memories and a lock of hair. She felt a surge of pity for this old woman who had nothing in the world but a phony medium to bring her consolation.

"May I hold it, Mrs. Malone?"

"You may."

It felt unusually warm, and she imagined Brigid held it often to get closer to Deirdre, to feel her presence.

"Now rest your hands on mine, please." The locket still within her hand, Kit closed her eyes. "Remember that those we have lost are always with us. All we need is to summon them by showing that we mean no harm, no recrimination, nothing but whatever love we may bring to them... Deirdre," she said quietly. "Deirdre, please show us that you're here."

There was a long silence before Kit felt something change in the atmosphere. It was happening again, with all the willpower drained from her and taken over by some other force. She opened her eyes slightly to see that Brigid was smiling so blissfully that she looked years younger.

"She's near," the woman told Kit, nearly rising from her chair.

"Deirdre, please give us a sign that you're with us," Kit said softly.

It seemed to come from inside her, the voice of a small child she'd never heard before: "I can't...find my way..." the girl said, her accent not very different from the imaginary Lucy's, though her voice was higher, more tremulous. And though Kit's lips were moving, the voice wasn't hers. "It's so…very dark. And cold. And I don't want to go back there."

Brigid gasped. Quietly she said, "Ah, my wee girl…"

Kit felt helpless as she voiced the words. She had been taken over completely by this lost little spirit. She could feel the draw of the child as she seemed to come nearer, like iron to a magnet. There was nothing threatening about it, or even frightening, only a sense of healing, of mending and joining.

"Where are you, Deirdre…?" Brigid said.

"Where the water is, where Fiona took me. I've been in the water for soooo long, Mam. I want to come out."

"I'm so sorry," her mother said. "I didn't know. And I didn't protect you. And then, when I came down Shone's Hill and saw you there, I was—"

"Who is this person with you here, Mam?"

The child was there with them, listening, watching, acknowledging Kit's presence. She'd taken her over completely.

"Do you see her, Deirdre?"

"I can see her because she is right beside me. She sits across a table from you. Is she a friend? What pretty hair she has." She giggled. "She can feel my fingers in it."

Kit felt a chill come into her as what felt like a breeze played in her hair.

"Her name is Kit—"

"Oh, I knew I'd seen her before. She has a little girl, too, and she misses her so much."

"She's a friend," her mother said. "A friend to you and me

both. You can trust her, my wee girl, if that's what's frightening you. She will be your friend forever."

"I've been so confused…lost… I didn't know… But," and there was a quick intake of breath, "I am out of the water now and I can see you so much more clearly, Mam. There you are, finally! And I see the sun! Finally the sun! And my da! He's here, too!"

"Brendan," Brigid whispered, her eyes brimming with tears.

It was as if the membrane between life and death had become flimsy and transparent, full of rips and holes. Which meant that Kit was now in both worlds, of the living and the dead.

The child's voice grew stronger. "I want Mam's hand. I want to feel it in mine again."

Kit watched as the woman held out her trembling hand to nothing. And then the woman suddenly rose to her feet. "I can feel it in my own hand, I can feel the warmth of hers. Oh, my little one. Oh, my lost little one," and she held her fists against her breast as tears rolled down her cheeks.

"There's someone else here, Mam," the little girl said. "She says she wants to say something to the lady sitting with you. I think she knows her. She's so unhappy. She's crying and holding her hands to her mouth as if she'd seen a terrible horror, a nightmare. I want to help this lady so much, because she's come to me, but I can't help her, she won't listen to me…"

"Who is she, then?" her mother asked.

"She's crying, and she makes me want to cry, too. Something has made her so very sad. Please stop your crying, because—"

"What has made her sad?"

"Something happened to her… And she keeps crying,

crying all the time. She's been so very hurt, and she's so afraid
for the lady with you..." Her voice faded until it could no
longer be heard. "She says... She says that something terrible is
going to happen to her, something horrible and frightening..."

"Is Dierdre still with us?" Brigid asked.

Kit felt the air lighten. "No," she said, coming out of her
trance. "She's gone. But she'll come back to you."

The candle flame wavered, then without a breath or a breeze
it went out all on its own.

"I think we're done now, Mrs. Malone. Now you know for
certain that your daughter is happy where she is."

But Kit knew for sure; it was inescapable: she would be the
next victim.

Or maybe, she thought, *it's just another voice in my mad head.*

29

I T WAS THE USUAL FRIDAY NIGHT CROWD, AND WHEN she saw there wasn't a free stool at the bar, she turned to leave. She always preferred the bar. Drinking alone at a table seemed somehow pathetic, attracting the wrong kind of speculation and unwanted attention.

Someone just walking in grabbed her arm a little too firmly, and at first she thought it was Ian, returned to make her life a misery all over again. She stiffened and felt her mouth go dry.

"Hey," the man said, letting go, and at first she didn't recognize him. "It's David. Dave Brier. Remember? We met here at the bar last week?"

She wondered if her life was getting just a little too complicated. There were coincidences, and then there were *coincidences*. "Hi. I didn't expect to see you here."

"I didn't mean to freak you out. You just leaving?"

"Place is packed," she said, rubbing her arm where he'd gripped it. Just as he had when he'd helped her off the street during the ice storm.

"Unless you're in a rush, let's wait for a table, okay? We can talk a little more."

"All right," she said. "It's fine." For a moment she felt as if she'd walked into a trap.

A table became free not long after. She ordered her usual, double vodka rocks, he a margarita, salsa and chips to share. The ambience in the room was a little frantic that night. The music was a degree too loud, and the clanging of silverware ricocheted between walls and ceiling. Kit felt something within her fracturing, splitting into pieces.

"I haven't eaten anything since breakfast," David said, raising his voice to be heard. Almost magically, the music level dropped a notch. "Long day, too much work." He looked at her. "You seem a little worn around the edges yourself."

"That bad, huh?" she said. "I thought I'd painted it over."

Seeing him like this had thrown her completely off-balance. That last time, up at the bar, it had been simple. She could ease her way into her role. Now she had no idea what she was going to be for this man.

"Hey. I'm willing to listen."

She took a moment. "Something I didn't mention the last time we talked. Which would have been the first time. I mean, I don't even know you, and I'm telling you all this stuff. Look. I have a daughter. Her name is Zoey. She's seventeen now. She's been in a coma for three years."

She felt almost ashamed to have said it, as though she had brought to light some dire medical condition of her own.

It took him a few moments to absorb it. "Oh my god. I'm so sorry to hear that, Kit. May I ask what happened?"

"When she was fourteen, we were waiting for a subway to take us to Carnegie Hall. I'd bought tickets for us to hear this famous musician. She was a... Zoey is a pianist. Taking lessons. She was good. She *is* good. Really good. She wants to be a professional musician."

He was listening intently.

"It happened so quickly that I missed it, and I guess pretty much everyone else there did, too, but she saw this, I don't even know how to characterize it... A woman fell in front of a train. And Zoey hit her head against the platform and lost consciousness."

"Jesus," he said, and it was as if the force of her words pushed him back from the table. "Where was this?"

"A few blocks up."

"So the Columbia University Station," he said, and she nodded. He thought for a moment. "I think I read about that. But you saw it happen?"

"Only just before. I must have turned away, and then the train pulled in, and people were screaming and shouting at the driver, and the woman was under the wheels, and she was still alive and the sound was...unbelievable, something I won't ever forget. The sound of a woman dying. The sound of a woman begging to live."

"You think someone pushed her?"

She shook her head. "I don't know. I didn't see it happen. But Zoey did. I thought she'd fainted. And then she went into convulsions—which had never happened before—and she's been in a coma ever since."

She lifted her drink. "It's one of those experiences that just stays with you, you know? I missed the whole thing. Whatever had led to the woman losing her balance."

"And your daughter... What's the outlook?"

Kit shook her head. "Nothing doctors can stand behind. She'll either spend the rest of her life that way or wake up one day and remember nothing. Or everything."

"Is that when you began offering séances? After what happened?"

Tread carefully, she thought, reminding herself what he was.

"Around that time. Zoey is... She exists in this zone, this place, it's not life or death. It's how I got into holding consultations. It's about reaching across to another world. And it can be done, I do it all the time. I sense Zoey can hear everything I'm saying when I'm with her. She dreams, because everyone dreams. So she has a second life within her coma. I like to think that she dreams about growing up. About what I used to tell her about her father. About her piano lessons and the kids she knew at school. Maybe she even dreams about the future. But at least she's alive."

Like a ghost, she thought. There, yet manifestly absent.

David looked at her with his sad eyes. And then he put his hand on hers and gave it a gentle squeeze, and to Kit it was something delicious. It had been so long since she'd been touched by a man, and now she felt something weaken within her.

She said, "One of the things I tell my clients is that the border between the living and the dead is thinner than they think. Sometimes, if the light is just right, we can see through it and catch the silhouette of those who've left us. So we're always just a few centimeters from our own deaths."

It was a good script, one she put together in the beginning;

she would try to remember to dust it off a little more and use it with new clients.

"And your husband?"

"I don't consider him dead. Which is why I can't reach him."

"Because you still don't completely believe it."

He actually seemed to hear and understand what she was saying.

"I know it sounds kind of morbid," she went on, "and maybe it's too much magical thinking, but sometimes I think that instead of looking back to the past, we're staring into the future. Today both our mates are still alive and we're just foreseeing their fates."

David looked at her slightly awry. "That means…what, that we're the dead ones? The ghosts?"

"And then we'd have all the time in the world with them, wouldn't we," Kit said. She leaned in. "But we don't, not really. It's like the woman and the train. It happened in the blink of an eye. I always think of what the woman had been planning for that night, and the next day, and the next month, and maybe deep into her future with this man. And then, in a moment, it was all gone."

30

DAVID SAT BACK AND LOOKED AT HER. "YOU'RE kind of amazing, you know that? You have this...power, this ability, to speak to the dead. As crazy as it sounds."

"It's my life, it's what I do."

Keeping up the act was the only way to gain credibility, she knew. The guy was probably waiting for her to slip up, and then he'd put her out of business.

"How about another drink?" he said.

She looked at her empty glass. "Yes. Please. Immediately, at once."

She looked up at him and they both began to laugh. They ate some chips and salsa as the waiter crossed the room to take their order. She was still waiting for him to tell her that he was a detective. How long would he carry on this seduction—until she was in too deeply?

Or maybe it already was too late.

"So do you think you can put me in touch with Caro?" he asked.

Now she had to venture into his territory. *Do it first,* she thought. *Gain the advantage.* She wondered how long it would take before he admitted what he really did. At least she now knew what this Tony DeLuca was all about. "I can try. Except that…I found out that I'm being investigated by the police."

She sat back. *Your turn*, she thought.

He didn't react. "Seriously?"

"One of my clients told me, this Irishwoman. I even know the name of the detective."

His eyes betrayed nothing.

"So what *do* you do, David? For work, I mean."

He smiled. "You mean you don't know? With this…gift of yours?"

"Actually, I've known it since I met you. You're a cop. Too bad you didn't get to say it first." Which would have put them on an even footing.

He sat back and looked at her. "Jesus. You really are good at this stuff."

Mouse, meet cat.

After he walked her home, they stood outside her building: the uneasy face-off, as she liked to think of it, the moment when everything could change.

"I'd like to see you again," he said. "You know, dinner or another drink…? Wait—am I jumping the gun here?"

She laughed. "Actually, yes… I'd love to have dinner with you." *Wrong word.* "I'd like that very much."

"I enjoyed myself tonight. I'm glad I ran into you."

She smiled. "I am, too."

She tried to will him to look back at her as he walked away. He stepped into the shadows and just kept walking.

31

WHAT WAS IT—THURSDAY? PASTA NIGHT, AS IT had been ever since they were first married, when everything was new to them.

Tony and Connie Cabrini's life had become an unchanging timetable of habits and customs. From their apartment in the Bronx to Tony's desk in the Special Frauds Squad at police headquarters was a long commute, subway downtown, subway up, same old crowded car, same old everything.

A little breathless, he reached the landing and unlocked the door and Connie, as always, had the chain on. "C'mon, it's me, open up."

He wondered who she thought might try to break in while she was making tomato sauce and listening to the radio. If he half closed his eyes, the scene looked no different from when he was growing up in an apartment in Queens, his mother stirring the sauce, listening to an oldies station, singing quietly along, her gaze turned back to the lost paradise of her own past.

Connie took her time coming to the door and left the chain in place. "Do the thing I like."

He pressed what he could of his face in the gap and pretended to be Jack Nicholson. "Heeere's Tony!" and she laughed and told him she was glad he didn't own an ax.

"Don't need it. I've got a gun," he said, stepping in and locking up behind him.

He took off his coat and holster and stashed his weapon away in the safe in the bedroom closet. "Where's Frankie?"

"Where else? Saving the world, one enemy at a time."

"Video game again, huh? The kid ever do homework?"

"Did you?"

"Sometimes."

As his father was fond of saying, Frankie was thirteen going on five, since he spent most of his time in the make-believe world of whatever game he was entranced by this week or month or, in one case, for almost a year, wiping away whole battalions of animated figures. The kid strolled into the kitchen while Tony poured himself a Scotch. He seemed to be growing an inch a week and already was taller than both his parents.

"What's new?" Tony said.

"Nothing," Frankie said.

"It's always nothing," Connie said.

"Because nothing's new anymore." The boy went back to his room and shut the door.

Connie said, "So. Another week, another séance?"

"Week's not over, remember. But, yeah, I'm just trying to get Dave to let me handle this one."

"She pretty?" Connie asked.

"Just my type."

"I thought I was your type," and she gave him a big smile.

"My *other* type."

She took a seat at the table, already set for dinner. "Ever cheat on me?"

"Lemme think," Tony said, and he started silently counting on his fingers. When he reached all ten he said, "Never." He joined her at the table. "How was your day?"

"Same as Frankie's. Nothing's ever new when you're a secretary for a carpet company. Wall-to-wall boredom and salesmen talking about piles. Did you make the collar at least?"

"Couldn't do it unless she takes the money. Didn't happen. Dave's already connected with her. Picked her up in a bar."

"She's a psychic and hangs out at bars?"

He shrugged. "Guess so. She lost her husband on 9/11."

"Oh, that's tough. This is the one with the Irish lady who used to live next door to us? Brigid?"

"That's all over. She doesn't want to help me make the bust. The old lady believes the woman. She said she wants to talk to her dead daughter."

"I'd like to talk to my dead father," Connie said. "Just to tell him how much of a bastard I thought he was."

He laughed. "I can arrange that," and she playfully slapped his hand.

"Aren't you getting a little tired of Dave taking all the credit? Why don't you tell that partner of yours to give you a break?" She picked up an envelope from the counter. "Maybe this'll get you to do it. Landlord pushed it under the door today."

He read what was in it before tossing it aside. "Another rent increase. Jesus H."

"Which is why, Tony, you have to reach your quota and get a step closer to a promotion. You think traffic cops don't bother handing out tickets? Just wait till the end of the month when they make up their shortfalls. More pay would be kind of nice just about now."

"I can't force the lady to take my money. I left her some, but the deal is to have her take it from my hand."

"Then why'd you give her something?"

He went to get another splash of Scotch. "Because I felt sorry for her. Maybe she's just harmless. Maybe she's really helping people, I don't know. And she's a widow. I mean, you know."

Connie put a hand over his. "Work on it, Detective Cabrini."

"I am working on it."

She got up to put on the water for the pasta. "So what was she this time, old, young…?"

"Medium."

Old jokes never really die.

32

KIT'S FIRST CLIENT THE NEXT DAY WAS A WOMAN in her fifties whose son had vanished while he was at summer camp some twenty years earlier. It took a few moments for Kit to take it in. *Twenty years.* The woman had spent all that time looking for his face in a crowd, praying, wishing, hoping, and now she'd decided to rely on a psychic. Kit saw this for what it was: a last resort, the magic of closure.

For a missing child she could do nothing; it wasn't within her imagination to make it play out. The cruelty of the scam would break her.

But she took pity on this person who seemed so distracted, her eyes everywhere but on Kit's face, her hands constantly fidgeting. She'd bitten her nails to the quick, and a few of them had become red and inflamed. She kept twirling a lock of her hair around her finger.

Kit read a kind of madness about her: not knowing what has become of your own child was the worst thing of all. At least Kit could see Zoey, talk to her, hold her hand, kiss her cheek. But this woman had nothing but a memory and the unending nightmare of speculation.

It was like Peter on that morning. Where was he? She knew where she wanted him to be. Was he coming back?

A part of her believed he just might walk through the door one day. And that was her insanity, her obsession, a mirror of this woman's.

"I'm afraid I don't do missing people," she told the woman.

"Please, Ms. Capriol. I've run out of options. I thought I saw him a few times in the past, in the subway and then on TV on this, this news report, the evening news, he was in a crowd in a street after some kind of accident, and then...I was told that it was just me making myself believe, it's what my husband said. That I was out of my mind, that I should be institutionalized."

"Is your husband still with you?" Kit asked, and the woman turned on a big bright smile.

"He's dead and buried, thank god. And then..."

"May I ask how you heard about me?"

"I saw you mentioned online. On some... On a website somewhere..." Her mind seemed to go adrift.

Kit waited. She tried to read her, but the woman was a kind of blur to her.

"What was I saying?"

Kit touched her hand. "I think I understand."

The woman shrugged. "Want to hear something absolutely insane? I mean really crazy insane?" and she laughed. "The psychiatrist I'd started seeing back then told me to let it go and move on. That my son was not coming back." She smiled. "Isn't that bizarre, though? *Let it go?* Like dropping off a favorite old sweater at Goodwill and just forgetting it? But I can't let go, do you understand? To let go is to..."

Let him die, Kit thought. And then the woman said those exact words.

"I understand that," Kit told the client. "I honestly do."

The woman told her what she knew of the circumstances of the boy's disappearance. "They never found a body. They never found anyone who'd seen what had happened. One minute he was there, on this raft in the lake, and the next... he was gone." She took a crumpled tissue from her bag and dabbed the tears from her eyes. "It was like he'd vanished into thin air." Her voice grew frantic. "Like in a horror movie. Like there was a seam in the world and he'd slipped into it. This little boy, my baby, my only one. And my husband and I were just supposed to carry on living. Like it was the most normal thing in the world. How did he get on that raft? I've been wondering that all these years. Because Joey couldn't swim, you see. And he was afraid of deep water. What was he doing there, I mean how did..."

Kit put her hand on the woman's arm to try to calm her. "I understand."

But it was as if the woman hadn't heard her. "And my son wasn't the first. They said there were other boys who'd gone missing over the years. Like twenty, thirty years. A few from the camp, from the town, from other places. They say there may even have been a girl or two that went missing. They never found any of them, either." She smiled a little crookedly. "Sounds crazy, doesn't it?"

Kit took her hand. She wasn't going to abandon this woman so quickly. "Let's go into the other room," she said.

33

I'M A LITTLE SCARED," THE WOMAN SAID IN A SMALL voice as she sat across from Kit, the lighted candle between them.

"You can tell me to stop at any time," Kit said.

"What if he's still alive and...suffering somewhere?"

"He'd be an adult now, of course," Kit said. "And I can't communicate with the living this way. So please understand that."

"Unless he died. Unless something horrible happened to him. He was just a child, and I keep thinking that he suffered." She put her hands to her face. "My own little boy in pain. Crying. Helpless."

Kit felt how cold the woman's trembling fingers were. She said, "It's important we both take deep breaths and see if he'll come to us." She had no idea where this would go. She kept thinking of the weeping woman. That was the one she feared the most, the phantom inside her life, the voice in her head.

"The people we love are all around us," Kit began. "They never leave our side. We have to remember and believe. That's what draws them to us. Faith and memory. Look at the candle. Think of your son. Of the moments you still treasure. Most of all, your love for him."

A tear rolled down the woman's cheek. She said, "I feel so close to him now."

Kit again felt herself being pulled down into a kind of vacuum. Sounds dwindled into silence and her fingertips grew numb as they held the woman's hands. This was nowhere, a negative space, the anteroom of death.

Glimpses. A low ceiling. Wooden beams. Wiring. A dirt floor. The smell of damp. The stink of waste. A place of history and ritual, where unfathomable things happened. When she opened her eyes, she was actually there. The consultation room had become this basement. Water trickled down stone walls marked by white scratches, as if people had been trying to leave something of themselves behind, a name, initials, a message for someone, a plea for help.

Scorch marks on the stones and bits of charred wood at the base.

Something in the corner, the slither of something moving, uncoiling.

A place of old anger and simmering vengeance. Clothing, shirts and jackets, lay in a pile beside a pyramid of dozens of old worn sneakers, as though it were a shrine to some unspeakable god.

Now she was outside, also in an unfamiliar place. Trees all around, the reds and yellows of the freshly fallen leaves of autumn. She looked up as one floated gently down, and when she reached out to catch it, the leaf went through her hand and settled on the ground among the others.

The land overlooked a lake, unnaturally blue in her vision. A raft in the stillness of an autumn day, the raft the woman had

told her about. Then she felt it, a presence, a warmth. She felt
compelled to press her hand to the ground, to the leaves and
the earth beneath them, and knew that she'd closed the circle,
the raft where the boy was last seen and now this, where the
boy now was, in the beautiful woods. No one would ever find
him, no one would ever learn the secret apart from her.

The boy's mother suddenly cried out, "He's here. He's
here!"

Kit opened her eyes, the spell broken. As if her touch to the
ground had somehow freed him.

"You can feel his spirit with us now," she told the woman,
sensing it herself. "He's finally at peace."

"Did he suffer?"

Kit looked at the woman. "No," she lied. She knew otherwise. The cellar. The threat that even after all these years still
hung in the stale air like a foul smell. But that was over. He'd
found a place of rest. Now he existed only in the woman's
memory. And she'd let his mother talk to him.

"Say what you've been waiting to tell him all this time. Say
it now."

The woman looked suddenly alert, her eyes bright and
hopeful as she told the boy how she missed him, how she loved
him, how she wanted to see him again one day. She spoke of
things they'd done together in the city, how she loved watching him in his school play. Her face glowed with a kind of bliss
that moved Kit to tears, and it came to Kit that the boy would
live forever in some other past, some fine magical place. A story
with a happy ending.

"I know I can't see him now," the woman said. "But I

know that I will, one day. Oh my boy. My poor lost little boy."

Kit stood and put her arms around her, comforting her as the woman wept against her shoulder. When she recovered minutes later, she said, "Was it over quickly, do you know?"

Kit thought of how real it had all seemed, almost like a movie set, every detail precisely crafted. Whatever the story, it was only half-understood by her. Someone evil had taken this child, someone with an appetite for cruelty and power. Someone who would make it last: a week, a month, longer. She imagined the child—maybe others—waiting and listening. A door would open. Heavy footsteps on the stairs leading down. The shadow cast upon them. It was all there.

"It was," she lied. "And there was no suffering."

The mother wiped her eyes. "Now I can finally rest. All these years of wondering. All these years of not knowing the truth of what had become of him. Do you think he could read my thoughts?"

"Oh yes," said Kit. "Those we've lost have that power. As I said, they're always with us. But this time you opened the door, let in the light and air, allowed him to find you. Now he's free. He's finally free. His loneliness is gone."

"Because I was apologizing to him," the mother said. "You see, we did this to him. We killed him, his father and I. We let him into the world. We sent him away that summer because we were selfish with our time. We hated each other, my husband and I," and she looked almost regretful for it. "Months after we divorced they told me he'd died, my husband, and when I heard that, I felt nothing." She looked up at Kit with a distant smile. "Now I can feel again. Now I have my life back."

She opened her hands before pressing them to her breast, as in a religious painting of great sorrow. "It would have been better had my son not been born at all."

"No. He brought you so much happiness for as long as he was here in the world. Thanks to you, he's now at peace. Take that home with you. Live with it for as long as you do so that you can have some peace of your own."

The woman smiled as if the heavens had opened for her. "Thank you, Ms. Capriol. You've made a miracle for me. I want to pay you," she said, opening her bag. But Kit could see there was nothing inside it except a pair of reading glasses, a few tissues, and a MetroCard.

"No. I will accept nothing from you. My reward is in seeing your face." She didn't want the woman to come back. Kit had seen enough to last a dozen nightmares.

She walked the woman to the door and once again embraced her. "Try to find happiness," she said. She closed the door and muffled her own cries with her fists.

But it wasn't over. She could still smell the damp of the cellar. She could still see the scratches on the walls.

Now she had a foot in each world. And both seemed like home.

34

S HE THOUGHT OF DAVID AT UNEXPECTED MOMENTS—
when she was riding the subway, or at the hospital with Zoey,
or coming out of the weekly acting classes she'd begun attending
downtown: little ambushes that caught her off guard and surprised
her in a pleasing but vaguely disturbing way. Perhaps she'd been
alone for so long that she'd begun to grow comfortable with her
solitude, protective of her privacy, this life she had created for
herself. She felt as though she had three distinct lives: her role as a
medium, her career as an actor, her life as a mother. And suddenly
David was introduced into the mix. That made four.

But she kept losing the memory of his face, as though it
were only a smudge on the surface of her world. It was the
kind of face you can't hold onto. Turn and he's there, turn back
and he's gone. He escapes your memory. As though he were
always half out the door. A face too easily forgotten. A face she
still couldn't read.

It wasn't an unattractive quality, she told herself. It was so
unlike Ian, who was always *there*, taking up space, siphoning off
the light; the kind of man who impresses you with his force of
character, with his intellect and his multitude of stories and his
bulk, yet whose whole goal in life is to absorb you, make you
vanish into his identity.

After the woman left the apartment, Kit checked her messages. A few clients wanted return visits, mostly widows and widowers, people who carried a little too much guilt over the deaths of their spouses. There were calls from people Kit had contacted after reading the memorial notices they had posted online or in the *Times*. Just not enough clients to help her with the mortgage.

She'd avoided thinking about what might happen should she lose the apartment, because it was too dark to consider about. She had no one she could rely on, no living relatives on either her or Peter's side. Her friends were like her, living from one month to the next, getting into whatever audition had been posted in the trades and online. One of her friends, in her twenties, out of desperation even showed up for the lead role in *Annie*, sitting amid seven- and eight-year old girls.

But there was nothing from David.

And now—here it came once more—she wanted to see him again. Right now, this minute, she wanted to tell him about this little boy who had vanished all those years ago and who had been buried in the woods.

She walked up to Broadway and looked through the restaurant window. For some reason it was quiet that night, with only a few tables occupied, and two people sitting at the bar. She walked in and took her favored seat at the end.

Louis held up a glass. "Same old?"

She smiled. It was like coming home. "And some nachos, please."

"You got it, Kit."

He poured in a little extra vodka. *I must look like shit*, she thought.

"Who's been around?" she said.

"You mean the cop you were with?"

"He didn't tell me that, Louis. You did. Let's keep it that way."

"Is it too much above my pay scale to ask what you do, Kit?"

"I'm the death whisperer," she said, and they both laughed. "Seriously? I'm an actor."

He laughed. "I get it. Horror flicks."

One day she would hand him her card. One day he would wander into her web.

She wondered if she'd hear back about that role as the war photographer, and then she stopped wondering, because she'd been through this too many times before. In the early days it was like practicing magic, you saw signs everywhere, the sun breaking through the clouds, the first flake of snow, a positive horoscope read online: *I'll hear today. I'll hear tomorrow. The delay is bad; the delay is good. The delay means they're seriously considering me. The delay means they've completely forgotten to let me know.*

And then a month later you'd get an apologetic email, half-boilerplate, half-bullshit, always ending with *We wish you all the best in your future endeavors.*

"Have I seen you in anything?" Louis said.

"Apart from this seat? I was in an off-Broadway *Crucible*. Long time ago."

"At the Cherry Lane? I saw that. My drama class went on a school trip when I was in junior high."

"God, I'm old," she said with a laugh.

"I kind of remember I felt like my head was going to explode."

"So did I most nights."

"Which one was you?"

She told him her character's name.

"You were amazing," he said.

She laughed. "Liar. You don't even remember me. But I was in Shakespeare in the Park at the Delacorte when I was twenty. Small role, alternating with another actor—Dorcas in *The Winter's Tale*. A lot of *whithers* and *neithers* and the immortal line, 'He hath promised you more than that, or there be liars.'"

"I was there, and you're the only actor I remember."

She laughed. "Then I deserve one on the house, don't you think?"

"Yes, my lady."

"I was a shepherdess, my liege, and I mostly traded lines with a clown."

He went to serve another customer. Now she was glad she had gotten out of the apartment. She needed to breathe the air of others, she yearned for mindless conversation and free drinks and David Byrne singing "Psycho Killer" on the restaurant's sound system, old music for happier times. For the person she used to be, when life was good and the bad was all behind her. And right in front of her was one for the road.

"Mud in your eye," she said, quoting her mother.

35

THERE.

A single note being played on the piano, and now she was awake, eyes wide open. *Blink.* Listen.

Listen.

Listen with your eyes. Seek out the sound in the darkness.

She turned her head to see the time: *2:13 a.m.*

The hour of suspension and silence, when people lose consciousness, while some quietly pass away and others find their victims, hunt them down, leave them to die. A time when people dream. A time when people wake and grow fearful.

She turned on her side. The door of an apartment down the outside hallway clicked shut. The lock was turned, the chain secured. Now all was quiet once more.

She drifted into a light sleep, when a few minutes later she was awakened again: another note on the piano.

Was it a dream? She sat up and listened, and now this: a third note sounded.

This was the fear. What she'd been expecting when things were no longer within her mind but outside it, as though she'd somehow set them free to wander, to look, to taunt, and to mock. Like the voice of the weeping woman. Like the sense of something about to happen.

Now it was in her home, unbidden by her.

She said, "Who is it?"

There was only silence. No one apart from Zoey ever touched that instrument. The keyboard lid had remained shut since the day she was taken to the hospital.

Then...

A different note was played and began to decay, growing fainter and weaker in the air. She could feel the heaviness of her breathing now.

Someone was in the apartment, someone had opened the piano, someone was touching the keys.

She quietly slipped out from under the duvet and, treading carefully, stepped to the doorway of her bedroom. Too scared to look into the living room, she listened hard, and heard nothing. No one's footsteps, no one breathing.

The air was unnaturally cold, and she shivered in the tank top she always wore to sleep. She crossed her arms over her chest for warmth, but her own skin was icy to the touch, as though it were the flesh of a dead person.

"Is someone here?" she called quietly, now gathering the courage to look into the room.

She stretched out a hand to feel the texture of the darkness, to see if there was something she could seize, or someone, or maybe no one at all. There was just herself, hearing things, notes that belonged to her daughter.

She switched on a lamp. The lid over the keys was open.

She tried to think back to the hours before, when she'd returned from the bar. She'd had two drinks and was feeling a little too merry, and when she came home she turned on the

TV, and the next thing she knew she was in bed, and it was 2:13 and she was wide awake. What else had she forgotten that she'd done?

She pressed the middle C. She waited for the sound to turn to nothing. She went back to bed and managed to fall asleep.

4:43 a.m.

This time someone smashed an octave or more, suddenly, angrily, and she woke just as instantly as she had those two hours earlier. Her clothes and sheet were soaked through with perspiration, and the muscles in her legs radiated pain, as though someone had been trying to hold her down. As though someone were doing it still.

She pulled the covers over her head. Please just *go away*, she thought. "Just leave me the hell alone!" she shouted.

There were no such things as ghosts. There was just memory and suggestion.

Somehow, just before dawn, she drifted into an uneasy sleep, waking suddenly three hours later to a heavy overcast and a steady rain. This time, when she looked, the keyboard lid was down.

She checked her messages and found one from a private number that had come in at 3:02 in the morning, when her phone had been muted. There was what sounded like the hiss of static between radio stations, and behind it someone—a woman—trying to break through as she spoke. Kit turned the volume up and held it to her ear when the weeping began. Then the woman said, *"Please save me…"*

The ghosts were finally coming home.

36

THREE HOURS LATER, JACKIE OPENED THE DOOR
after buzzing Kit into the building. "What's happened?"
she said when she saw Kit's face.

Jackie listened as Kit told her about the piano incident.

"You're sure you didn't dream this...?"

"Definitely. I woke up, I went into the room and found the
lid open, the one over the keyboard. It's always closed. Always.
And then this morning I found this message on my phone."

She took out her phone and scrolled through her voice messages. She said, "I wanted you to hear it for yourself."

She scrolled through it again with growing frustration. "It
was here this morning. I swear it was." She looked up at Jackie.
"The same voice I heard during the séance. She keeps asking
for my help, begging me to save her."

Jackie looked at her. "Go on."

"That's it. It was here earlier."

"Okay," Jackie said. "So who is she?"

Kit shook her head. "I don't know. I don't know where she
came from, what her name is, whether she's real or not. But I
heard it."

"And now it's gone."

Kit nodded.

"So she's a dead woman," Jackie said flatly in the voice you use to placate a child who insists there's a monster under his bed. "Do you trust it?"

"I don't know," Kit said after a pause.

"Are you afraid...?"

"Part of me is, at least since I had what I was told was one genuine summoning with a dead girl."

"But the dead belong to time past. Logic tells us they can't come back."

Kit remembered what she'd tell clients: that the dead can see all, past, present, and future. She knew all about the power of suggestion and saw it now for what it was: she was talking herself into this zone of dread.

"And so there was a message on your phone. Same voice?" Jackie asked, and Kit nodded.

"That's why I called. I wanted you to hear it. I wanted you to tell me that I'm not going out of my mind. I didn't want to be the only one who heard the voice."

Jackie said nothing. As if she were hoping something sensible and sane might sink in.

"You think I'm losing it, don't you," Kit said.

Jackie said, "What's this really about, Kit? What's going on with you?"

"I'm scared. I mean, it wasn't supposed to be like this. The whole medium thing was just an act, and then I saw that I could maybe help some people, and now...somehow I've touched this place, this...I don't know, other place, where the dead are."

Yet part of her knew that was impossible. It was where

survivors spent too much of their time, remembering, regretting, unable to forget and always willing to forgive.

"So do you think your apartment is haunted?"

"My life is. I've carried death with me ever since I lost Peter. And then there's this man I've been seeing. That I'm interested in. Who makes me want to just move on, think about someone else other than me and Zoey," and she told Jackie as much as she knew about David.

"And you're in love with him?" Jackie asked.

"Not yet." She took a breath. "Maybe not ever. I just don't know."

"An open door doesn't always mean we have to walk through it," Jackie said.

"I know, I know."

Jackie took a moment. "Okay, so with all this talk about voices you're hearing and the piano being played, I think there's a problem. But I don't think you're suffering from some sort of mental distraction."

"What is that, another euphemism for insanity?"

"No, I meant it as I said it. I don't think you're entirely losing your grip on reality. But I think it would help if you stopped pretending you're a medium and get back to the land of the living. Audition, take classes—teach if you can find a job somewhere. Go out and meet people. But this, what you're doing, it's not doing you any good, Kit. And I'm seriously concerned."

"I told myself I'd give it up if an offer came through. I had an audition last week, and it went really well, and I think I have a shot, but I know this business, I know what they're going to say, I—"

Jackie raised a hand. "Okay, Kit, please stop. Everything is running away with you and you'll end up thinking yourself a failure. So stop, okay?"

"Now you're going to tell me I'm manic." And for some reason Kit smiled.

"Look. I know you've had to deal with a lot of very serious things over the years, and I know these can wear us down when they start to pile up. But you need to think and act clearly now. You're holding séances. You're hearing voices. Weird things seem to be happening in your apartment, you've got a daughter in a coma, and now you tell me you're becoming involved with a detective who because of what you do can potentially make your life a living hell. See a pattern here at all?"

"He's *not* Ian."

Jackie raised her voice a notch. "You barely know this man, Kit. And now you're telling me you've fallen for him. Or he's made you feel that you have."

Kit took it in. "I know, I know. It's just—"

"Is there a chance he might actually arrest you for what you're doing?"

"I've thought of that. It's not so much that he could just be doing his job. It's that I don't know how much faith I can put in him. In us."

"But you're attracted to him."

"Well, yeah. Very much so."

Jackie looked at her for several long moments. "He may just be leading you on."

Kit nodded. That had come to her a number of times. She looked away.

Jackie said, "It seems to me you're looking for a handhold, something secure to grab on to. My advice? Get to know him better. Use your intuition. And cut down on the booze, okay?"

"I'll try."

Jackie smiled. "Liar."

37

THIS ONE WAS AT HER DOOR EXACTLY AT SEVEN that evening, just as arranged. She introduced herself with only her first name, Leslie, and shook Kit's hand. Well dressed, well spoken, a woman of means.

"I almost didn't come up," Leslie said. "I'm... Well, I have to confess I'm a little embarrassed."

Kit smiled. "I understand. But once you become comfortable with the concept and the practice, you'll see just how consoling it will be. And, of course, you may leave at any time."

An attorney with a long-established law firm in the city and an address on the Upper East Side, Leslie told Kit that years earlier she'd had an affair with a much younger man who died of brain cancer four years into a relationship built on stolen moments and furtive phone calls. Her husband had known nothing about it.

"Yet I love my husband," she told Kit. "I always have. I mean, we've known each other since, oh my god, college? And I can't imagine not being with him. And we have two wonderful children, now adults, of course. But this other man, this exquisite young man I'd met at this charity function at the Met, he simply stole my heart away. I was flattered, deeply flattered, and he made me feel young again." She shrugged. "I think about him at least once a day. It's funny how weak people can be."

"You're human," Kit said. "We all succumb sometime in our lives. And we all wish things had happened differently in the past."

"And of course, here I am hoping to speak to the dead." A brief laugh, then: "Part of me is saying, don't be an idiot, be practical. I'm an attorney, I live in the land of facts and evidence—so this is a kind of way out for me. As if I could speak to the dead." And she made a dismissive noise.

"But that's why you're here, isn't it? Because I can. And you're curious enough to give it a try."

"I know that people like you and trust you," the client said. "And to some I know I'd look foolish, but...there was so much that was left between us. We never had the chance to say goodbye."

"And what's left unfinished just lingers on, doesn't it."

The woman told Kit that, ridiculous as it may sound, she wanted to see if she really could reach him, wherever he was. "I mean, I don't especially believe in all this mumbo jumbo, but I've had these odd things happen to me."

"Tell me," Kit said.

"I keep seeing him. Not all the time, just, you know, at odd moments. Passing a store and seeing him there. Or across a crowded restaurant. Once my husband and I were at the opera, and on the way out I could swear he was in the crowd ahead of me. I mean, it was the back of his head, but when he turned to talk to the person he was with it was him, I'm certain of it.

And he *loved* opera." She put a hand to her breast. "I could hardly catch my breath."

"It's happened to me, too," Kit said. "I see my husband from time to time. Even though he's been gone now almost eighteen years. Seeing him on a bus, in a museum, wherever."

As though she and Peter existed at the same time on different planes of reality, passing now and then with only a brief wordless acknowledgment.

"May I ask who referred you...?" Kit said before they walked into the room with the candle.

"Dave Brier. He said he was a friend of yours."

38

LESLIE HAD GIVEN HER ENOUGH INFORMATION about her dead lover so that Kit could improvise her way through the session, playing off of this detail or that. Upon leaving, the attorney pressed five one-hundred dollar bills into her hand.

Kit felt herself wavering. It was a larger donation than she'd been given lately, and she was tempted to keep it, especially as she had until the end of the month to pay the previous month's mortgage. But she remembered that David had sent this person to her, just as Tony had referred Brigid Malone to her, and something went *click* in her head.

"May I ask why Detective Brier referred you to me?"

The woman smiled. "He said you were the real thing. And then, of course, I asked if he was intending to charge you with anything." She laughed. "Because then I'd have to give you my card and suggest I represent you in court. He said no, you were just good friends."

"I can't accept this," Kit said, handing the money back. "As I mentioned, the first session is always free. If you return after this, a donation is appreciated." She pressed the money into the woman's hand. "This would be most welcomed. Just not now."

And no one could arrest her for *that*. Not even David Brier.

Peering out between the curtains, she waited until the woman left the building and crossed the street.

"Happy day?" Louis said when she came by the bar the next night.

"Are you nuts?" she said, and he laughed, because that was their act, the bartender and the sad lady in her forties, even though she was feeling pretty good.

He lowered his voice. "By the way, that cop you were talking to? He was here like an hour ago."

She looked around. "Really."

"With a woman. Having dinner," and he nodded toward a corner table. The same one where she and David had been sitting only a few days earlier.

Now, for some reason, she wanted him even more.

He called three days later. At first she had no idea who it was. She didn't recognize the number. Client? Salesman? Pervert?

He said, "It's Dave. Brier."

"David. Yes," and she felt her heart beating hard within her chest.

"I think we left off by me saying that I'd like to take you to dinner. I hope you didn't think I'd forgotten."

"Yes. Yes, of course. I mean, no, I didn't think you'd forgotten," and she laughed. Already she'd blown it, sounding so eager. Playing hard to get wasn't in her nature. Jackie was right: she was grabbing onto anything even mildly promising. A man at a bar; someone with an attentive ear and a kind word. Someone like her who had lost a spouse.

She had tried hard to make friends over the years, reliable

people, people she could confide in, people she could relate to. There was a group of other actors with whom she'd worked in past productions, some going back as far as ten or fifteen years, that would get together once a month or so for drinks or a meal, each time at a different restaurant or bar, mostly in Manhattan. Conversation would quickly become an outpouring of professional woes. This director was an asshole, that leading lady was a drama queen, this one was kind to me, this producer tried to grope me. Everyone there knew they were in competition for the next role in the next production. Little was revealed. Mention a forthcoming audition and everyone was making a mental note of it.

And if one of them had actually landed a decent role, the others, Kit included, would consider their day completely ruined by this horrible news.

But David was the first man who showed genuine interest in her.

"I know this is kind of short notice," he said, "but I have to be in the area until just before seven tomorrow, and I was thinking that maybe we could meet at the South Street Seaport afterward and walk to the restaurant?"

"Let me just check my schedule," she said, then sat back and silently counted to ten. Slowly, backwards, and in French. "Yes, I can do that. That would be nice. I look forward to it."

She heard the smile in his voice. "Me too." He told her where they would meet. Then he said, "All okay with you otherwise?"

"Yeah, good. Fine. Really." She had no idea why she'd added that.

"Good. See you tomorrow, then."

Kit looked in the bedroom mirror and did a quick assessment. Forty-three, not sixteen, on this day looking closer to fifty. But a good fifty, a fine fifty. Flinty and cool and in serious need of a full makeover kind of fifty. Okay, forty-three.

When she returned from her run the next morning, she showered. As she was about to dry her hair someone rang her buzzer, a woman who said she was a case worker with an assisted-care facility on the East Side. "I wonder if I might have a word with you regarding one of our residents?"

"You must have the wrong person. Sorry." Kit was about to walk away to comb out her hair when the woman said, "It's about a woman who came to see you the other day." And she gave the name.

Kit buzzed her in. *Knock-knock, and you get nothing in return*, she thought.

The visitor introduced herself as Jessica Dowd, and immediately Kit began to read her. Midforties. Polished. Shiny and up to a point unreadable. A chilly exterior. Possibly unmarried, probably divorced. Then she saw the cracks and flaws: the woman kept scratching at a rash on her neck; the knuckles on both hands were as white as bone. Nerves, she guessed. Right on the edge. *Temper, temper.*

The woman held up a laminated ID lanyard confirming her as an employee of the facility, and asked if they could speak "just for a few minutes. If another time would be better, then we can—"

"Fine," Kit said, and let her in.

They sat in the living room. The woman said, "How long

had you known the woman who saw you quite recently? Mrs. Proctor?"

"I hadn't met her before then."

"And her purpose for coming here?"

Kit smiled. "That's confidential."

"I see," the woman said, pausing for a moment. "Had you somehow gotten in touch with her in the first place? I'm only asking because she'd wandered off from the building, and when she came back some hours later she said she'd been here. At this address. Meeting with you. She said you had put her in touch with her dead son."

Like a bird trying to put things in focus, the woman tilted her head to one side and the other and waited for Kit's explanation. Already Kit hated her.

Kit said, "I took no money from her, nor did she offer any. It was a conversation, not a transaction."

"So...you profess to be a medium of some sort?"

"You said it, I didn't."

"Then what would you call yourself?"

"Kit. Kit Capriol. Actually." She sounded like James Bond, sans suit, gun, car, women, and license to kill. The martini would come later. Once again, she must have come off as crazy as this woman probably thought she was.

Like her image on the lanyard hanging from her neck, Jessica Dowd smiled without showing her teeth, as though out of pity for Kit. Sad, delusional lady. Sad, lonely, and nuts. Kit could read it all in her look.

"What you do here in your home isn't my business. But Mrs. Proctor is my responsibility. Maybe I should make myself more clear. Our facility is for people with Alzheimer's. Mrs. Proctor has a rather fragile grasp of reality. She speaks of this child often. Sometimes she believes she's speaking to him. Sometimes she does it for hours on end. We have no idea whether she even had a son, though she may believe she did. And now, it seems, you also believe in this boy. Because when—and I can't imagine how—she found her way back to us, she was in a manic state. Animated beyond anything we'd seen in her before. Laughing and jumping up and down and twirling and singing and telling everyone what she thought you had done for her. So much so that she had to be escorted to her room and sedated."

She sat back and looked at Kit. "If I may say so, that was one of the cruelest things I'd ever seen, to leave her so deluded, especially in her condition."

"I had no idea that—"

The woman eased up. "I know that—"

"But she was genuinely happy," Kit said. "Whatever you may think of me, I did nothing to hurt the woman. I simply put her in touch with her dead son, even if he only exists in her mind, even if he is just a work of fiction. A character in her story."

"So you imply that you actually saw him, then."

"I was where he died. Where he's buried. It was a long time ago. And now he's at peace. That's what she wanted to hear. That there was no suffering, no pain."

Kit decided it was best to spare this woman all the details: the cellar, the scratches, the pile of clothes and sneakers. The squalor. And yet she'd felt that nothing of it could touch her.

She wasn't a trespasser on the past; she was a presence in someone else's past.

"And you believe this," the woman said.

"Belief doesn't come into it. I was there."

"And you believe it," she said again. "You're just like her. You believe in every delusion that comes into your head. Or maybe you just made it all up."

"I believe in my clients, not necessarily in what I hear or see."

The woman took a breath. Clearly she had no patience for this fruitcake.

Kit had had enough. "I think it's time you left. And I'm not sorry I left that poor woman happier than she'd been in a long time."

The woman walked to the door. She looked like she was thinking about murdering Kit.

"Leave the psychology up to us, okay?" the woman said. "I know who you are now, and I know where you live."

"That's not very nice. No wonder your husband left you."

Dowd had opened the door a few inches and now she closed it. "How did you know that?"

It wasn't hard to see. This was someone nearly impossible to live with, and Kit imagined the terror her Alzheimer's patients must experience every day as she thundered her way down the hall, keys clanking from her belt, going from one room to another, flinging open doors, staring them down and talking to them as if they were five-year-olds in a lifelong time-out.

"Because I just saw him."

"You are a very strange woman, you know that? Now mind

your own business." The case worker walked to the elevator while Kit held open her door and watched her. Just as the woman was about to step in Kit said, "I was right about your husband, wasn't I," and the woman gave her a stony, dismissive look. "Oh, and hold the door," Kit added. "He's right behind you."

Now she felt a lot better. Now she was ready to go on a date.

39

RETURNING FROM CLASS THE NEXT AFTERNOON, Kit saw she had a voice message from Rita Daly, the casting director from LA.

She sat on her bed and tried to temper her anticipation. Casting directors didn't call unless they had good news; actually, most people in Hollywood skipped the calling part altogether. They simply expected you to read their minds. Silence was almost always the default, because they'd already forgotten about you.

She tapped to listen and her hand holding the phone began to shake.

"Hi, Kit, I was hoping to speak directly to you, but I guess you were busy, so I thought I'd just leave a message. Two things. First of all, the video I made of you was a little strange. It's a new camera and it's been super reliable, but when I tried to show it to some other people here... I mean, it was odd, because Blake and I viewed it after we saw you, but when I sent it out to others, the footage was just, well, black... The picture was gone, and the sound was a kind of white noise. Like the audition never took place. I had the camera checked out, but they couldn't find anything wrong. So I'm very, very sorry about that. But the other thing, which is more important, and obviously not a reflection on you, is that the people behind the project really want to go with a

more established name and revert back to a male lead, because, well, it makes the project all that more viable. You know the business. I'm sure you know how tough it is for a woman in this industry. I just want you to know that I really liked your reading, and I'm keeping your contact info for my files. I wish you all the—"

And then it turned into the peppery hiss of perdition.

Kit sat for a minute more, trying to absorb the news. She played it through once again, then deleted it. This time, almost as if it had been when she was younger and first starting out, tears came to her eyes. She was sure she'd nailed the audition. She had pinned more than a few hopes on it. She could envision herself in the role, she could see getting up before dawn to get to the makeup trailer, she could imagine grazing the craft-service tables at lunchtime, sharing small talk with the other actors, making friends. But that wasn't going to happen; not this time. Now she wondered if she really had a future as an actor.

She had been erased from her audition as though she'd never existed.

40

WHEN KIT LOOKED ACROSS THE RIVER TO Brooklyn from the pier, she sensed him approaching from her left, a looming figure out of the corner of her eye. *Be cool*, she thought. *Don't smile*. And then he was there, alongside her.

"Hey," she said with a big smile. A lame start to the evening.

"Been waiting long?"

"Two hours work for you?"

He stared at her. "Are you serious?"

"More like five minutes."

"Everything all right?"

"Yeah," she said, trying to keep the smile. "Fabulous."

Except that what had been happening at home had left her dreading the gathering night, the two o'clock solitude, the four-in-the-morning anxiety, the phantoms that wandered uninvited through her apartment. Lately sleep had come late and remained shallow, as though she were waiting for it to begin all over again: the sound of the piano, the unnatural cold, the sense of another.

A barge moved slowly downriver, sounding its horn as it cleared the Brooklyn Bridge. "The last time I was here was on Zoey's twelfth birthday," Kit said. "She invited three of her friends. We went out for lunch here on the pier. Then she insisted on going to the 9/11 Memorial. I was dead against it, but it was her birthday, and I really couldn't say no."

"So did you go?"

"Zoey stood there and said to her friends, 'This is where my dad died,' and I burst into tears. Made a real scene, people staring at me, turning away in embarrassment. And then I felt this weird sense of peace. Like going down there and actually standing at what would have been the base of the North Tower somehow brought me closer to Peter. I've gone a few times since alone. Just to think and remember. And avoid the souvenir sellers."

He put a hand on her back. "I'm glad it turned out okay for you," he said, and again tears began to well in her eyes. She laughed a little as she wiped them away.

They made their way to the restaurant, a few minutes' walk from there. Though it was crowded that night, David had made reservations. Once they were seated outside on the terrace and had ordered drinks, she asked if he and his wife had had any children. It occurred to her that she had no idea who he really was, while she'd been telling him almost everything about herself.

"We'd planned on it. I mean, we talked about it, not a lot, but every once in a while, you know. She wanted five kids. She grew up with four siblings, so I guess she wanted to copy that. I told her it was four too many. So we went back and forth and settled on three." He paused and looked away. "Figured I'd talk her down to two. But she died before we could even have one."

She put her hand on his. "I'm so sorry, David. I am, really."

The waiter brought their drinks.

"By the way," he said, "I went back in the files and looked up that incident your daughter witnessed at the Columbia station three years ago. Looks like the victim suffered from depression and was under treatment by a psychiatrist, and it was concluded that she'd committed suicide. So"—he opened his hands—"case closed."

He lifted his glass to her. "Cheers."

"It's good to see you again, David," she said, and he reached over and brushed his fingers lightly along her cheek.

"So what's been happening with you?" he said.

"I've been busy. Oh... Before I forget, that lawyer, the woman you referred to me—?"

"Leslie Palmer. Right. Yeah, she was really happy with her session with you. I don't know what it was about, who she wanted to connect with, but she said she was really, really pleased."

Kit still didn't understand the connection between the two of them. Had this Leslie Palmer approached David? Or had he set it all up?

She looked out the window, then back at him. "And then there was this mother. Her son went missing at his summer camp."

When she described what she'd seen, it caught David's attention, as she knew it would. No cop ever passes up hearing about an unsolved crime.

"So, basically, you viewed a crime scene?"

"All I know is that it was some sort of basement or cellar and it was obvious someone had been there."

The pyramid of shoes and piles of clothes had really gotten to her. Trophies of someone's obsession. Souvenirs of the darkness.

"Something terrible happened there, and whatever it was, it hung in the air like a fog. You could taste it. Feel it. You just couldn't see it. A long-ago memory that refuses to disappear. Like a photo that doesn't fade."

He looked at her for a long moment. "When did this happen?"

"A few days ago—"

"I mean what you were seeing."

"According to the mother it was over twenty years ago. She thought he might still be alive. But the boy was already dead. He was buried in the woods near a lake. Because that's where I was next. I could feel a breeze coming up from the lake. I could see hills in the background—"

"It was that real?"

"I was *there*, David. I saw the leaves floating to the ground. The whole area was carpeted with them. It was one of the most peaceful places I'd ever been to. And when I knelt and touched the ground it felt warm to me. Not the warmth of grass in the sun, but some kind of deeper warmth."

"Dead bodies are cold."

"But I was feeling some kind of life there, as though something remained of him. And all of it seemed natural to me. Not scary at all, as if I were meant to be there. And nothing could touch me, nothing could hurt me. I was there and not there. I was safe."

"Did you report what you saw to the authorities wherever this was?"

She shook her head. "I had no idea where it was, and, anyway, what's the point? I'm not a private eye, I'm a medium. They wouldn't take anything I say seriously—"

"Not always true. Usually police departments won't rely on psychics, but sometimes investigation units listen to what they have to say. Especially if a case has gone cold." He smiled. "Hey, I watch cop shows, too, you know."

"And the boy's mother suffers from Alzheimer's. A shrink from the facility where she lives told me they know nothing about a son, or even if she had one. They think she's delusional."

"But you saw him—"

"No. I saw *something*. It isn't the same thing." She sipped her drink. "But there have been other things that've happened to me. Weird things. Things I also can't explain."

She told him about the piano, and the audition video that had somehow vanished.

"And then there was this voice message. I'd been hearing this crying woman, especially when I'm with a client. They don't hear it, but I do."

Now he just stared at her. He opened his hands. "The voice was the same?"

"Exactly the same."

"Can I hear it?"

She had to laugh. "The message? That disappeared, too. It was there, I listened to it a few times, and when I went to play it again, it was gone."

He narrowed his eyes. "So only you heard it."

"Well, yeah. But it was there, I heard it, I played it."

"And now it's just...gone?"

She could read his look. *Crazy.*

"These things ever happen to you before?" he asked. "Mysterious sounds in the night, a phone message that erased itself...?"

"No. Never."

For some reason she felt embarrassed by it all. Shamed by his look of mild disbelief. As though she were a child again, making one dumb mistake after another.

"And you live alone," he said.

"What are you saying, David?"

But she knew what he was saying. No one else had witnessed these things. No one else could vouch for her. There was just Kit among the invisible, her word against the truth.

41

THE WAITER WANDERED OVER TO RECITE THE SPE-cials. They hadn't yet opened their menus.

"Actually," David said, "I think we'd like another round of drinks before we order."

"So let's have it out before we even think about dinner," she said. "When do you intend to arrest me, after dessert? Otherwise we can just get it over with now." She held her wrists together, ready to be cuffed.

"Okay, look."

"You aren't really interested in me for who I am. You're just interested in bringing me to the station and booking me, like in the movies—fingerprints, mug shots, and all. Round one goes to me just for knowing stuff like that. Like you said, everyone watches cop shows. And, to be honest, I really enjoyed costarring with you. But it's looking like a limited series, isn't it."

"All right… I'm a detective with the Special Frauds Squad. Yes, we became aware of your work through what we've heard people say on the web. Everyone thinks you're good at the game, everyone thinks you're real. But there really aren't any genuine mediums, are there."

"Not in your world there aren't," she said. "There it's just the good guys and the bad guys. Except you leave out the big gray area between them."

"That's where you operate."

"It's a lot more interesting there. Might want to pay a visit someday."

He laughed. "I don't know when you're being serious or when you're just screwing with my head."

She lifted her glass. "Just keeping you on your toes." And she took another sip of her drink. "So what's your interest in me, really?"

He took a long, deep breath. "Honestly? When my partner and I first heard about you, we thought we'd landed a good one. They're always on our backs down at the office. Especially as all of a sudden there are a lot of so-called psychics out there. More than usual. When times are bad, when people don't know what's going to happen next, it's these scam artists who take advantage and drain them of their life savings. We've seen lonely seventy-year-old widows with nothing left in their bank accounts and a dresser covered in trinkets and spells they were talked into buying. But with you, we don't have a real case. You don't ask for money, not directly. You don't promise anything, you don't sell anything, and you don't grab people off the street. You know your way around the law. And that's kind of admirable in a strange way."

The waiter appeared. He clearly didn't have the patience to be put off again. "We'll be closing soon," he said.

"What's soon?" Kit asked.

"Two hours." The waiter looked as grim-faced as when he had first come to their table.

"Guess we'd better order, then," David said.

Once they were alone, she spoke slowly and clearly, looking him straight in the eye. "Let me be clear with you, David. If we're honest with each other, if we can each respect what the other does, we'll get along really well. But here's the thing. This woman—this voice... She's reaching out to me for a reason..."

He shrugged. "Like what?"

Kit sat back and fixed him with a look. "If I knew that I'd tell you, David. But let's talk about the cop investigating me, Tony Cabrini. I'd bet money he's your partner."

Now it was her turn to wait. She had all the time in the world.

42

WITHOUT HESITATION DAVID SAID, "LOOK. Tony's a good guy, but he's desperate to close the deal on an arrest. He's hungry to move up."

"So I'm the proverbial sitting duck."

He nodded. "In his eyes you are. He's kind of impulsive. He's a little obsessed with arresting you. As his partner, I can deal with him, I can make sure he doesn't bother you again. You have my word on that."

"So he's been aiming for entrapment. Which could cost him his job, right, since that's illegal?"

He smiled. "How do you know all this stuff?"

"Because, as you probably already found out, my day job is acting. Stage work, mostly, a little TV. I had a small role in an HBO detective series three years ago. Working undercover. Couple of scenes, a few dozen lines, entrapment galore, here one minute, gone the next. Just like half the cast who ended up in bayous and woods. They found most of my body in the fourth episode, decomposing in a swamp. They found my head next to a six-pack in a guy's refrigerator in episode six."

"Looks like they managed to put you back together pretty well."

"So the bottom line is, what, you'll protect me from this guy?"

"I really can't act on this just because of your intuition. You need solid evidence. Some way of proving he's overstepping his bounds as a detective."

"I just want to be sure that partner of yours leaves me alone."

She could see him assessing what this meant to him. "I'll absolutely do what I can," he said. "As long as it's within the law. On the plus side, you have a police detective looking after you." He smiled a little. "That would be me."

She looked at him for several seconds. "Were you ever going to tell me you're a cop?"

"You tell people you're a cop, and they're already half out the door," he said. "But you'd already figured me all out. You're not bothered though, I guess."

"If I were, I wouldn't be here with you."

"Look. I like you, Kit. I mean, I *really* like you."

"It's just that since my husband's death, I've had some pretty miserable experiences with men. Men who lied to me, guys who hurt me, and trust really does have to be earned—"

"I know that—"

"And if you want to continue with this, if you want to turn this into a relationship, you have to be completely open with me. So I need to know... Are you seeing anyone else right now?"

"Why do you ask?"

"Because Louis—you know, the bartender at the place where we met—mentioned that he'd seen you with some woman there."

He laughed. "Maggie, you mean? Maggie Fergusson? She's an old friend from the Baltimore FBI office, in for a few days advising us on a case we're dealing with. Anyway, you can't be jealous of Mags. She's already spoken for. By her wife."

"Sorry. But I just wanted to be sure I wasn't going to get in too deep and end up in a bad place. It's just...I'm still a little fragile, especially now with all of my money worries. Please just be patient with me. Meaning don't rush me."

"I won't. And if this woman who keeps telling you things bothers you again, let me know, okay?"

She laughed. "What're you going to do, arrest a disembodied voice?"

He said, "It kind of concerns me. What you're going through. Hearing things. Seeing things. I'm just wondering if maybe you should slow down with the dead people thing."

"So you don't want to see if you can communicate with Caroline?"

"Soon. When I'm feeling up to it. Before I forget...let me give you my cell number."

She entered it into her phone: *David Brier*. As though making him official.

The waiter brought their meals and they made small talk as they ate.

After their meal, she excused herself and walked to the ladies' room.

She pushed open the door to find herself alone. Now she could feel the effects of two martinis, one more than she should have had. That had never ended well before, so clearly she felt she had to give it another try, with the same lousy result. She went to a sink and washed her hands and dabbed water on her face, turning off the water as she looked up to see a woman, her face in shadow, standing a few feet behind her, a hand extended toward her as though in invitation.

Kit said, "Hello? Can I help you?"

When she turned to see who it was, the figure was no longer there.

She hadn't heard anyone come in. And all the stall doors had been open. The door swung open and one of the waitresses walked in.

"Is there a Kate here?" she said, and Kit said, "Do you mean Kit?"

"I guess. The guy you were with was worried about you." She looked as if she had expected to find Kit passed out on the floor, a syringe in her arm.

"There was a woman here... I think she needed help."

The waitress looked around. "It's just you. Your friend asked me to see if you were okay."

"I only just walked in a minute ago."

"He said it was like fifteen, twenty minutes."

"He said that...?" The woman nodded. "I don't understand. I came in to splash water on my face and brush my hair and—"

"It's what he said."

Jesus... "I'm fine. Tell him I'll be right out."

I'm really, really stinking miserably drunk. What had she been doing in there? How had she become lost in time?

She needed coffee. She needed to go home and get some sleep, she needed to wake up and forget it all, she needed to be anywhere but there, on a sloppy, boozy date with a man she liked too much for her own good. Because every time that happened, someone would die or turn on her, or vanish like a ghost into the ether.

She looked again in the mirror as she dried her hands. No one. Just herself.

David stood as Kit made her tipsy way back to the table. "Everything okay?"

"Apart from me being a little drunk? Sorry I was so long. I thought I was only in there for a few minutes. I'm still trying to figure that one out."

"I was worried about you."

"I'm okay now." She conjured up a crooked smile.

"Come on, let's get out of here." He took out his phone to order an Uber. "There's a driver just up the street."

Distant thunder, and the air grew electric, crackling, chemical, the ozone sky a deep charcoal.

A white Kia pulled up just as the rain began to fall in torrents. David told the driver to take Kit home first. "I live about fifteen minutes from there," he said.

The driver was unusually quiet, and when Kit looked at his rearview mirror from the back seat, she could see his eyes shift to take her in. She looked away, then back, and his gaze was again meeting hers, almost insistently, as if he'd seen her before and was trying to think where. She reached over and took David's hand. "I really enjoyed myself tonight. Thank you for that. And for being honest. And I'm sorry I took so long."

"I'm just glad you're okay. I'd like to do it again."

She smiled at him. "Me too."

They made it to her building in just over thirty minutes. "It's the one on the right," she said.

Before getting out, David turned his head to kiss her. "Come up with me?" she whispered in his ear.

"I can't, Kit."

"Just for a little while?"

Once again the driver was staring at her reflection, narrowing his eyes as though trying to tell her something.

"Let's save it for another night. When we're both a little more sober."

She smiled and squeezed his hand. "You're right. And thanks."

He leaned over and kissed her again, lightly, lips to lips. Finally, she felt alive again.

And she didn't trust him for a moment.

43

FIRST THE SUMMONING, THEN THE UNFOLDING.
She let herself in, switching on the lights as she went from room to room.

When she came into the living room, she stopped and stared. The keyboard lid was open, and on the rack was some sheet music. She stepped closer. It was Beethoven's *Moonlight* sonata. That hadn't been there before. It hadn't been *anywhere*. Zoey still hadn't reached that level of playing when she fell into her coma.

She looked around. "Is someone here?"

She thought, *This is crazy*. It was as if someone had been in there, played the piano, and walked away.

When she turned on the light in Zoey's room, the temperature dropped precipitously and she began to shiver. Although Kit had closed it the last time she found it open, Zoey's closet was now open. Once again, the drawer of her nightstand was also open, not an inch like last time, but halfway.

Kit looked in the drawer, then stopped dead when she saw it.

She closed the drawer, took a breath, opened it again. As if it were a magic trick. Close your eyes and it's gone. Wake up and it was all a dream.

But it wasn't something she imagined or saw in her sleep.

She picked up the single earring, a diamond stud, and turned on the bedside lamp for a closer look. Zoey had never had her ears pierced. And what had been in the drawer before—the earbuds, the gum, the photo of Kit and Peter—was no longer there.

She looked over at the open closet. Instead of the clothes of a teenage daughter, they were items she'd never seen there, clothes that had to belong to someone older.

It was as though she'd walked into someone else's apartment, or as if the previous tenants, the Frenchman and the wife who heard voices and went mad, had never left. She stepped back and looked around at the walls. Most of the posters Zoey had put up had been replaced with framed prints and photos of people and places Kit couldn't recognize. She felt like a trespasser in her own home.

"Enough," she said loudly. "I'm done with you." She turned off the light and shut the door.

44

K IT WOKE SUDDENLY, AS IF SOMEONE HAD LOUDLY called her name, and it was as abrupt as a slap across her face.

The bedside clock read 2:03 a.m., and now, *click*, it was 2:04, dead silent in the apartment. Hours had gone by since she'd passed out on her bed. Now something had awakened her, a shout in the street or a police siren.

She rolled onto her back, stretched her legs, and closed her eyes. Her head ached, though not unpleasantly. *Hangover*, she guessed. She would pay for her boozy night in the morning.

Tomorrow she would visit Zoey. She would talk to her daughter, she would speak all the words she'd been saying for three years, the same hopes and wishes and bits of unimportant news, to the point where it had seemed to have run out of its own usefulness.

When the weather was warm, in the spring and summer, after spending time with Zoey she would cross over Fifth Avenue into the park and follow the path. Same path, same crows, same routine: as though she were walking into her own past. It was all beginning to feel like a ritual, a miscellany of obscure gestures and words, a form of magic, its ultimate meaning beyond her grasp, the trick never completed. One day she would complete the maze, she thought; one day she'd reach the end.

She breathed steadily, sensing her heartbeat slowing, waiting for sleep to embrace her once more. And now she heard it, a shifting of the silence, a whisper in the darkness.

She opened her eyes to a figure standing at the foot of her bed, its head slightly bowed, its face unseen. More a shadow than a person.

I miss you...it seemed to whisper. *I miss you so much*...

And now it put its hands to its face, as though to weep.

"David...?" she whispered, and when the intruder didn't move Kit cried out, though it was more an exhalation, a sharp expression of breath, and still the figure remained there.

This is not happening, she thought. *I will not believe a moment of it.*

She closed her eyes and tried to think of anything but this, random things, banal things, honest memories, better times, and she wondered if this manifestation in her room could read her mind, back away, and vanish. And when she next opened her eyes, it was to the gray uncertain morning light and a day like no other.

45

BEFORE HER SHOWER, BEFORE THE ADVIL HER head was begging for, before coffee and the routine of the obituaries and memorial notices and the red pen, she called his cell.

"David Brier."

He actually sounded like a detective, all business and just the facts.

"Hi," she said as brightly as she could on this ragged morning. She looked out her bedroom window: the rain had started to taper off, and already she could see a few scattered patches of blue in the sky where the clouds had begun to tear away.

"Hi?" He seemed to have no idea who the caller was.

She could hear voices or a voice in the background, and then a shift as he must have walked the phone out of the room. "Yes?" he said.

"It's Kit. Remember? Dinner, drinks...?"

There was a lengthy pause. "Look, I'm sorry, but who is this?"

"Dinner at the Seaport?"

"And when was this?"

She couldn't believe what she was hearing. It was David's voice, or at least it sounded like him. She said, "Maybe I have the wrong number." She apologized, he said nothing, and she clicked off.

When she tried it again a moment later, she was sent to voicemail. *David's* voicemail. "Hi, I don't understand what's happening, but—" She ended the message. Something had gone wrong. Or was this what they called ghosting…?

She looked at the screen: *David Brier.*

It was no wrong number.

She had become the stranger.

She tried to rerun the night before in her mind. They'd arrived at her building at just past ten. She remembered the curious way the driver looked at her, and David's smile through the window as she turned to wave from the door of her building. A sequence of details that remained crisply defined amid all the cloudiness, like a series of steps that would lead to an answer. Then something else came to her: there was nothing on the car—no decal or other markings—that indicated it actually was an Uber. He'd only been up the street, David said, and by the time they left the restaurant he was there, idling by the curb.

It meant nothing, obviously, a matter of perception. Just like her seeing things that hadn't been there before. Zoey's room: the earring, the closet full of someone else's clothes, the missing posters.

She checked the apartment door. She hadn't locked it, and the chain was off. And when she walked into the living room, the keyboard lid was down, the music rack empty.

She opened Zoey's nightstand drawer. Half a pack of gum. Earbuds. A crumpled tissue. The photo of Kit and Peter.

Nothing else. In the closet the clothes were all Zoey's: her jeans, a few skirts, the black dress she wore for recitals, what she had been wearing the night she'd fallen into a coma—everything as it had been three years earlier.

There was no point in talking to Jackie. No use in trying to appeal to logic and common sense. Kit knew what was happening. She'd seen it all before.

46

TONY CABRINI WAS ALREADY WINDED BY THE TIME he reached the first landing in his apartment house. He wondered what he'd be like when he turned sixty-two, the same age his father was when he dropped dead behind the wheel of a crosstown bus. A hell of a joyride, Tony sometimes thought, picturing the bus careening into parked cars and delivery trucks as it made its way west on Fourteenth Street. The cops thought he'd been drinking and had passed out. Instead they found a corpse slumped over the wheel and 122 stunned passengers wondering what had just happened. One day Tony would take a bus ride himself, and there wouldn't be a return trip.

He steadied himself for a few moments, his hand on the railing, before going on to conquer the next flight. When he looked up, Connie was already outside their apartment door, peering down at him.

"What?" he said.

"C'mon up and I'll break it to you gently."

She was already inside the apartment when he got to the door.

"We got a problem," she said. "Too bad you weren't around to do anything about it. Now it's too late."

"Hey. It wasn't my idea I had to work on a Saturday."

"Your partner, too?"

"He had a day off."

"So you could spend it behind a desk thinking up ways of arresting crazy ladies with crystal balls while he's off playing golf or something?"

"Dave doesn't play golf."

"You know what I mean."

But he knew what Dave was doing, and he pictured him riding the elevator up to Kit Capriol's floor.

He sat at the kitchen table. The day had turned hot, and no one had reminded the evening to turn it down. Connie had brought the window fan, the noisy one he'd never bothered to replace, to the kitchen. He closed his eyes and felt the hot city air and a whiff of garbage wash over him.

"They turned off the gas," she said. "I can't cook. I can't even take a hot shower."

"It's too hot for a hot shower."

"You want to take a cold one? Be my guest. You wouldn't last three seconds in that."

"Didn't you pay last month's bill?" he asked.

"I thought you did... Jesus... Know what? Frankie and I are gonna spend the night at my sister's. You want to eat? Go get a couple slices of pizza or something. I don't care what you do. Just pay the bill, for chrissakes."

He stared at her until she stopped staring back. He walked out the door and she slammed it shut behind him.

47

DINNER WAS THE LAST THING ON TONY'S MIND. He headed to Angelo's, a few streets away from their place. The bartender that night was the usual guy, Sal.

"Place is dead," Tony observed. A Mets game, the sound muted, was on the TV. The jukebox hadn't been fed. And the only other customer, at the end of the bar, looked like he was going to walk out and kill himself after he finished his beer. *Maybe he'd take out a few people first*, Tony thought, and laughed a little at the notion.

"Give it time, Tony," the bartender said, opening his hands. "It'll get busy. Hey, it's Saturday, right? Having the usual?"

"Bud and a shot. Make it two of each to start with."

"Tough day in the naked city?" Sal asked.

"Sat on my ass, mostly. Homicide had all the business."

Sal set down Tony's beer and his shot. "Yeah, I heard something about that. What was it, a block party in Queens and someone got goofy with his six-shooter?"

"Five people," Tony said. "Just another day in a city with eight million stories."

"Nine, Tony. Nine million. Keeps growing exponentially. See? They already made up for the five people that were lost today."

Tony threw the bourbon down his throat and laughed. "Anyway, what's a million between friends, huh?"

Other customers began to drift in over the next half hour, all regulars. Tony was on his fourth round. He watched the game for a little while, then grew bored as the Mets were down six-one at the bottom of the fourth. "One more," he said, "then I'll call it a night."

"You driving?" Sal asked.

"You crazy?"

He had places to go, things to do, lives to interfere with. After he paid his tab, he took the five-minute walk to the subway. He felt more than a little drunk, pleasantly numb. And deeply pissed off. It seemed that every step he made or decision he'd arrived at led to nothing but Dave coming up with something better. Or that he liked more.

The subway platform wasn't as busy as it usually was at this hour. He stood back and waited for the train. And that's when he saw her.

She was too close to the edge of the platform, just on the yellow line, distracted by her phone and whatever she was listening to through her earbuds, and as a train began to approach, he quickly crossed the platform, grabbed hold of her arm, and as she jerked away toward the tracks, he pulled her back just as the train pulled in. One more step and she would have been under the wheels.

He displayed his shield as she glared at him. He said, "I'm a police officer. You were standing too close. You were lucky this time. From now on, stay well back behind the yellow line."

Next time, he thought. But he wouldn't be there to save her.

48

AFTER RETURNING FROM THE HOSPITAL AT THREE in the afternoon, Kit lay down for an intended few minutes that turned into hours of a profound and dreamless sleep. Slowly and reluctantly rising out of it was like surfacing through murky water, resistant and viscous, and when she blinked herself awake, she turned her head to look at the digital display on her bedside clock: 8:03 p.m. Now 8:04.

With no plans to fulfill, no one to see that night, she closed her eyes again. Five hours gone. Five hours shot to hell. As if she had had other things to do. No auditions. No clients until two days later. No messages from David. What had she missed? Five hours when she simply ceased to exist in her world.

She drifted back into sleep until an hour later, at nine, when she was woken by someone playing the opening of Beethoven's *Moonlight* sonata, over and over, and then in frustration smashing the keys before starting over again.

She walked warily to the entrance to the room. She was no longer afraid, as though everything that had been happening, that was happening, and would happen in the future had become perfectly normal. As though she were in that world and not her own.

Her back to Kit, the woman at the piano continued to play

the same measures, one time, two times, then again. Kit whispered, "Zoey..." and when her daughter began to turn, the tiny diamond in her left ear catching the light, someone began knocking on the apartment door and Zoey faded into nothing.

Kit could barely catch her breath. "Who is it?"

"David. It's David." A quiet voice, a hallway voice.

She leaned against the wall, thought for a moment, then let him in.

"I was in the neighborhood." He looked curiously at her. "You okay?"

She took a step back. Something about it seemed completely off. "I don't understand..."

"Someone was walking out when I was on my way in. It's why I didn't buzz first. I think I left my watch here earlier tonight."

She looked at him. "Watch?" She had no idea what he was talking about. Her eyes went to his left wrist: no watch where there usually was one.

"Remember?" He laughed. "Couple of hours ago? I dropped in at seven, ten past, whatever. I wanted to surprise you, and we ended up in your bed. Let me go check." He walked into the bedroom and came back with his watch in his hand. "I knew I'd left it on the floor." He strapped it on his wrist.

She remembered none of it. "But I was sleeping the whole time."

"Not quite the word I'd use," and he laughed again.

"I came back from seeing Zoey, and then I was just too tired to keep my eyes open." She couldn't understand how something like this could have happened—again—without her remembering any of it. Was she genuinely losing her mind? How had she lost such a significant patch of time?

And then the matter of the call. She accessed the directory in her phone and showed him the entry. "Is that your number?"

"It's the one I gave you."

"When I called you and you answered, you didn't seem to know who I was."

"I couldn't talk at that moment."

"You couldn't just tell me that?"

"It would have been...difficult. Awkward. I'm sorry."

"Sure of that? Because it sounded as if you had no idea who I was."

"Just bad timing. I'm sorry, it's been a crazy week."

She told him about the piano being played. "A piece Zoey was looking forward to learning. She was here last night, David. She was at the piano, practicing."

"But you'd seen her at the hospital."

There was no point in trying to make sense of it.

"Did you try to record any of it on your phone?"

She shook her head. "No."

"So maybe you only imagined it?"

She sat at the kitchen table. "But I saw her, David. She was...different. Older, maybe. She was playing the opening over and over again, and then she turned to say something to me when you knocked." She heard exactly what she was saying; she knew what she had to say next. "And then she wasn't there."

She put her head in her hands. It seemed impossible to her, blanking out whole blocks of time, something she'd never done before. Was she going mad again, just as she thought she'd had after Peter's death?

He sat beside her on the sofa. "Look... I'm a cop, I deal in hard evidence. I'm not saying you're wrong or lying. I'm just suggesting that without any solid proof it may have all just been dreamed. Or imagined."

She knew what he was implying: *Or just made up.*

She reached for his hand. "Maybe you're right. It's been rough for me for too long. And I've been alone for most of that time. Maybe I'm just going a little stir-crazy here."

"You may have finally ended up spooking yourself with your séances."

She smiled. "Maybe I just need to get out a little more."

"Any chance I can get that session with you? Your grand finale, since you're thinking of giving it up?"

"Caroline?" she said. "I can try, I suppose."

"Now?"

She laughed. "With me like this? There's got to be preparation. I like to dress properly—it's kind of a formal procedure. I have to get the room in order. Spend time beforehand composing myself."

Finding my center: it was what she used to say to impress a certain type of client.

He put his hands on the table. "So when?"

"Choose a day and time. I'll let you know if I'm free."

She wondered how she was going to fake this one. She knew nothing about his wife other than her name. There was no obituary, no reference to anyone with her name remotely her age. But she knew from experience that people grieve in similar ways. They remember little things, the defining details others would have missed. A certain look at a particular time, a gesture that aroused one's attention, the words that carried meaning only for the other. The way to do it, she'd come to learn, was to summon the spirit, claim she was in the room with it, and that alone would disrupt the sitter's way of thinking. *She's right next to me. I can touch her hand.* It was a subtle form of seduction, a gradual chipping away at doubt, until the light in the client's eyes sparked with acceptance, mirroring her own. And then the vocabulary of the afterlife would pour out of them, this one-sided conversation with the past. *I miss you. I love you. I think of you always.*

Once a connection was made, it was rare for a client not to return a second or third time. Everything depended on the machinery of the con.

"How long does one of these séances even take?"

"I prefer to call them consultations. All depends on how successful I am in reaching the subject. Sometimes it's over in fifteen or twenty minutes, sometimes it takes an hour. It's all about how receptive the sitter and I both are. Like a magnet— the more powerful it is, the better it draws things to it."

"And then I'll pay you."

"I told you… I don't ask for anything, and the first session is always free. After that it's a matter of donations. In your case, though, there'll be no charge, of course."

He sat back and looked at her. "So people actually do come back."

"Almost always. They have things to tell the person they've survived. For them, life has moved on—"

"Do the dead ever answer?"

"Almost always."

He looked at her. "Now you're scaring me."

"And then, when our lives are coming to an end, the voices begin to fade, memory starts to wear down. And they wait for us to join them. Patiently. They have all the time in the world, don't they."

He gazed at her. "That's also a little spooky for me."

"We don't see it that way."

"'We' meaning—"

"The spirits and I."

He laughed again. "Okay, I'm starting to feel a little creeped out. See you tomorrow." And he kissed her.

She saw him to the door, and when she heard the elevator descending, she put on the chain. She went to the fridge, found nothing worthwhile, unless week-old iridescent roast beef counted as edible. She put on her shoes and jacket, grabbed her bag, and headed up to the bar for something to eat.

And that's when she saw him.

49

HE'S THERE, JUST WAITING FOR HIS MOMENT ON A night thick with cloud, a time of something impending, gathering, swelling, preparing. She can taste it in the air; she can feel it crawling beneath her skin, between an itch and a burn. She doesn't know what time it will be or how it will be done, but she knows it's here. All dying people and animals go to ground, bide their time, close their eyes against the encroaching darkness. And so would she.

He crossed the street and came up beside her like an unshakable bad memory. She kept her head down and her feet moving.

"Hey, it's me...Tony, right? Tony DeLuca? I was on my way to see if you were free to talk. Then I saw Dave leaving, and I figured you'd be—"

"Yeah, well, I'm not seeing clients tonight. So please go away. I don't want to be disturbed right now."

She took out her phone as she sped up ahead of him, and clicked on David's number. It went straight to voicemail—

"It's Kit. He's back—Tony—and I think he's drunk and—"

Once again he was alongside her. Without ending the call, she held tightly to the phone. She wanted Dave to hear it all.

"I have to talk to you," Cabrini said. "It's important."

"Make an appointment for another time."

He grabbed her arm to make her stop, and she turned on him. "Take your hand off of me."

The man stank of drink, his eyes watery and wandering in the streetlight. He found his nerve in the bottle, just as she sometimes did. At another time she might feel sorry for him. Just not now.

"I'm not leaving till I finish my business with you," he said.

"I'm not seeing any clients, especially on a Saturday night without an appointment. So why don't you go home, sober up, and get some sleep. And leave me the fuck alone. Got it?"

He seemed to find this amusing. "As a cop I could bring you in right now."

"On what charges? Using a naughty word?"

"Resisting arrest."

It was almost too laughable to believe. "But you haven't charged me with anything. And we're on a city street, people are out walking. It won't look so great for New York's finest if you make a drunken scene with me. So goodbye, Detective. Leave me alone and save your career, okay?"

But he kept pace with her. She caught a glimpse through the window of Louis behind the bar and kept walking north on Broadway. She felt as if she were on the losing end of a hostage crisis.

He said, "Five minutes of your time, it's all I'm asking for."

"I can't do that now, Detective Cabrini. Call to see when I'll be available. And then we can talk."

Anything to send the guy away.

"Listen to me. It's one thing being a fake medium. A whole

other story when the medium's fucking over 9/11 survivors and Gold Star families. I'm right, aren't I. If it gets to trial, the jury's gonna hate your guts, big time. Especially here in New York." Now he was shouting for all the world to hear. "And there's something else you should know. My partner—Dave Brier? Bet you fell hard for him, didn't you. He's been playing you the whole time. This is a game you cannot win, lady."

She stopped to confront him. "You came to me, I provided the service you asked for, and we were done. I never once asked for your money. Sounds like you got the better end of the deal. Considering that Angela DeLuca has nothing to do with you."

"That's why I'm here. See?" And he held up some folded bills. "Take it. Put it in your hand. Make this work for me."

"I can just as easily report you to the police, can't I. Last I looked, bribery was against the law."

She kept walking north on Broadway. She was only a block away from the subway station. She'd take a train, get off after a few stops, and return to the apartment. But he kept walking alongside her. "This is the deal," he said, then he seemed to be running out of breath, and his words tumbled out. "I'll take you down to the station, book you. They won't lock you up if you can meet the bail. It won't be a lot. First offense? You'll get off easy with probation and a fine. But I need this, and when I get my promotion and I'm back on my feet, I'll make sure no one bothers you again about what you do. That's fair payment, isn't it?"

"So I take the fall and earn a police record for you getting a promotion, is that it?"

"You help me, I help you."

"Then bring me in. You'll regret ever getting into my life, Detective. I can play my role better than you think I can. But I can get any number of people who'll vouch for what I do. And will say it's legit. Like the Irishwoman you sent to me."

He laughed a bit crazily. "What, Brigid? She's dead," and Kit slowed down and looked at him.

"They found her body after a neighbor reported a bad smell. They say she'd been dead in her apartment for almost a week. So forget about witnesses to back you up. None of the living ones will risk the embarrassment in testifying at a trial. Threaten me all you like, but you're screwed, lady. Just remember that I can make it a lot easier for you."

She thought of Brigid sitting on her sofa, a woman at the end of her life just wanting to reconnect with her long-dead child. She thought of her tears when she heard the voice of the daughter who'd drowned.

And Kit began to run, just like she did most mornings when fleeing from her memories. A UPS truck was barreling down 115th Street, the lights were against her, she paused a moment and then ran across the street as the vehicle was upon her, its horn blaring, nearly getting herself killed when for a moment she seemed about to stumble. When she reached the other side, she looked over her shoulder to see Tony waiting on the corner to cross.

In two minutes she was on the subway platform. Oblivious passengers checked their phones, lost in a world of LOLs and emojis.

When she looked back, she saw him walking onto the

platform, looking for her. She edged her way closer to the yellow line, and now she could hear it, she could feel it rising up through her legs, an approaching train, when she turned to see him pushing his way through the others toward her.

Please hurry, she thought, *please let me get away, let me save myself.* Now he was trying to grab her arm, and the heat and noise of it, the screech of brakes as the train began to pull up to the platform was the last thing she remembered, the heat and the noise.

And then it was over, except for the screaming.

50

SHE LOOKED UP AT THE POLICEWOMAN FROM A bench at the back of the platform. "What did you say?"

The platform was noisy with people shouting back and forth and the squawk of police radios. A group of firefighters and EMTs joined the uniforms and plainclothes cops as they looked down at the tracks, a few of them talking into their cell phones, while the driver of the train was sitting on the platform, holding his head and rocking back and forth, inconsolable.

"I asked if you were okay, miss," the policewoman said.

"What happened?"

"You don't know?"

Kit shook her head. There was a commotion by the tracks, and the officer turned to it. She said loudly, "Are you bringing him up now? Because if you are, I'm taking this lady right out of here before she has to see it."

"We'll let you know," someone said, and she turned back to Kit. "You definitely do not want to hang around for act two of this thing. Anyway, what was I saying just before?"

"I don't remember."

"Oh yeah... I asked your name."

"Kit Capriol," she said, spelling it out, and the policewoman nodded and made a note of it in her pad. "What happened here?" Kit asked.

"You said 'Kit'? That short for something? Or a nickname, maybe? Because I need a legal name, the whole deal, name, address, everything."

"Catherine." It was as if she were speaking of a woman she barely knew or had forgotten. "I've been called Kit for most of my life." She gave the woman her address and then her phone number.

"That's the best one to reach you at?"

Kit looked up at her. "It's the only one."

The woman wrote it down and closed her pad. "Consider yourself blessed," she said. "Because the life of Catherine Capriol could've come to a bad end about an hour ago. One day you'll tell your grandkids about this."

Kit very much doubted that. "I'm just not understanding any of this," she said.

"You really didn't see it, did you."

Kit shook her head.

"Lucky lady. Some man fell under the train just as it was pulling in." She looked over her shoulder and shook her head. "Not a pretty sight. Haven't identified him yet. There isn't a lot to work with down there."

Kit could still see Cabrini beside her, desperate to make the grade. She prayed he wouldn't revisit her, a ghostly voice endlessly badgering her.

"If it's the same person I'm thinking of, his name is Tony DeLuca," she said. "No, that's not his real name. He's a cop,

a detective. Cabrini," she said, suddenly remembering. "Tony
Cabrini."

"You *know* the guy? And you say, what, that he's a cop?
That sounds way out of left field."

"He's been threatening me."

The policewoman turned to the others. "Hey! I'm gonna
need someone senior to talk to this lady."

Now Kit knew it: she was on her way to becoming their
prime suspect.

51

DAVID WALKED BACK FROM THE EDGE OF THE platform. "I'll talk to her," he told the policewoman.

Kit stared at him. "When did you get here?"

"You two know each other?" the policewoman said, shaking her head as she walked away.

"After I left your place I came here to get the subway home," he said.

"So you were here when it happened?"

Someone on the tracks called for a body bag. "Better make it two. There are a lot of moving parts to this one," the guy said, and some of the cops laughed.

Funny how death becomes just another day's work, she thought. Both for the cops and for her.

"There's a detective here from the local precinct who's going to want to question you," David said. "But only if you feel up to it. You're probably in shock."

She just looked at him. "So you were here, is that what you're saying?"

"I'm guessing that Tony went after you, and he somehow ended up on the tracks. Couple of witnesses say he was pushed."

He lowered his voice and came in close. "My advice is not to mention anything about Tony—especially that you'd spoken to him, and on no account should you say anything about the séances. Tony Cabrini's a complete stranger to you, okay? I told you I'd protect you, and this is all part of it."

"Except the policewoman who was just questioning me—I told her I knew he was a cop."

He pressed his lips together. "You're going to have to stand behind that somehow."

"And you know what he was saying to me. I called you, and it went to voicemail and—"

He nodded. "Yeah, I've got most of it on my phone." He lowered his voice even further. "If that call ever got out it could be a problem for you. What you said to him could be taken as a threat."

"Because he was trying to bribe me for his own career prospects?"

"A threat's still a threat."

Once again, with David everything seemed just a little off to her, though she couldn't quite see why.

"So you'll erase it?"

"I promise I'll do everything I can to look after you."

They were joined by an older man in a yellow polo shirt, navy blazer, and khakis who identified himself as Lieutenant Woodson. She noticed a small stain on his shirt, ketchup, she guessed. Barbecue night shot to hell.

"We've got two witnesses being questioned at the moment, and you'll be the third." He looked at his pad. "Your name is Kitten?"

"Kit," she said. "Catherine," she added.

"The police officer who took your information first wrote 'Kitten.'" He shrugged. "Noisy in here," he said, looking around.

"I really didn't see anything. So I guess I'm not your best witness."

"One of the others said that you and the victim were together. That the victim was talking to you. And you told the officer that you knew the person in question. That he was a detective here in the city."

David asked the lieutenant if this was really the best place to question her.

"You know each other?"

David said, "We're friends. Can I be present at the questioning?"

"If you think it'll be useful," Woodson said. By now a number of EMTs were on the tracks in what looked like hazmat suits, masks and gloves. Woodson looked at David. "You want to ride with us?" he said, and David nodded.

The drive took all of five minutes. Woodson opened an interview room and they took seats at the table, the two men sitting across from Kit. It was just like in the movies or on TV: ugly furniture in an ugly room with bad lighting, the words *Fuck me* carved into the table. He said, "First of all, Ms. Capriol, would you like to have a lawyer present?"

"Why should I have a lawyer? I haven't done anything wrong."

Woodson made a note of that. "As with all interviews, this will be recorded. A formality, nothing more. But anything you say will be on the record, is that understood?"

She looked at him. "Am I being charged with something?"

He said nothing. She looked over at David, and his look back was blank, as if he'd never seen her before in his life.

52

WOODSON SAID, "GIVE ME AN IDEA OF THE sequence of events that led to your coming to the subway," and now David's eyes shifted to hers.

"I was out walking and this man started talking to me—"

"This man meaning—?"

"The one who died. If it was him."

"According the notes I was given, you identified him to a policewoman as a detective."

"He told me he was."

"Someone you already knew."

She paused. "Yes."

He opened his hands. "Did he say why he wanted to talk?"

"I think he'd been drinking. I really couldn't understand what he wanted from me. He kept trying to make me take his money."

The lieutenant stared at her. "So he propositioned you."

"I didn't say that. He was trying to force me to take his money."

"For…?"

"I have no idea."

Woodson said, "There's a witness who states that she saw the two of you loudly arguing on the street just before the incident."

"He was bothering me. And he wouldn't leave me alone."

He looked at his notes. "You first identified him as Tony DeLuca, is that correct?"

She nodded. "Yes."

"But according to the policewoman who questioned you, you said that wasn't his real name."

Kit said nothing. The lieutenant glanced at his notes. "The victim has been identified as Detective Anthony Cabrini, with a unit investigating fraudulent enterprises." He waited a moment. "Can I ask what you do for a profession?"

"I'm an actor."

David said, "I think the lieutenant is trying to see how Detective Cabrini and you had come to know one another."

She sat back, unsure of where David was leading her. "He had approached me before and I had turned him down."

"Approached you...why?"

Now David was looking pointedly at her. She said, "For sexual favors." It was her only way out.

"And what was your answer?"

"That I'm not a prostitute."

Woodson leaned forward. "But why would he proposition you in the first place?"

She shook her head, as though trying to rid herself of all the confusion inside it. "I don't know. Honestly...I just don't know."

"Had you seemed...inviting to him?"

She had to laugh. "Do I look inviting?"

Woodson ignored her and looked at David. "Was the victim also known to you?"

"He was my partner."

The lieutenant seemed overwhelmed by all the coincidences bouncing around the room. He laughed a little. "Why do I think there's a whole other story here?"

53

SCATTERED ACROSS DAVE BRIER'S DESK WERE photos from the forensics team: what was left of Tony Cabrini after the train had run him over, his head several feet away from what remained of his torso.

When the funeral took place, eight cops in dress blues who had never known Tony carried his coffin out of the church and to the hearse, followed by Connie and Frank Cabrini, as well as what looked like half the diocese of New York City in their robes and finery. A lone bagpiper played "Amazing Grace." David watched impassively and reminded himself to give the widow a call a few weeks later. A formality, the usual thing.

His death was being initially considered an accident, though the file remained open. A few witnesses spoke of a woman with Tony who seemed angry. There was talk of raised voices.

Other witnesses had been taking selfies on the platform at the time, and one photo that was brought to Dave's attention had caught Kit and Tony behind the smiling, shiny face of the photographer. Kit seemed to have her arm in the air, as though about to strike him.

On Dave's desk was a file labeled PROPERTY OF FEDERAL BUREAU OF INVESTIGATION, beside it a small, detailed map of the United States, a number of different cities—from Los Angeles to Palm Beach to Baltimore, Philly, and New York—having been flagged with red marker.

On his monitor was an array of mug shots and composite drawings. Only one stood out for him, a sketch sent up from the archive at the Wilmington Police Department in Delaware, though the hair color was lighter, and the woman in it wore black-framed glasses. And yet. And yet.

He looked up to find another detective in the unit, Rosie Vargas, coming toward him.

"Okay, so…" She opened her laptop so they could both view it. "I've found a couple of things I was able to put together for you over the past few days. Kit Capriol checks out as having traveled under that name primarily to Los Angeles. Auditioning for acting jobs, sometimes getting some. Her maiden name is Catherine Covell, by the way."

"Already knew that."

"Anyway, before that the only serious travel was a semester studying in London. Third year of college. Vassar. And then what looks like a honeymoon in Greece and Italy."

He nodded. Rosie found a chair and dragged it over beside Dave.

"Any priors?" he asked.

"Not even a speeding ticket. Completely clean record."

"I hear a 'but' coming."

She smiled. "There's one possible lead. Sifting through thousands of cases nationwide of fake mediums, this is the one the computer came up with. Maybe it's a long shot, but I thought I'd bring it to your attention."

She clicked to a file supplied by the Metro DC's Fraud

Unit. "They've renamed it the Financial Crimes and Cyber Unit. They're a lot less interested in psychics and a lot more concerned about identity theft."

David nodded. "Which I'd really prefer covering to what I'm doing now."

"So, speaking of identity, there was that case"—she pointed to the top half of the monitor, as two open cases were displayed at once—"which you were already told about. Anyway, I did a little more digging. An unidentified Caucasian female in her late twenties to early thirties was working the Maryland-Delaware-DC area."

"I knew about that one. I met with Maggie Fergusson from the field office in Baltimore when she was in town on bureau business. She really had nothing definite for me to use." He glanced again at the composite sketch.

"Probably because this was what, fourteen years ago—? And your person of interest is now forty-three? So she would have been twenty-nine at the time, and the statute of limitations has already kicked in. That would have been two years after Catherine and Peter Capriol were married. Here's the thing, though. Before he was hired by a restaurant in Westchester, Capriol had been working for a few different chains—Olive Garden, Chipotle, Panera—four months here, six there. He had a good reputation, a solid work record, and it was obvious he was waiting for a big break."

"Which came when Windows on the World hired him."

"Right. But before then there were sometimes several months between jobs. And that went for both of them, the cook and the actress. Lots of lean times."

Just as, David knew, there was now. A little digging had showed her seriously in arrears on most of her monthly payments—mortgage, medical bills, the credit cards she'd long ago maxed out. So resorting back to being a medium was her natural way to deal with it. It was all starting to come together for him.

Rosie clicked on another link displaying two police artist's renderings of several witnesses' descriptions. "It turned out to be a husband and wife team. They were described as young, attractive, and full of charisma. I remember reading... wait..."—she took out her pad and flipped to a page—"what one witness told the police. She said, 'She could have sold me the key to Fort Knox, and I would have paid plenty for it. She was *that* good.'"

David knew she was. She had almost—almost—sold him on her so-called gift.

He said, "You have a detailed description of the couple?"

"Nope. Apart from what a few witnesses told the artist," she said, gesturing toward the monitor. "Looks like they might have done the whole wig-and-makeup thing. Like in that TV show, the Russians, the spies—?"

"*The Americans*," he said.

"Right, right. Like I indicated on that map, the same team popped up a year later working the Palm Beach area. Bilking rich retirees missing their dead spouses. Apparently, the woman was good at working with widowers. She'd dress a little sexily, and I guess just being alone with her gave the old men a lift. A sense that someone pretty was paying attention to them." She looked at him. "Yours pretty?"

He couldn't help but smile. "Yeah. She's very attractive. Let's get back to the couple. What was the MO?"

"Right. While she was conjuring up the spirits at her hotel room—because clients always came to her—"

"How did she get away with that?"

"She told them that she'd once gone to a private home and was sexually assaulted. So she's naturally cautious."

"People bought it?"

"Wouldn't you have? Anyway, she'd be talking with dead people and the husband would be breaking into their homes. Wouldn't take anything too noticeable, like TVs or laptops. He'd go through the drawers and lift what looked valuable. Turns out a lot of these widowers kept their wives' jewelry they never bothered to check on. Said jewelry put a lot of money into the couple's pockets." She looked at him. "Where'd you say she lives?"

"Morningside Heights."

Rosie laughed a little. "Ain't cheap up there, is it."

David quickly read through the police report from the Palm Beach County Sheriff's Office. It seemed that clients became so dependent on the medium's abilities that she was sometimes able to get them to sign over their life savings to her.

Rosie went to another page in her pad. "Looking at the Capriol timeline, this whole sequence in the DC area would be just before Catherine and Peter Capriol moved out of their New Rochelle apartment. The woman in question strictly worked weekends. Like I said, it was always at a hotel."

"So traveling down from the city wouldn't have been a problem for them," Dave said.

"Three hours on Amtrak and they're ready to start work. Anyway, Catherine and Peter then moved to the co-op in Morningside Heights. By then Peter was working for Windows on the World, and the rest of it everyone knows. But here's the interesting bit. In December 2001, Catherine Capriol was admitted to a private clinic outside Hartford."

She clicked on another link, and the hospital's website appeared on the monitor. It resembled a small private college in Vermont or Ohio.

Dave looked at it. "I don't know the name."

"Loony bin," Rosie said. "But for a higher class of loony. People with depression. People who hurt themselves. Moneyed schizophrenics hearing voices." She shrugged. "Anyway, she was there till the end of January 2002. So, a little over six weeks. It's a dead end, Dave. Records there are sealed."

He slid over a pad and grabbed a pen. "Do we have a police contact?"

"Yeah, in DC. A Detective Albert Mendoza. Second-in-command of the frauds division."

"I'd like to talk to him."

"Then you'd better ask your medium. Mendoza's dead." And for some reason she laughed.

"Natural causes?" Dave asked.

"Only if you consider getting run over by a DC Metro train natural. As for Palm Beach, the detective in charge of the case retired to Nova Scotia. Long way from the palm trees and humidity." She closed the lid on her laptop and put away her pad. "Your suspect is either really, really good, or maybe just good at making us think she's really innocent. You may be in way over your head here, cowboy. She could be playing you just like she does the suckers that come to her. I wouldn't believe a word she says."

Rosie dragged her chair back to where she'd found it. "But here's the third possibility: maybe you're dead wrong and she's none of these people and not guilty of anything. Except being just a little too shrewd, maybe. Just to keep us on our toes."

54

WHEN THE PHONE RANG THE NEXT MORNING, far too early for Kit on most days, she groped around blindly on her nightstand—not the glass, not the Advil, not the book, here it is—and she managed to get out exactly half of *good morning*, mostly the second part.

There was what sounded like static, then fragments of a voice, as if the connection were breaking up, and then—

"Doing okay?" It was David.

"Yeah. I'm fine."

"You don't sound it."

"I feel half-dead, to be honest," she said.

"Look out your window."

She lifted the blind. Standing under the scaffold on the opposite sidewalk, exactly where Tony had been that night, was David in a tie and jacket, his phone to his ear. It felt less like a pleasant surprise than an intrusion. She wondered how long he'd been staring at her window while she lay in a heavy sleep, and for a moment she felt her skin prickle with something like fear.

"Thought I'd surprise you." He held up a paper bag. "Breakfast. Minus the coffee. Too tough to juggle. And then I have go to work downtown."

She wondered: at the police station he hadn't seemed to acknowledge her existence. Now he was bringing breakfast?

"I'm just going to jump in the shower," she said. "I'll put on the coffee and leave the door unlocked. Let yourself in. I'll be out in a minute."

She only remembered when she turned off the shower that she'd forgotten to unlock the door. She dried off as best she could, wrapped the towel around herself and went to the door, leaving behind a trail of wet footprints.

It was unlocked. And he was right behind her. "Hey," he said.

She turned and stared at him. "How did you get in here?"

"Guess you'd forgotten to unlock it. But..." And he held up a key.

It was like a zoom shot from a movie, meant to pull all the strands together with one simple image. Now it seemed like just another layer of a more complicated mystery.

"Sorry to have startled you like that." He put his arms around her. "That was really dumb of me."

"Where did you get that?"

"You gave it to me when I was here with you. You said you wanted me to have it." He looked at her. "Don't you remember?"

She couldn't even recall it. They'd slept together? She hadn't a single memory of it, as though it had never happened. And as for the key, she had two of them—Zoey's, a tiny grand piano still on the key chain in a dresser drawer; and a spare Kit kept in a kitchen drawer with the knives.

"It's too soon for that, David." She held her hand out, and he dropped it in her palm.

They'd known each other for almost three weeks. She'd never seen where he lived, and knew only that he was a detective whose wife had died. Yet things were moving too quickly for her, as if she'd already lost the thread of the relationship. As though there was another version of her in another timeline, bearing her name and history, living a different life in some other place, glimpsed by her only in the half sleep of three in the morning, or in a phone message that had somehow vanished.

It made her think of the first real role she had played, the one that had given her the passion to do it again and again, in a high school production of *Our Town*, as a young woman come back from the dead to revisit her youthful self: *Do any human beings ever realize life while they live it?—every, every minute?*

She was fourteen then and had puzzled over the line during the three weeks of after-school rehearsals, its meaning eluding her. She asked the drama teacher what it meant, and the woman said, "One day it will all become clear as day, as it does for Emily in the play."

"But she's dead when she says it."

And her teacher smiled in that knowing way she had.

55

KIT WENT INTO THE KITCHEN AND OPENED THE drawer where she kept the spare key. She dropped the key in and slid the drawer shut.

"Coffee's done," she said. "Pour yourself a cup while I put on some clothes."

"I've got blueberry muffins, if that's okay."

"Perfect, yes, thanks. There are plates in the cabinet above and to the right of the sink."

When he came close to kiss her, he hooked a finger in her towel and let it fall, and looked at her as for the first time.

"I was thinking that maybe if you're free, we could take a drive up the Hudson on Saturday. Might be good to get your mind off everything that's been happening to you. Good for me, as well. We can spend the night there at a great little inn I know. It's up near Storm King. Do you know the sculpture park there?"

"I've been there, yes." The coincidence struck her as odd. She remembered the photo in Zoey's drawer that she had thought was in a box in her closet. She thought of the crow, unnoticed until she had a better look at the photo in Zoey's drawer. If a flock of crows was called a murder, as Peter had said, what was a single crow?

"I'll reserve a room and a table for dinner. We'll drive back on Sunday. And we're still on for tonight, aren't we?"

Dinner at a restaurant near Lincoln Center that she'd already agreed to, and now was beginning to regret.

"Yes, of course. And the weekend trip sounds nice, David."

"It will be," he said.

Kit went into the bedroom to get dressed. She combed out her wet hair and returned to find him in the kitchen, standing over the table with her computer and research materials, along with the *Times* from the day before, with a single memorial notice circled twice. She knew exactly what he was reading.

Alison Ingalls. Lovingly remembered on what would have been her thirtieth birthday by her family, as well as colleagues at NYU's Institute of Fine Arts, where she was an assistant professor. At the time of her death Alison had been completing a study of Vermeer's *A Maid Asleep*, on display at the Metropolitan Museum of Art.

She had also printed out a paid obituary, posted in the *Times* three years earlier on a day in April. Alison came to life for her as a fleeting memory the moment she'd read it.

Ali, as she was known to everyone, is survived by her parents, Howard and Barbara Ingalls of Croton-on-Hudson, New York. Born in Cambridge, England, she came to America when her father took a teaching post at Columbia. She acquired her passion for Dutch painting when she worked as a docent at the Metropolitan

Museum of Art while also completing an art history
degree at NYU.

There was no accompanying photo. Yet Kit remembered
her as if she'd been with her only a day earlier.

In the doorway was once a man, Kit remembered hearing the
docent say when she was at the museum months after Peter's
death. Now the man was no more, painted over to become
an empty doorway in a world filled with symbols and omens.
Had the man just been drinking wine with the young woman?
Had he broken her heart, told her he was leaving for good? Or
had the woman in the painting, the maid dozing at the table,
dreamed the man, and, when the dream faded, had the artist
simply painted him out? Who was the man? Would he return?
Or was he gone forever, now just a threadbare memory in
the mind of the artist, a fleeting, wishful dream of the young
woman?

Kit felt as though her and Alison's lives were intertwined,
that some strange twist of fate had brought them together
briefly once before, and now, in death, had reunited them.
When she saw the obituary, she wondered if she and the docent
had exchanged glances, as though each knew a secret about the
other.

On a separate sheet of paper she'd written down an address
and phone number for the woman's parents.

After the usual condolences she would say: *I wanted you to
know that Alison has been in touch with me...*

Summoning her would be just like summoning herself. But
all that remained was a ghost in a doorway.

56

USUALLY IF I KNOW SOMEONE'S COMING I PUT A tablecloth over it," Kit said, startling him, and she picked up a folded cloth from one of the chairs and draped it over the table.

He said, "How long were you standing there?"

"Long enough."

"These...things on your desk—the 9/11 book, the newspapers..."

"I have to know a little something about the person I'm supposed to summon, don't I? I mean, all I know about your wife is that she liked cookies from Magnolia Bakery. You've given me very little to hang a consultation on. But that's up to you." Baked goods never led to ghosts, just a few extra pounds.

He picked up the Alison Ingalls obituary. "Why this one?"

"I'd seen her once, at the Met. Something like three or four years ago. She was giving a talk in a gallery, and something about her... I don't know what, exactly, but something she said moved me, connected with me. Maybe one day I'll know why."

She decided not to mention her sighting of what she believed was Peter.

"And you're going to, what, contact the parents?" It was

more a statement than a question. "I have to say, it's a nice little operation you have going here. The first few times we got together you really had me believing you."

But he didn't seem even mildly shocked. Was this, then, the nature of his game?

"Why stop believing me now? Like I said, I have to do some research before I can hold a consultation. Just having the name of the deceased isn't enough. I need something to show that I'm aware of what they were in life. The empathy factor," she added. "It draws them to me."

"And you're an actor."

"But I also have the gift. Sometimes it takes me to good places, peaceful places where I can reunite people with those they've lost. And sometimes it takes me to really scary places. Especially if someone's trying to tell me something. Or warn me."

"Did you look up Caroline?"

"I will soon enough," she lied. Like the man in the doorway in the painting, his wife had become like the air, painted over and invisible, leaving no trace in the world.

"Another reason I'm here is to tell you there's a problem," he said. "There's been a complaint filed against you." He looked at her. "It doesn't look good, Kit."

57

H E SAT ACROSS FROM HER. "A CASE WORKER AT an assisted-living facility here in the city claims you'd misled one of the patients. That the patient still hadn't recovered and requires daily monitoring and treatment. After she filed the complaint, she gave me an earful. Said that until she'd seen you the woman had been doing well. Now, she says, the woman is out of control. She talks to her invisible son, sometimes for hours, apologizing to him. She needs almost constant sedation."

"I know who you're talking about. The case worker was crazier than the patient who came to see me."

"A complaint is still a complaint, so it has to be addressed. Sooner or later it'll come up and maybe even be handed to someone else. But I'm going to see if I can take charge of this now. At this point I can't guarantee anything."

She reached over and took his hand. "David...I told you before, I saw where this boy died. And where he may be buried. I don't know what town or state it was in, but I did see it and kept it to myself, because I didn't want to distress the woman. But I told her he was at peace, and when she left she was satisfied."

"Calm?"

"Happy," she said.

"And you really saw all this."

She looked at him. "I swear I did."

She thought it might just be the cop coming out, but there was something of the stranger about him now. As if this were his obverse: a different face, a darker, more distant mood.

She touched his hand. "Hey... I'm still here, you know."

He sat back and looked at her. "But here's the issue. We get all kinds of complaints—there's a whole range of cases we handle, from identity and insurance fraud to phony psychics and plastic surgery clinics promising miracle makeovers. In the end, most of them can't prove that they're the real thing. And people keep handing over their money, or actually dying from these quack treatments. It's why we have to keep after them."

"But I gave Brigid Malone time with her daughter. That voice—the words of this little girl—showed her that I had broken through. And she believed what she'd heard."

"You convinced her, you mean. Talked her into it."

"No. It wasn't coming from me. It was coming through me. Not my voice, not my words."

"Maybe the old lady was just playing along. I mean, you know now that Cabrini was using her."

"Not after Brigid told me about him."

"She wasn't well off, you know, and Tony was paying her. You have no idea if this woman really had a dead daughter. No proof, no facts, like in those newspapers and books of yours," and he waved his hand toward the table.

Now a speck of doubt had been planted in her mind. "You know that I'm an actor. I can assume all kinds of roles. I can do accents, I have a good ear. I did it for money, I'll admit that, to help cover Zoey's expenses and what I owe on this place every month, but I also saw how I was reaching people. Bringing them comfort—"

"Comfort that you just plucked from the air—"

"Doesn't matter. I learn a few things about the deceased and improvise off of them. And for the most part, people believe me. Because it's what they want more than anything in the world. But now I really have been able to reach the dead, now it's really happening. And I think they're somehow taking over my life. Living in this apartment, playing the piano, moving things around, making me see things that aren't there."

"Ghosts," he said.

58

THE DAY HAD BROKEN UNSEASONABLY HOT, ninety-four by eleven, and Kit waited on a crowded subway platform already reeking of sweat and cigarette breath and an overdose of someone's cheap cologne. Already she felt as if she'd bathed in a sewer.

She looked at her watch: forty minutes before she had to be in class, in a church basement in the Village, after which she'd pay a visit to Zoey at the hospital. Too much subway time, too little living.

She glanced warily down at the tracks. Not a scrap of fabric or a shard of bone to speak of remained. A news item, stark in its brevity, stated only that Tony Cabrini had been involved in a fatal accident. His obituary published in the *Daily News* two days later mentioned nothing about it. What else were obituaries but a kind of fiction, the editing of a reality to reduce thirty, forty, eighty complicated years to fifteen or twenty anodyne and inoffensive words?

Much missed. Forever loved. The silent, empty spaces of the unwritten were where life was lived in its most interesting and unexpected ways.

Son of the late Camilla and Francis Cabrini. Married to Connie (Abato) Cabrini for eighteen years. Father of Frank Cabrini. Graduate of DeWitt Clinton High School in the Bronx and Pace University, with a BS in criminal justice. Distinguished career as a detective in the Special Frauds Squad, NYPD.

She perversely wondered if this Connie might one day stumble into her life and demand to be reconnected with her husband, and the idea made her smile from the sheer polished irony of the whole thing.

The platform grew even more crowded, filling with people caught in the media smog, oblivious to those around them as they watched videos or scrolled through threads or flicked out words with their thumbs to their friends or lovers. She seemed to be the only one there not listening to music or checking a screen, and now a train already packed with commuters came into the station.

She stepped into the car and grabbed hold of a pole, sticky from someone else's palm.

The train negotiated a sharp curve, people leaned slightly to the left, and there by the door was Tony Cabrini, calm and detached, gazing out into the dark tunnel with a smile on his face. He was about to turn to look at her when she lost view of him behind the figure of a man in a Yankees cap and Banksy T-shirt with the image of a rat holding a boom box. Kit recognized him as being the Uber driver from the other night, and wondered if he had been following her, or if he'd even recognized her. The man was staring at his cell phone, and as though he'd seen the devil, he crossed himself and looked up at Kit before getting off at the next stop, putting Tony once again in view.

As if she had thought him back to life. He was wearing the same clothes he'd had on the night he died, a blazer and white shirt, his tie loosened, his collar unbuttoned.

And now Tony was looking directly at her. She wondered who was looking at whom, which of them was dead and which alive, and for a moment she felt vertiginous and weak, her sense of reality sabotaged.

Of course it was impossible. She had last seen him when she'd reached the platform on Saturday and turned to see if he was there. He grabbed her arm and then he was gone, people began screaming and shouting, and the next thing she knew she was being questioned by a policewoman because he was dead. What had happened between the time she spotted him and the questions? That was gone, too.

He was alive. Except that he wasn't.

Perhaps this was someone who only looked like him, as in the past others had come to resemble Peter, coming into her life over the years: her husband in the Met, with a new family; her husband on a bus, smiling at her in that funny crooked way he had, his mouth curving up a little on one side.

She reached her stop and stepped onto the platform. She knew it was just her imagination, just like everything else that had been happening lately.

And when she turned to look back, Tony lifted his hand a little, the dead greeting the living.

59

THE EMAIL CAME AS SHE WAS LEAVING THE STA-
tion. It was from the casting director from her last audition. All it said was *Call me when you have a chance ASAP.*

Rita picked up after three rings. "Kit. Thanks for getting
back to me. So there's a new independent company in Santa
Monica that's developing a limited series I think you'd be
perfect for. Financing is in place, the leads have been signed,
and they'll be shopping it to the big cable companies. HBO's
already expressed interest in it. As has Netflix. Now they're just
putting together the remaining cast. Do you have a moment?
I'd like to run this by you."

Kit left the station and walked into the open air.

Rita went on, "It's based on a true story about a missing
child. A kid who disappeared years ago. They're looking for
someone to play the mother. It's a supporting role, but from
what I've seen in the script, it's going to be emotionally sub-
stantial in the kind of story that does really well with audiences.
The dialogue is solid, and I think you could easily knock this
one out of the park. I told them a little about you, they've
seen your headshot and some of the ones I took in New York,
which thankfully didn't disappear, and they'd like to meet
with you. And—by the way—you're the perfect age for it. I'll

email you the pilot after the next revision is finished, probably late next week. Read it, and let's talk. Oh, and I also just left messages for your manager and your agent. Looks like you may need to fly out here to audition—"

"That's not a problem," Kit said.

"Great," Rita said. "I'm keeping my fingers crossed for you."

When that evening she arrived at the restaurant by Lincoln Center, David was already seated and looking at his phone. He glanced up and smiled. He seemed almost surprised to find her there.

"You look happy," he said.

She told him about the phone call. "It's just the kind of break I've been hoping for," she said, and for the first time in years felt herself fully relax.

After they ordered drinks, she sat back to watch the people at the bar, young couples, a few singles. Those days were gone, she hoped: the clients and their communing with their dead; the boozy, lonely nights alone at the bar; the blankness that always seemed to come after. As though she had somehow lost track of herself. Now she felt weightless, buoyant, apart from herself.

She looked at him: "You know, I only know that you're a detective, you live ten blocks from me, you're a widower. There's a lot of blank space there, mister." She put on her TV cop voice. "So, come on. Spill it, pal."

He laughed, he said, "Okay, here are the highlights of a pretty dull life. I was born in Philly. I'm forty-three. I like to sail when I can wrangle a boat from a friend for an afternoon. I like to travel. I like meatball pizza, I like my coffee strong, I sleep naked and usually on my right side. I don't snore. At least I don't think I do."

"Well, I do," she said, and they laughed. "Not really. Maybe sometimes."

Their drinks arrived. He said, "And just to add to that list, I'm beginning to think that you'd be really good for me."

She knew what he'd said earlier about her was right. That she was forgetting things, imagining things. And she convinced herself that she'd been the one who gave him the key after one too many drinks. Everything had a rational explanation.

Except the ones that didn't.

He lifted his glass to meet hers.

Click.

And it was sealed.

60

FOR THE FIRST TIME IN MONTHS—YEARS, REALLY—
she was feeling truly alive. No longer alone in the world,
with a chance at reviving her career, and looking out the
window, Kit saw only the bright colors of the lives of others as
people walked across the plaza to the opera house. Once again
she felt part of it all.

"Yes," she said suddenly, finishing her thought aloud, "it's
all going to be good. And I've decided I'm not going to try
to contact Caroline for you. I know that you and your wife
were happy in your marriage. I know that you miss her. I also
know that you have your doubts about my abilities. None of
that is relevant, because this is different, this is you and me. It
doesn't mean there's no room for Caroline in your life. But
it's only for your life, not ours. Just as Peter belongs to my
life, my past, and what remains of him is my memory and the
daughter he helped to create. So I think instead of looking
to the past, we think of the future. Of where we're going.
Whatever happens."

"I understand. I really do."

But his mood quickly darkened. "What?" she said.

He took a breath. Then: "Probably not the best time to
bring it up, but I finally did a face-to-face this afternoon with

the case worker, the one who came to see you. You were right. She really does come off as flaky."

Not quite the term Kit would have chosen. More like *batshit raving mad*.

"I explained that if the resident of her facility had come to see you on her own volition, without in any way being invited or tempted by you, then there is no case. She showed up, she asked for a consultation, and she left satisfied. You're positive she gave you no money, right?"

Kit shook her head. "Not a penny. I wouldn't have taken it, anyway."

"Good. Anyway, this Jessica Dowd said that residents typically didn't keep any money on the premises. Money too often in the past went for little walks with other residents there. Who had no memory that they'd done it."

"So she'll drop the complaint?"

"I spent forty minutes with her, Kit. You met her, you know what she's like. But I think I convinced her that pursuing this would be time-consuming and, because her employer would need a lawyer, expensive."

"And the woman who came to see me...?"

"She's reached that stage when she doesn't even know her own name. And she doesn't talk to her dead son anymore. She just sits in front of her window, saying nothing."

So Joey may have already been forgotten. With the boy's father dead, it meant there was no one to remember the child who'd disappeared. Kit didn't even know what he looked like. But she knew that she, at least, would think of Joey from time to time, at rest in a clearing beneath a grove of maple trees.

Later that night, after David had left her apartment, she drifted into a sleep so thin and precarious that part of her remained aware she was still half-awake. The sound of distant fire engines and police sirens faded into the distance as the neighborhood finally grew quiet, and she was pulled into a deep sleep filled with ambiguous messages.

Her mother was walking up the steps of a subway station, leaving her daughter at the bottom. Kit watched as she kept walking without turning back, until, becoming a silhouette against a bright oblong of sunlight, she turned to look down on her child. She said, "If you don't hurry up, you'll have to die all over again," and now Kit woke suddenly, eyes wide open, to see the softly glowing digits of 3:13 a.m.

She let her eyes slowly close as she took in the sound of the apartment. This was a different kind of silence, not the heavy soundlessness she had experienced in the past, but something wiry and acerbic, a tone pitched so high that you felt it more than heard it.

She thought: *This is what it's going to be like when I'm no longer alive.* It came to her as something certain, undeniable.

She didn't hear it, but sensed it: she wasn't alone. She thought: David had left just past eleven. She sat up on the side of the bed. *Focus. Think.*

Listen.

Someone was in Zoey's room.

Without turning on the lights, she made her quiet and cautious way there. She carefully opened the door and saw her daughter lying in bed, only the top of her head visible under the covers, trying to muffle her sobs.

Kit walked around to the foot of the bed and looked down. Quietly she said, "It's Mama, Zoey. There's no need to cry. You probably just had a bad dream."

And when she stretched out her hand to comfort her daughter, just as Zoey was about to turn and lift her head from the pillow, Kit opened her eyes to see the morning light from her bed. And it sounded as if the front door had clicked shut.

She lifted the blind: bike riders, a taxi, other cars, a FedEx truck. A woman walking up toward Broadway, a black knapsack over one shoulder. Kit told herself over and over that what she'd experienced that night had been only a dream. Yet she remembered waking to the idea that she was no longer alone.

She switched on the coffeemaker and opened her laptop on the table in the kitchen to check her emails. She wrote her manager and agent, stating that she was looking forward to the audition in LA. And then she closed her laptop, grabbed her bag, and as she stepped out of the building, Jessica Dowd crossed the street and confronted her.

"What do you want?" Kit asked.

"A minute of your time."

"I know that you contacted the police. I also know that they talked you out of pursuing this. So why are you here?"

"Just to update you on the patient who came to see you. Mrs. Proctor died last night. Now there's no one left to remember the son she kept talking about. If he even existed. Our thinking is that he was just a figment of her imagination. Something she'd invented to make people feel sorry for her. A character in her storybook."

Kit remembered the woman's wild eyes. "But she did have a son. I saw where he's buried."

Now the woman laughed a little more. "So if you run into her ghost, you might want to send my regards."

As she turned to walk away, Kit yelled, "Get fucked, you psychotic bitch!" in the loudest way possible, only to realize people on the sidewalk were staring at her, the crazy woman she appeared to be, alone, unmoored, and in disarray.

"Anyone know who that was?" she said calmly, before strolling away.

61

SHE PUT HER ARM OUT THE WINDOW AND FELT THE wind against her hand, and when she looked over at David he was smiling at her.

"I used to live not too far from here," he said, nodding to the windshield. "Stony Point."

"I thought you were from Philadelphia."

"I was four when we moved to New York. My father was transferred to the office up here. Insurance," he added with a shrug.

"So you grew up in the area."

"Graduated from North Rockland High," and he gestured to an exit sign with the school's name on it. "Class of '94."

"So no brothers or sisters?"

"I've always been on my own," he said.

"Are your parents still alive?"

"My father's been dead for ten years. My mother died three years later. Now there's just me."

The inn was located at the end of a long drive that ended in a small parking area. A discreet sign in a window by the entrance displayed the words No Vacancy. He took out their bags, locked the car, and went into the lobby.

The woman at the desk recognized him. She looked from

David to Kit, and back to him. She said, "Good to see you again, Mr. Brier."

"You've been here before?" Kit said once they were alone in their room.

"My father used to take us here for dinner, usually on Sundays, when we lived in the area. So I still come when I can. It's a nice place to get away and clear your head, enjoy the river views. Even for a detective it's good to get out of the city. You spend too much time behind a desk, trying to track people down to build a case. It's kind of a dark life, you know? I guess I got doubly lucky with you, though. No case to develop, and here we are, right?"

He laughed as he fingered a button on her blouse.

They arrived at the sculpture park at two, after a quick lunch at a diner along the way. After he paid their admission, they walked in and at once it bore down on her: coming there with Peter, having someone take their picture. The crow with its beak open behind them. As though time had vanished, and she were about to see her husband waiting for her under the same tree. And everything that had happened afterward was still to come.

She leaned against it. "Let's take a photo, okay? The two of us?"

"There?"

"Right here. One day I'd like Zoey to see it."

She asked someone walking by if she'd take the photo, and handed the phone to her. She put her arm around David's waist, while he draped his around her shoulders.

When later she looked at it, she noticed the flaw: on her face was a flash, a flare of reflected light in her right eye, its corona nearly obscuring her face. And David was looking at anything but the lens. She was there; but then she wasn't. And neither, it seemed, was he.

62

WHEN THEY WENT DOWN TO THE BAR AT FIVE there was the same woman who'd greeted them at the front desk, now serving drinks. On a stool at the far end was an older woman looking at her phone. The skin on her hands was mottled and her nails were painted purple.

Kit and David placed their order, and the older woman set down her phone and looked at them with narrowed eyes. "I know you," she said. Her voice carried a trace of a pleasantly soft Southern accent, and out of habit Kit tried it out in her mind. *I know you*, it said.

David said nothing. Kit said, "Me?"

The woman shook her head. She looked a little drunk. She pointed at David. "Your friend there. Seen him here before." Her eyes shifted back to Kit. "Good luck," she said, and laughed.

Good luck?

The woman's empty glass was replaced with a full one. She lifted the little straw and sipped demurely from her cocktail. "Now that's what I call pleasure," she said, mostly to herself.

"I left my phone in the room," David said. "I'll be right back."

"There goes my lucky streak," the woman joked. After he left, the woman said, "Known him long?"

The bartender ignored them both as she polished some glasses.

"Not really."

"He's been coming here for years, but don't quote me on that. *I've* been coming for years, only because I live across the road, and I don't like to drink alone. Makes me bitter and antisocial."

"I get that."

"You're the third one," she said.

Kit looked at her. "The third what?"

But David had returned and slid onto the barstool, putting his phone down before him. "Two missed calls already."

"You need to return those?"

"Not on a Saturday, I don't." He lifted his glass and quietly offered Kit a toast.

She said, "Not just to me, to us."

He smiled. "Yes. To us." And when she went to sip her drink, she saw the woman at the other end of the bar staring at her.

After dinner they went for a walk in the garden behind the inn. "Thank you for dinner," Kit said. "It was wonderful."

"They have an amazing chef. Once the *Times* had given the place a great review, people began to drive up from the city just to eat there. I'd already made the reservation before I asked you. They tend to book up quickly."

She came to a stop and looked at him. "What if I'd said no?"

He looked at her. "But I knew you wouldn't."

"And if I had?"

"Well," and he smiled, "then I just would have had to insist upon it."

63

WHILE DAVID WAS IN THE SHOWER THE NEXT
morning, she checked her phone to find a text from
the hospital, time-stamped 7:37 a.m. *Please come to the ICU
ASAP.*

Kit sat up suddenly, and nearly breathless she called the
unit and was put through to the nurses' station. There was no
answer, and she tried twice more with the same result. And
once again, when this time someone finally answered, Kit
identified herself and asked for Diane, the nurse who had been
with Zoey since the beginning.

"She's on break at the moment. Breakfast, actually, for her."

"I received a text a little while ago saying that my daughter was
back in the ICU. She hasn't been there in a few years, and—"

"I just need to stop you there. I'm actually not permitted to
discuss individual patients with any callers," the woman said.
"A matter of protecting our patients' privacy."

"But I'm her mother."

"I don't know that, do I," she said, and Kit abruptly ended
the call.

David stepped out of the bathroom. "Hungry?"

She was already up and starting to dress. "I have to go back
to the city. Right now."

"What's happened—?"

"It's Zoey…"

David said, "Did she…?"

"I don't know what's happened. But I have to go now."

"Let's dress and get out of here."

He pulled the car around to the front of the inn and she opened the door. "Hang on," she said. "I need to use the bathroom before we leave. I'll just be a minute."

She'd noticed that the woman who'd checked them in and then made their drinks was again working the front desk.

Kit said, "Can you tell me—I'm just curious—when the reservation was made by David Brier for the room we were in?"

"I can do that." She looked at her monitor, pressed a key, then another, then gave her the exact date.

"Are you sure of that?"

The woman turned the screen around. "See for yourself."

It was almost exactly a month before David had taken the barstool next to hers that first time. He'd been in her life before she'd ever known it.

64

S HE SAID NOTHING FOR THE FIRST FEW MILES OF
the drive back. The more she thought of it, the less sense
it made. The chronology—their chronology—seemed not so
much broken as somehow skewed.

Finally he said, "What do you think? About Zoey, I mean."

"I'm her mother. Wouldn't I be thinking the worst?"

He put his hand on hers. "We'll get through this. We'll do
it together."

David drove as quickly as he could before he was caught
speeding by a radar gun on the Palisades Parkway. He slowed
to a stop, and when the trooper reached the car, he already
had his license and registration in hand. Right out of central casting, the trooper looked stony-faced, first at David,
then at the documents. David said, "I'm a New York City
detective."

"And I'm Santa Claus."

"I'm going to reach into my pocket to get my ID. Is that
okay?"

"Are you carrying a weapon?"

"I'm off duty and unarmed."

"Then please step out of the vehicle while you do it." Kit
watched the man take a step back, gently brushing the butt of

his holstered gun with the heel of his hand, as David shut the door and slowly took his shield from his pocket.

She couldn't make out what he was saying, but it was over in a minute. When David opened the door, the trooper ducked his head and peered at Kit through his sunglasses. "My condolences, ma'am," and he handed the documents back to David.

He got in and waited till the guy drove away.

"What was that about?"

He took her hand. "Nothing. It was nothing."

"No ticket?"

He smiled. "Of course not."

And after the trooper pulled away, David reached under his seat and retrieved his gun.

65

THE HALLWAY WAS DESERTED WHEN DAVID AND Kit stepped off the elevator: no doctors, no one at the nurses' station. And when she reached what had always been Zoey's room those first months after she'd fallen into the coma, it was empty.

She knew what that meant. Chased by adrenaline, she started to run.

A nurse stepped out of one of the rooms and Kit staggered to a stop. "What's happened, where's my daughter? Zoey Capriol?"

"They've been trying to reach you. Dr. Roman should be here any minute now."

Kit grabbed her arm. "Tell me now. Is she dead?"

The nurse looked over Kit's shoulder. "Here's the doctor now."

David said, "I'll wait down in the lobby, okay?"

Dr. Roman asked her to join him in his office one floor below. He shut the door and took a seat behind his desk. She felt herself beginning to tremble. He said, "The nurse didn't tell you? Zoey woke from her coma about two hours ago. And not just for a minute or two. We tried to get in touch with you, but—"

"Say that again?"

He said, "Zoey seems to be out of her coma."

He let it settle between them.

"This can't be real," she said. "I was expecting—"

He nodded. "I imagined you might think that. But we don't typically leave status updates in emails or texts. And I'm sorry Diane wasn't able to speak with you directly. Typically a patient is first brought to the ICU to be tested and, if needed, stabilized. But we were able to move her off the floor fairly quickly, as it was clear she didn't need further intensive monitoring."

Kit felt time come to a halt. She closed her eyes as they filled with tears: of relief, of exhaustion, of all the too much she'd been living through. In this one long moment her life had changed. The center had shifted.

"I'm sorry," she said and reached for a tissue.

"I see a lot of tears, Kit. I'm only glad these come from some other place this time."

She asked how Zoey was responding.

"This is a new reality for her, of course. She has no awareness that she'd been in a coma. Probably her last memory is of standing on the subway platform with you. It'll hit her sooner or later, and it could be difficult for her. It *will* be difficult. Getting to grips with having lost a significant piece of her life will take time and patience. And in terms of her physical state we need to see further signs of stabilization. Three years ago we had to address the physical trauma. But an MRI taken an hour ago revealed no visible injuries. So we're keeping her on a monitor for the time being. After her discharge we'll also provide you with support from the neurocritical care team for post-recovery assistance at home."

"How soon—?"

"Maybe a month, probably more. But," he went on, "I must caution you, Kit. We don't know if this is temporary or permanent. Further tests will have to be run for a day or two before we have a better idea of her condition and what we anticipate will follow. But right now this is very promising news."

She could hardly put her mind around it. "How did it happen, I mean, what—"

He opened his hands. "It may have just run its course."

She still couldn't take it in. "Will she know how long she was under?"

"She doesn't even know that she's seventeen. A lot has happened since that night, and it'll be up to us and you to carefully and gently draw her into this whole new world. Could take a while."

Which meant that in Zoey's mind she was still in middle school. Over three years lost.

"Can I see her now?"

He smiled. "Just for a few minutes, okay?"

When they left the office, Dr. Roman and Kit walked briskly toward the elevators. The doors slid open and David stepped out. "Everything okay?"

Still overwhelmed by the news, still not quite believing it, she said, "Zoey's out of her coma."

He took a moment. "That's great. It's amazing."

"I'm going to see her now." As they waited for an elevator, she introduced him to the doctor.

Dr. Roman said, "I think it's best you go in first, Kit. If all seems well, I don't see why you can't introduce her to your friend."

Without thinking, she grabbed David's hand and held it tightly. He leaned over and quietly said to her, "I feel as if I'd known Zoey for years. I'd love to finally meet her."

"Just remember that she may not recognize you at first," the doctor said to Kit when they reached the door of her room. "That could take time. After we've determined her status, she'll be in the hands of therapists. Essentially she'll have to relearn to walk and begin to strengthen and train the muscles she hasn't been using all this time. We just need to be patient."

Diane and one other nurse were in the room. The bed had been adjusted to allow Zoey to recline, and the light in the room had been dimmed and the shades drawn so that her eyes could adapt more easily to it. Seemingly asleep, Zoey looked calm and peaceful. Radiant, even. It was as though Kit had dreamed her back into life.

"Look who's here, Zoey," Diane said quietly. Zoey's eyes fluttered open. When she saw her mother she managed a weak smile, and when she tried to sit up, she fell back into the pillows. But Kit could see recognition in her eyes. Dr. Roman put a hand on Kit's back as she began to cry again.

"It feels like a miracle, doesn't it."

Kit nodded and wiped the tears away with her fingers. Zoey tried in vain to lift a hand. "She doesn't look a day older," she said to Diane.

"She's been well looked after. By us, and by you."

It was hard to believe Zoey was now seventeen. Kit sat in a chair beside the bed. She said, "I missed you so much, baby. I came to visit you a few times a week. To tell you about what I was doing, and—"

Zoey's lips began to move, but no voice filled them.

"She also has a story to tell," the doctor said. "Soon enough you'll hear it. I think it's okay for you to introduce your friend to her now. Just don't stay too long."

66

"I'D LIKE YOU TO MEET SOMEONE, ZOEY."

What Kit had heard that morning at the inn dissolved in this important moment.

"Would that be all right…?"

Now Zoey seemed a little lost.

"His name is David," Kit said. "Is that okay?"

Kit opened the door and returned with him. She said, "This is David, Zoey." And then she introduced him to Diane, as Zoey tried to push herself back in the bed, her eyes shifting from David to her mother, then to him, then back to Kit.

"Your mom's told me a lot about you," he said, taking a chair next to Kit's. "Especially about your music. I'd love to hear you play someday soon," and he looked at Kit and laughed. "That's pretty much all I know about Zoey Capriol."

Zoey looked directly at her mother, her eyes widening. "What is it, baby?" Kit quietly asked, and then Zoey's monitor started beeping as her heart rate surged and they were asked to leave until the doctor could come in.

"It's best she rest, anyway," her nurse said.

67

A FTERWARD.

After Zoey's collapse three years earlier, after the EMTs came and put her on a stretcher and the police cleared the subway station of passengers; after Kit rode in the ambulance with her daughter; after Zoey was taken to be examined and Kit waited by the nurses' station; after a nurse there asked what had happened, all Kit could say was, "There was an accident." The words themselves carried no real meaning. She felt her voice as something apart from her. "A woman... I guess she fell in front of a subway train." She lifted her arms as if to indicate she had nothing more to tell, she'd missed it all, and if you missed it all, had it really happened?

Two detectives came in, quietly identified themselves, asked a nurse if there was a room they could use, and, because there was none, ended up talking to Kit in the hallway.

"We're sorry to have to put you through this now, but we're trying to get statements as soon as we can from as many witnesses that we've been able to identify."

He spoke in a quiet, reassuring voice, and Kit felt herself relax a bit as she was told to have a seat.

"And can we get her a bottle of water, please?" the officer asked anyone within hearing.

"What's the last thing you remember?" the other officer asked.

"My daughter—my daughter, of course. She's never suffered anything like this before. I mean, she's a normal teenager. She's always been healthy." She didn't know what else to tell him. *Zoey's going to be fine*, she thought. She could sense it deep within herself.

"I mean, what did you see on the platform?"

"It was...crowded. People were going downtown, to the theater, to restaurants, I guess."

"Did you notice the woman?"

"There were a lot of women there."

"I mean the...victim. The woman who suffered in the accident."

"I just remember noticing this couple. I only saw them from the back. He wore one of those wool caps, beanies—"

"Beanies, yes," and he made a note of it. "By any chance do you remember the color?"

She shook her head a little, as if to dislodge the memory. "I don't know. But I remember the woman was blond."

"Did you see her face?"

"No. Their backs were to me. I mean, that's all I remember. Was she the one who—?"

"And did you notice how the couple was behaving with each other? What I mean is, why this couple in particular? What made them stand out for you?"

She took a few seconds to consider it. "They were affection-ate, I guess—"

"You noticed that, then."

"I'm an actor. I'm interested in people's gestures. Body language, you know."

"Do you remember anything more?"

She had to smile a little. "I remember thinking how lucky the woman was. I'm a widow, so you notice things like that."

"I'm divorced," and he smiled a little sheepishly. "I notice things like that, too."

"The man had his arm around her shoulders—"

"Okay…" he said, continuing to write.

"And she had an arm around him, his waist I think, and he whispered in her ear, and I remember he kissed her on the side of her head, and the train was coming, and that's when my daughter collapsed."

"So you did see the man with her."

She thought for a moment. "I just can't remember what he looked like, I can't describe him."

He looked at her. "But did your daughter actually see what happened?"

"I guess she did. I mean, she must have, otherwise we probably wouldn't be here. But she began to convulse and then I looked up and a woman said she'd already called an ambulance—"

All she remembered, though, was chaos: people fleeing the station, people screaming and crying; the curious solitary ones staring down at the tragedy.

She shrugged. "Sorry if I'm not being helpful."

"Once she's been discharged we'll need to question your daughter. As she's a minor, it's only with your permission and with you present. But you understand that anything she can say would be helpful to us."

"Okay," she said. She gave him Zoey's name and age.

"And I'll need your address and phone number."

He made a note of both. "Okay, so this is what's going to happen. I've added you and your daughter to the witness list. Don't worry, it won't be made public, it's for law enforcement only, so it only circulates within the department. So that if we need to, we can question you and the others at another time. It's not a long list, but every witness statement helps."

"It's fine," she said, still a little dazed by what had happened.

She unscrewed the top of the water bottle and took a long drink. "My daughter. I need to see my daughter." It was as if she'd just realized where she was and what had happened, and a nurse standing nearby asked if she was talking about the Capriol patient, and when Kit said she was, the nurse said that it would be a little while before she could see her.

"What's going on?" Kit asked her.

"I don't know, ma'am. I'm not assigned to the ER at the moment."

"Can you find out, please? I need to know that she's okay. That she's—"

"Why don't I go ask someone. I'll be right back."

The cop said, "I'm sorry to keep going over this, but is there anything else you can remember from the platform? Did you see the man again?"

She thought for a moment. "No. I was only paying attention to my daughter."

"So she may have seen it all," she remembered the cop saying.

68

N ORTH ROCKLAND HIGH SCHOOL
Kit found it on a website devoted to high school
students of the past and their yearbooks. But there wasn't a
yearbook available for 1994, the closest being 1993, when
David would have been a junior.

Scrolling through the pages, she found a Robert Brian and a
Rosemary Brunswick in his class. But no one in between. And
David didn't show up in any of the photographs of the school
clubs or teams.

After three rings a woman answered the phone, sounding as
if she wanted to do anything but speak to Kit.

"My name is Rosie Brunswick," Kit said. "I'm trying to
organize a reunion of the class of 1994, and—"

"So you're an alum?"

Kit put a smile in her voice. "I am. I've been able to locate
most of my class—maybe two-thirds of it—but I'd like to get
the current contact info on David Brier, if you have it."

She heard the woman's fingers on her keyboard. "You say
David Brier...?"

"That's correct." And she spelled it.

"Give me one sec... Are you sure he's class of '94? Because
I have no one by that name showing up."

"Hmm. I wonder if I have the wrong year for him. But I distinctly remember Dave in our class."

"Let me do a wider search." It didn't take long. "It seems that no one by that name ever attended North Rockland High."

"No one."

"That's correct."

First the summoning, then the unfolding.

Now the unraveling.

69

L ETHAL SUBWAY ACCIDENT, SHE TYPED. EXCEPT
she'd forgotten the exact date it had happened. She pictured her and Zoey walking down the stairs to the platform.
She remembered where they stood, what they were wearing,
everything but the date, and it was only then she remembered
the unused tickets she'd put in Zoey's drawer.

The only item the search yielded for that date was a brief
report from NY1. The victim was called Alison Ingalls, twenty-
seven at the time of her death. It had happened at the Columbia
University Subway Station. She remembered the memorial
notice in the *Times*. The obit from much earlier. The woman
in the museum talking about the Vermeer.

Alison Ingalls.

"Found you at last," Kit said to herself. It was like closing
the circle, she thought, thinking back to that afternoon at the
Met. As if the scene in the painting were but *a moment in time,
a place between life and death, dream and oblivion.* Alison Ingalls's
words had stayed with Kit all this time.

She put on the coffee and was rummaging for something
edible in the fridge when the phone rang. When she saw it was
David she waited until the call ended, only to be replaced by

her outgoing message. She put it on speaker and listened carefully. The words. The tone of his voice.

"Hey, it's me, David. Just wanted to see how you were doing. Where are you, anyway?" She paused the message to take it in.

Where are you, anyway? As if that made a difference?

"It was really nice meeting Zoey yesterday. Actually...I've just arrived at the hospital. I was in the area for work, and I thought I'd drop in and spend a little time with her on my own. I'd like to get to know her better—"

She thought of how Zoey had reacted when he walked into her room, and it took her a moment to follow the trajectory from beginning to end, her heart racing as it all unfolded in her mind. She ran out of the apartment and on Broadway grabbed the first taxi she found.

And then got stuck in traffic on 110th Street.

"Moving van," the driver said with a shrug. When horns started blowing, he looked at her in the rearview mirror. "How are we doing today?" he said brightly.

She sat up and leaned forward. "Please...I need to be at the hospital as soon as possible." Again she stared at her watch. "Like right now."

His eyes met hers in the rearview. It reminded her of the driver who'd taken her and David back to her place, still an unresolved mystery. "You're sick, maybe?"

"It's my daughter. Someone's going to hurt her."

"In a hospital...? Are you joking or something?"

She pushed some money through the slot and began running like she did most mornings, cutting through Central

Park, passing other joggers, people pushing strollers, nearly knocking down an elderly man with a cane, until, a few minutes later, bathed in sweat on this hot, humid day, she reached Madison Avenue. Moments later she was riding the elevator to Zoey's floor. A nurse stopped her as she was heading down to Zoey's room.

"My daughter… I think she may be in danger."

"Her name, please?"

Kit told her.

"And you're her mother?"

"Please. Let me just see that she's all right. I know the room she's in."

Diane stepped out just as Kit reached it. She said, "Your friend was here to visit. The man you brought with you last time."

"Is Zoey all right?"

Diane took a breath. "We had a bit of a crisis. We had to ask your friend to leave, David, is it—?"

"What happened?"

"We don't know exactly. The doctor's in there with her now."

"What did he do to her?"

"Your friend, you mean? I don't know. Nothing, I guess. I mean, the door was open, as it usually is. He knew where the room was, and when one of the other nurses asked him if he needed help, he said he was in the neighborhood and wanted to visit Zoey. He said he was your fiancé."

"He's not—" But then Dr. Roman stepped out and Diane left the two of them alone. "What's going on?" Kit asked.

"It looks like something had frightened Zoey. The man who was with you the other day came to visit her and closed the door, which is contrary to hospital procedure for visitors. The monitor at the nurses' station registered a spike in her heart rate. We had to go in immediately. Something must have disturbed her."

"And the man? My friend?" Now it sounded strange even to say it.

"He just disappeared. I assume he just got on the elevator and left the building."

"But she's okay?"

"She's sleeping now. Let's let her rest, Kit."

Now she remembered what the cop at the hospital told her after the woman had fallen in front of the train three years earlier. That they were taking her and Zoey's names for possible later witness interviews. And that only the police would have access to it.

David had known who they were long before he'd sat down beside Kit in the bar that first time. He'd been playing Kit all along, just as Tony Cabrini said he was. Being a medium had nothing to do with it; Zoey as a witness was far more dangerous to him.

When she was back on the street, she phoned David. She didn't bother to start with *Hello*. "I just need to know. What did you say to my daughter today?"

Offhandedly he said, "I talked to her. Told her a little about myself. Told her how much I liked you. That I wanted to be part of her life, too."

She couldn't believe what she was hearing. "You said that? You went there without asking me first? Zoey's *my* daughter,

David. The only people who get to talk to her apart from me are the people at the hospital. You had no right to do that. Or call yourself my fiancé."

"Okay, okay, sorry. I was just trying to be friendly. And—while you're here—that case worker who brought the complaint from that facility...? Now that the patient is no longer alive, her facility's attorneys are considering charging you with negligence as having contributed to the woman's death. My thinking is that they're looking for a payday."

She put a hand to her face. "Jesus, David, I thought this was all settled. The woman had Alzheimer's—"

"I suggest you find yourself a good lawyer, Kit. The case worker said you verbally assaulted her in public. Called her names, swore at her. She said she thinks you're delusional and out of control, probably in need of professional help. If it ever goes to trial, I'll be called to testify under oath. It could get a little dicey."

She thought of what she'd sent to David's phone that night on Broadway when Cabrini was killed.

"You said you'd protect me," she said.

There was a long pause. She said, "David...?"

She was left saying his name, over and over again, until she realized he had already ended the call. She felt as though she had been trapped in someone else's nightmare, a story full of ambiguity and dead ends. A room with a door that she couldn't unlock.

Now there was no way out.

70

KIT HAD GONE TO BOARDING SCHOOL IN THE AREA for three years, and as the train followed the tracks along the river she caught sight of landmarks from her past—the Tappan Zee bridge spanning the Hudson, the red train station down the road from her school, where as cocaptain of the track team she would run a three-mile loop to the station with her teammates, downhill to the river, all uphill back to the school; and from where, on some weekends, she'd catch a train into the city to see her mother.

When she called Alison Ingalls's parents the day before, to offer her condolences and ask if she could come up and meet them, Mrs. Ingalls was more than gracious. "Did you know Ali?"

"Not personally," Kit said. "But I once heard her speak at the Met, and I was moved by what she was saying. It's always stayed with me. I'd like to know more about her."

"And you said your name was…?"

"Kit Capriol. I was very taken by what your daughter had to say about a particular painting to her group. I was there on the anniversary of my husband's death. It was just a brief moment or two, but it touched me personally, this sense of loss in what she said."

"That would be the Vermeer she'd been writing about. Ali could be very persuasive," the woman said a little brightly, remembering in the moment the best of her daughter. "Well, I don't know what Howard and I could possibly tell you. And this is for what...?"

"Just that I felt a connection between us. Between your daughter and me. And I really just wanted no more than a half hour of your time. I don't in any way intend to distress you, and if you say no, I will respect that."

The woman explained that she and her husband were retired. Her husband was a professor emeritus at Columbia, and she was a ceramicist. "Still firing up the kiln and throwing clay, but it's a lot slower these days. Some days I'm too tired even to bother."

Kit could hear a man's voice in the background. The woman said to him, "Shall I, then?" and then to Kit, "Where are you living, may I ask?"

"Not far from Columbia."

"If you have a day off from work, we'd be happy to talk to you here. It's not a long train ride from Grand Central. Rather pleasant, actually."

"I'm an actor, Mrs. Ingalls. I have lots of days off."

"How does tomorrow work for you? Come up around three, say. Does that suit?" She gave Kit her email address and asked her to let her know what train she'd be arriving on. "Howard can pick you up at the station."

"Please don't trouble him. I can walk."

"Not to where we live," and the woman laughed again. "In the back of beyond."

As the train pulled into the station at just past three, Kit checked her phone, set to mute. There had been three calls from David, the third of which brought a voice message. *Hey, it's me. Listen, um, I'm a little concerned that you're not answering. I'm in the neighborhood, and I'll stop in and make sure you're okay. I'll try again later on.*

When she stepped out along with a handful of other passengers, most of them fanning out to find their cars, an old green Volvo wagon with an aging muffler drove around to the front of the station. An elderly man with a neat mustache and trimmed white goatee peered out at her through the open window. "Ms. Capriol? Kit—?"

Getting into the car she said, "How did you know it was me?"

"You're the only one who looked lost." He laughed. "Pleasant ride up?"

She smiled. "Actually, it was. I went to school not far from here."

"So a trip down memory lane," he said. He pulled away from the station. "We try to get into the city a few times a month. See a play, visit a museum... It's not a bad life."

"I appreciate you allowing me to come and visit you and your wife, Mr. Ingalls."

"That's Howard and Barbara to you. We don't stand on formality much these days. Never did, actually."

"I mean coming here, especially under the circumstances."

"You mean our Ali...? The mourning ended long ago. It's the missing that lingers, even after three years. All the things she had to say about art have enriched us over time." He smiled. "In that way she does live on."

He drove faster than Kit would expect of someone his age, and seemed comfortable negotiating the blind corners leading away from the town. Occasionally she'd close her eyes to the apparent fatal crash awaiting them around every bend. "We live in Mount Airy. Just above Croton. Used to be known as Red Hill."

"I've heard of it."

He smiled. "Not many have these days. Old Communist neighborhood. Lots of artists. Writers. Eugene O'Neill. Louise Bryant."

"My school's drama teacher lived up here." She mentioned the name, and he said, "We knew her a little. Nice woman. She moved a few years ago to Western Massachusetts."

"When did you and your family leave England?"

"Let's see... Ali was fifteen. Absolutely hated the idea of it. Leaving all her friends behind in Cambridge. Her school. Her riding lessons. But it had to be done," and he looked over at Kit and smiled. "She adjusted soon enough. Loved the museums in New York, so she learned how to be happy here. We first lived in the city, though. Morningside Heights."

"That's where I live."

"You're...with the university, then?"

"I'm an actor. My husband and I moved there in 2001."

Howard said that they'd first had an apartment on Riverside Drive, but it was too small for Barbara's work. So they bought— "Well, you'll see for yourself in a minute"—a white Cape, not far from it a small detached cottage painted a deep red. "That's Barb's studio. I daren't go in there," and he laughed.

Ali's mother stepped out to the porch. She had shoulder-length white hair and wore jeans and a crisp white shirt and yellow Converse sneakers. Kit guessed she was in her late sixties.

"I see you survived Howard's driving," and she held out a hand. "Some haven't. I'm Barbara. Very pleased to meet you, Kit. Join us for tea, will you?"

The screen door swung noisily shut behind them. A brightly colored ceramic pot was already on the table along with a plate of English biscuits.

The Ingalls spoke of everything but their daughter. Before coming to America they'd lived in Cambridge. "Our old university town," Howard said. "Trinity College for me."

"I was at Newnham," Barbara said, "reading English. It's how we met. He was driving like the lunatic he sometimes appears to be, sideswiped my bike on Trumpington Street and knocked me to the ground. Told me I was a clumsy old cow, and I told him to fuck off. In just those words."

"And she fell in love with me there and then," Howard said.

"And since we'd both ended up teaching there, we decided to settle down and make a life for ourselves."

Hanging over the mantel was a framed reproduction of Vermeer's *A Maid Asleep*, the subject of Ali's project.

"We bought that for her when she was a docent at the Met," Howard said. "It was her favorite painting, but she very much specialized in Dutch art generally of that period. After she died, we decided to keep it here. In her memory. In her honor."

Kit looked at the disarray of the overturned wineglass, the overripe fruit in the bowl, the folds in the tapestry on the table. And perhaps a memory of someone once loved, now lost, in the young woman's sleeping face.

"She's dreaming," she said. *She's hearing voices, imagining faces, in this other world.*

"That's what Ali always said. I suppose it's up to us to give this mysterious young lady the dream she wants."

"Except in a minute or two she'll wake up with a nasty hangover," Howard said.

Barbara looked at Kit. "So why not tell us what your visit is really about. No one travels from Manhattan just to talk to two over-the-hill academics."

She told them just what she'd said over the phone: that she had been moved by what their daughter had said in the museum and was sorry to read of her death. She didn't mention the odd, vaguely undefined sensation that something of her had died along with Alison Ingalls. She just hoped they'd get around to what she really wanted to hear.

71

S OMEHOW WE FEEL THAT SHE HASN'T LEFT US," Barbara said. "Sometimes…" and when she took a breath, Kit could see a twinge of pain in the woman's face, "sometimes I wake in the night and sense that she's watching me. Once I woke—it was very quiet that night, as it usually is up here, isn't it, Howard?—and I could hear pages of a book being turned. In this room, in fact. Nothing loud or intrusive, it wasn't like that, and Howard was beside me in his usual heavy sleep and I thought, well, she's back, she's downstairs looking through a book, as she often did when she visited us. It was comforting to think that, somehow. And I went back to sleep."

"Tell her about the next morning," her husband said.

"And have this nice young woman laugh at me?"

"I'd like to hear," Kit said.

"So I came downstairs first to put on the coffee, and on this table was one of Ali's old art books from university. It was open to a page with a reproduction of *Las Meninas*—"

"The one by Velázquez—"

"Where the painter depicts himself looking directly at us from behind his easel. It's a painting of reflections and gazes, as Ali once told us. A painting where we're in the eyes of the artist himself, as though we were the subject of his painting.

Both the watcher and the watched. And completely invisible to him. Quite eerie in its way when you think of it like that."

"Ali thought it was a painting about death," Howard said. "She never explained why. Once we thought we might have understood, but then it just eluded us." He looked at Kit. "I think it's starting to become clearer to us now that we're getting on in years and beginning to fade."

"Anyway," Barbara said, "I told Howard that he had probably taken the book down from the shelf before bed and completely forgotten about it."

"But I hadn't, you see."

They lingered a short while at the table. Kit steered the conversation to Ali's life as a teacher and her time in the city.

"It's funny," Barbara said. "The only people who think about those we've lost are the ones who loved them. But you think about her, don't you, though you'd never exchanged a single word with our daughter."

"I think about how our lives have crossed without us knowing each other."

"And now," Barbara said, her mood darkening, "we come to the real reason you're here, Kit, and please tell me if I'm wrong. The man Ali was involved with... He's in your life now, isn't he."

Kit took a breath. "It's also why I'm here."

72

S O HE'S STILL OUT THERE," BARBARA SAID TO HER husband, "and there's not a thing we can do about it."

She turned to Kit. "Ali first met him at a restaurant where she sometimes had a meal or a drink with friends. She'd gone alone one evening after a day's work, and he took a seat next to her at the bar. She was never a big drinker—wine, mostly. One thing led to another, and she was seeing him regularly."

"His name is David. David Brier," Kit said.

Barbara looked at her. "Exactly. And I expect you met him the same way. Seemingly by chance. But we believe he had seen her before and made her his target. It's a bit dramatic, I know, but I don't know how else to put it. And yet," Barbara went on, "he appeared to us to be an honestly nice man. She'd take him around the museum and talk to him about the paintings, and he always listened to her, he always seemed interested in her work."

"Did she ever see where he lived?"

Barbara smiled a little. "That was the question we always had. She didn't even know the address. So they always met either at a restaurant or her apartment. Never his. Which made us wonder, because he seemed such a genuinely decent man— intelligent, thoughtful, kind. And he paid attention to Ali, to what she was saying to him. She'd never encountered that before with other men she'd been seeing."

"He's a detective," Kit said. "But I guess you knew that."

"He was completely upfront about that with Ali. And it gave her a sense of security, as one might imagine. But I think at times she felt a little overwhelmed by him. She'd been shy all her life, a little unsure of herself. When it came to men, she always felt slightly out of her depth, she was always a little naive. She only began to gain confidence with her work. Then she began catching him out on simple lies. You know, he'd claim they were supposed to meet somewhere at such-and-such a time, of which she knew nothing. Or that she'd told him something she never remembered saying."

"She began to feel she was going mad," Howard said. "That she was starting to lose her sense of reality. Of identity, really. Missing whole blocks of time. To the point that she asked her doctor to put her on an antidepressant."

"By that time it was too late in the relationship to do anything about it," Barbara said. "She'd grown reliant on him—he gave her whatever she was looking for. Comfort, probably. Security. Certainly a sense of safety. She was deeply in love with him. In too deep, as we discovered."

"How long were they together?" Kit asked.

"Long enough for her to get pregnant," Barbara said.

73

S HE WANTED THE BABY," HOWARD SAID. "WE
were delighted for her. We'd be grandparents, finally, and
she and Dave would settle down together."

"All we wanted was for our daughter to be happy," Barbara
said. "She was a brilliant young woman who loved her work.
Having a partner, having a family, would have completed the
circle. And she was happy—things were finally going her way.
The man she loved, the baby she so wanted, her work on the
book... We hadn't seen her so content with life as she was then,
even with her bouts of depression. But nothing lasts, I guess."

The atmosphere in the house grew oppressive.

"Maybe it's time for me to go," Kit said. "You've been very
kind to me, and I'm sorry I made you both uncomfortable."

Barbara looked at her. "You said you're involved with him
now," and Kit nodded. "Then I think it's important you stay
and hear the rest. Some two or three months after they'd first
met—this was before she knew she was pregnant—Ali and I had
a day out together in the city. Shopping, lunch, the usual things.
She told me that she felt she didn't really know David. That
she loved him, but that she couldn't quite grasp him. I couldn't
understand what she meant by that. They seemed such a happy
couple, and we liked Dave from the start, didn't we, Howard?"

"But I think I know what Ali meant," Kit said. "As if he were hiding something. Keeping something back."

"Which, in fact, he was," Howard said. He looked over at his wife. "But go on, Barbara."

"They spent a weekend at this inn he liked, up the river from here. She may have confronted him about her concerns. Because when we spoke on the phone the day after she returned, she seemed distracted. Troubled. It was more than her depression. It was rather frightening, wasn't it, Howard. We thought she might try to harm herself in some drastic way. She told me that when they were at the inn, he was in the shower when his cell phone rang. The name on the screen was Caroline. And on impulse she answered it. This Caroline kept asking who she was, and finally the caller demanded to speak to her husband."

"He told me his wife had died of pancreatic cancer."

Barbara smiled. "I would bet she's still very much alive and ignorant of what her husband gets up to. We realized later that being a New York City detective lent him protection. Status. Power. He could go through life pretty much unchallenged."

It all began to make sense to Kit. Your lover gets pregnant, you have a wife, and the solutions run out until only one remains. Which meant their relationship, as his had been with Ali, was built on lies. On the same kind of fraud David was meant to be investigating, as though trying to outplay anybody who crossed his path. The woman who stood before a painting and talked about a man in a doorway, about betrayal and abandonment, had come back to warn her.

"A few days later she confronted Dave about it. He laughed

it off and said that he'd never been married, that this Caroline was a woman he'd been involved with a few years earlier who wouldn't let go of him. A person who made things up, fantasized about him. He said she was obsessed. Crazy, even. And then it seemed that everything was fine between Dave and Ali. He was even starting to talk about their baby and settling down to a new life together. And she believed him."

She took a breath. "I guess it had all just become too much for her."

"That was the last we heard from our daughter," Howard said.

And he lifted a hand because there were no words for the rest.

It wasn't suicide. And Zoey had seen it all.

74

BEFORE SHE LEFT, **B**ARBARA AND **H**OWARD GAVE Kit a printout of everything Alison had completed for her book. "She'd only reached page fifty-three, and was hoping to expand it into a book-length work that would touch on things apart from the painting—her own career as an art historian, and her other passion, the relationship between the viewer and the work itself. Read it, and that voice you heard in the museum will hopefully come back to you and bring you the kind of inspiration it always brought to us."

If there's a window, it casts no appreciable light, she read on the train back. *The table, on which lies a rug or tapestry in disarray, stands in a small, seemingly airless room: suffocating, claustrophobic, a catchment of fever, a place of no true escape. This is a room full of omen and clue, a rebus that, if solved, might tell us the full story of this young woman who sits alone in the wine-fueled sleep of late afternoon, dreaming of what had been, what might have been, or what may yet come. Her story; or perhaps only ours.*

Kit unmuted her phone and found two texts and a voice message from David. The usual thing, him checking in on her, something he'd do daily anyway; something that had made her feel wanted, needed, loved. Now she was beginning to feel hunted by him.

The voicemail was more frantic.

"Hey, me again. I stopped at your building, but no one answered, and then I got as far as your door after I slipped in after someone else, and I knocked, but no one was home. So I'm a little concerned. Anyway, let's get together in the next few days—any chance for dinner and maybe more?"

It all sounded a little too contrived, almost scripted. As though he were hinting at what he was capable of doing. Coming unexpectedly to her apartment, catching her unawares, rearranging her expectations: the subtext of their relationship. Just as it had been with Alison Ingalls.

She called him when she got off at Grand Central. He answered after two rings and asked where she'd been. "I was starting to get worried," he said.

"Visiting friends in Westchester," she told him.

"Bet it was good to get away for the day. By the way, I had a meeting a few blocks from Mount Sinai this morning at the 23rd Precinct house. So I dropped in again to see Zoey," he said, and Kit felt herself suddenly go cold.

"You shouldn't have done that, David."

"Yeah, I kind of got that. I took the elevator up, they took my name at the nurses' station, and then they told me Zoey's doctor wasn't allowing visitors that day. I'll come back another time."

"Know what?" she said. "Maybe you can come with me to visit her sometime soon. But the last time you were there her ECG spiked, and she needs a lot more rest."

"Oh, and that case worker from the Alzheimer's facility? She said they'd found a lawyer to represent the place. I know the woman—actually she's something of a friend. Wait... I think she came to see you once for one of your spooky sessions. Leslie Palmer...?"

Kit remembered her: the woman had wanted to communicate with the spirit of a young lover. And this was how it was going to end, in a courtroom and a conviction. And David's role would probably never come into it.

"That will complicate things, David."

"I know. Leslie knows me, she knows you—"

"Which means that if she wants to try to prove me a fraud when I testify, I'll bring up everything she said to me during our consultation. And this married attorney will suddenly find that her past infidelity will be part of the court record."

"*Infidelity?* Leslie? Really?"

"And now you know, too, David."

By the time she reached her building it was already growing dark. She let herself in and locked the door behind her, securing the chain. And when she walked into the living room he was sitting there, in the dark.

75

"HOW DID YOU GET IN HERE, DAVID?"

He switched on a lamp and lifted a hand to show her the key chain dangling from his fingers. Zoey's key chain, with the tiny grand piano. The one that had been in her dresser drawer.

"How did you get that?"

"Cops are good at this kind of thing. I've had it for a while now. Ever since you took the other key from me."

He tossed it to her, and before she could snatch it out of the air, it fell to her feet.

"And how long did you have the other one?"

"Long enough," he said, and smiled.

It was almost too much to absorb. He had been in her life possibly for months. "So you've been in here when I wasn't home."

"Maybe even sometimes when you were," he said, a little too cryptically. "You talked to them, didn't you. The Ingalls?"

"What makes you think that?" she said.

"I know your MO, Kit. I know how you go about things. All that research. Memorial notices and obits. Addresses, phone numbers. Saying all the right things to lure them to you. Remember how you pitched me that first time in the bar?

Yeah, I get it, I felt myself being sucked in by the whole act. I was almost there, Kit, I really was. But that's where you were today, doing the same thing with Howard and Barbara. Am I right?"

"That's my business, isn't it." She didn't need to summon Alison. She was already with her.

"Nice people, aren't they, the Ingalls. I suppose they told you about me and Ali."

"All they said is that you were a couple and that she suffered from depression. To the point where she couldn't go on."

"And what do you believe, Kit?"

"I just want to know why you're here and what you want from me. Because, frankly, all I want is my daughter here at home, my acting career back on track, and my life to be my own again."

He rose suddenly to his feet, frightening her. "Tell you what. How about one last séance? A final summoning? Then we can part amicably. As friends, of course. I'm not going to hurt you. Because how would that look—you, a woman I'm investigating? That would put me right in the spotlight, wouldn't it. Now I just want to hear from Caroline."

"So she really is dead."

She could hear the smile. "You tell me," he said. "In fact, I insist."

The curtains were drawn, the candle lit. She slid her hands across the silk, *shhhh*, palms upward. He put his hands on hers. She would give him Caroline, just as he asked. She would end this nightmare on her own terms.

She reverted to the usual script: "Know that the people we

love are all around us and never leave our side. We have to remember and believe. That's what draws them to us. Faith and memory. Understand that the curtain separating us is only as fragile as the breaths we're taking right now. I feel certain Caroline is not far from us. So let us summon her now."

She could see him smirking a little.

"I can just about sense her... She's near... She holds a hand out... Caroline, do you see who's with me here...?"

Her head seemed to slump. "Yes... Now I see her, yes... Caroline's—she's in this...place..." she said. "She hasn't yet passed over. She feels as if she's in danger... Caroline, talk to me... Tell me what frightens you..." She fell silent. "Yes... Yes... Yes, yes, yes," she said frantically, "Caroline's still here. With you. With me. She knows. She knows everything, and she's afraid, terribly, terribly afraid..." She opened her eyes. They seemed to look inward as the candle flickered, died out, and then burst into flame once again, when another voice came from inside her, that of a young Englishwoman: "*You leaned over and kissed me... You said something about our baby... I loved you, David...right up to the moment you killed me.*"

David was alert now, vigilant. And once again she was falling, being pulled into some greater depth, a dark undefined place.

This time the voice came in a whisper: "*But I'll always be here, David. By your side. Watching. Waiting for your time to come. Just like you did with me.*"

76

DAVID WAS STANDING AND LOOKING DOWN AT her as she rose up out of her trance, blinking a few times without seeing him.

"You're good, Kit," he said. "You even have the accent down cold."

He looked upon her with a kind of pity. She felt drained again, as though something essential had fled her. She stood and turned on the light before extinguishing the candle.

How perfect it now seemed to her: Alison and Kit, two vulnerable people looking for a sure thing. They never questioned him, never doubted him. A young art historian unsure of herself. A medium ripping off innocent people, just waiting to fall for the bait: the con artist forever in thrall to the cop. Married, she could never be asked to testify against him, and he would never put her life in jeopardy. All that remained was the silence of complicity.

And Zoey. Who would have to be silenced. Another accident, probably. He would find a way. He always did.

Followed by him, she'd made her way out of the consulting room into the little hallway. She would never reach the door in time. She would never be able to get out. She'd just be the victim of another break-in who'd struggled and was killed.

Got to get outside, she thought. *Other people. Witnesses.*
Go now.
Run.

"Let's go up the block for a drink," she said. "Just let things cool down for a while, okay? I'm thinking that maybe taking a little time out might be good for us. I just need to feel I can trust you again. And that has to be earned back."

Her trust and her silence: something he understood, because then she could never say a word about what had happened to Ali Ingalls.

"Fair enough, Kit," he said.

When they walked out onto the street she felt herself breathe again; she was now finally free. Away from the dead, from the candlelight, from the voices and the fear.

They walked up to Broadway and waited to cross. Suddenly the words came to her in the voice she so clearly remembered, a voice that hadn't been hers: *I loved you, David…right up to the moment you killed me.* And she saw the look in his eyes while they waited to cross. He knew what she knew, whether she had actually channeled the dead woman or only made up the words. There was only one way the evening could end.

They would attribute her suicide to her legal difficulties with an Alzheimer's facility. *It had all become too much for her*, David would testify.

She said, "I'm finished here, David," and began to walk briskly back to her building.

He grabbed her arm and swung her around toward him. He said, "You're coming with me. You know too much."

"I won't give you that pleasure. Go home to your wife."

And without bothering to look back, she broke away and ran blindly across Broadway back toward her street.

"Missy," someone called out, and when she looked up she saw Brigid Malone on the opposite sidewalk standing beside a little blond girl. "Missy," she said again, and Kit came to a stop in the middle of the road.

"But you're dead," she shouted, and the old woman smiled and held a hand out to her just as the light changed.

The driver said he hadn't seen her. He hadn't seen anything at all.

CODA

IT WAS AS IF SHE HAD NEVER LEFT.

She returns occasionally, dropping in, so to speak, knowing that her daughter finds comfort in sensing her presence, just as others had found solace in her words at the little table with the silk cloth and the candle.

Sometimes she comes upon Zoey sobbing, and though she'd like to be beside her, holding her, saying *Shhh, baby*, she can't console her, waiting instead for her daughter to sleep and dream, when she'll know that all is well. And there are the times when Zoey comes into her mother's room and stands over the empty bed, left exactly as it had been that day, as though to summon her back to the living.

Six weeks after Dr. Roman told her about her mother's death, Zoey moved from the hospital's rehab center to her nurse Diane Carlson's home to live for nearly a year afterward, coming a few times a week into Manhattan to continue her physical therapy and resume working with Mrs. Fischer. It felt good to be part of a family. She liked Diane's kids and husband, and when able even did some babysitting for the children, and it helped her find her balance once again.

There was an upright piano in the living room, and she was free to use it whenever she liked. At first it frustrated her, as if she had to start all over again. She'd hit a note, listen to it fading into silence, then press another key. Slowly her fingers began to remember, and single notes became phrases, an opening to a Bach prelude, the first measure of the Mozart sonata she'd been studying when everything had gone black.

Sometimes she thought of the father she had never met, and remembered—but from where?—a funny story about him taking his aunt's car when he was just a kid. Had she made it up out of nothing, or had it been with her all her life?

When she was completely recovered and resuming her piano lessons, she was living in what was now her Morningside Heights apartment. Sometimes Kit watches from the doorway as Zoey plays the opening of the *Moonlight* sonata, brow furrowed as she tries again and again until she gets it exactly right.

It's perfect, Kit once whispered, and Zoey turned to see who'd said it. But no one was there.

Yet the words lingered with Zoey, as though they'd come from deep inside the young woman's heart: an intuition, a private certainty.

Early on, Zoey would remember the man who'd said he was her mother's friend, the man who visited her at the hospital, who closed the door and sat on her bed and smiled. *One day when you're not expecting it*, she remembered him whispering in her ear.

And then, over time, she forgot him, a distant memory lost amid the notes of her music and the richness of her new life.

But not for her mother. Because now she has all the time in the world.

Now in her third year at Juilliard, Zoey has inherited Mrs.

Fischer's practice. Zoey had begun noticing it for herself once she'd resumed lessons, her teacher forgetting the names of pupils, unable to remember what they'd been asked to practice. She once called Zoey by the name Klara, and then, when Zoey gently reminded her, she laughed it off and said Klara had been her sister, "And maybe, I don't know, you remind me a little of her."

Zoey knew that Klara had been dead since 1957.

Now Frida Fischer has vanished into a nursing home. She has forgotten her students. She has forgotten her sister. She has forgotten her name and her life, just as others have forgotten her. She sits by the window and watches people walk by. She watches the cars pass. She looks to the sky and watches the clouds gather. And when Zoey comes to visit, as she does quite often, Mrs. Fischer just looks vacantly at this stranger sitting across from her in the lounge, while they sip tea and nibble on cookies and say very little to each other.

Now, as for both Mrs. Fischer and Kit, there is only one tense, the here and the moment. Close your eyes: blink, and it's gone.

Once a year, at the end of June, Zoey takes the subway into Brooklyn to visit her mother's grave, near a blossoming magnolia tree at Green-Wood Cemetery, and quietly reads the lines she herself had chosen for it, as though the words might bring her mother back to her.

> *Though I am old with wandering*
> *Through hollow lands and hilly lands,*
> *I will find out where she has gone,*
> *And kiss her lips and take her hands...*

She has no idea why she'd selected the verse, this fragment from a Yeats poem, waking one morning to find the lines in her head, sensing that her mother would be pleased. And then she brushes away the leaves from the headstone and with her fingers traces a few of the letters engraved on it.

Zoey is engaged to be married. His name is Joel, a recent Juilliard graduate, a cellist newly hired by the Metropolitan Opera Orchestra. He will be moving in with Zoey soon, and then it will be time for Kit to let Zoey have a family of her own. Sometimes she'll visit them, too, quietly and discreetly.

But now it's time to settle accounts. It wasn't hard finding him, sitting across from a woman much younger than himself in the restaurant near the South Street Seaport, at the same table he and Kit were seated at on the terrace in the evening warmth not many months earlier. A man of habit, she thinks; a man who knows the lay of the land, who keeps it all on his own turf.

She listens to the conversation, all too familiar to Kit. He talks about his wife, who died young. He talks about how life has been hard for him since then, "Coming home to an empty apartment," and the young woman puts her hand on his to comfort him.

The woman gets up to use the ladies' room. She goes to the sink when she senses someone else is there. "*He'll kill you, you know,*" the stranger whispers, dissolving into nothing as the woman turns to look at her.

Not long after—however short or long it might have been, for time means nothing now—Kit finds herself alongside David, walking along Broadway in Morningside Heights. He hasn't appreciably aged. But then again, neither has she. She wants to run the back of her hand along his cheek, because she's missed that, the feel of another's skin, the stubble of an unshaven man.

As she walks she sees others like her, just like in the newspaper memorials, *sorely missed, still loved, never forgotten,* crowds of them, translucent, glittering shadows in the slant light of this August afternoon, unseen by the living; and more than once, just as she had all those years earlier, she has seen her husband, Peter, walking toward her among the others, as spectral as she is, a shimmery mirage in the city air. Their eyes meet; their hands brush; there's a sense of promise, of future encounters, of thoughts to share, and each walks on knowing that they'll meet again someday when the time is right.

She follows David into a subway station, and when he reaches the platform he puts on his killer smile and moves quickly to greet someone he expected to meet there, the same young woman who sat across from him in the restaurant, her eyes full of happiness for being with this man at that moment. Kit thinks of Zoey on this same platform. She thinks of what her daughter had witnessed. She thinks of what Zoey still knows. And she knows what this man will one day do to her.

A train is about to arrive, and she steps up behind the couple, walking through David and looking back to see the shadow cross his face as he pauses: as though he'd suddenly caught a glimpse of his own end. The chill of death is upon him, and it'll stay with him for the last moments of his life.

Goodbye, David, she says sweetly in his ear, brushing her fingers along his cheek, stealing his attention just as the train is pulling in, and it's only when he falls that the screaming begins.

Reading Group Guide

1. What was your first impression of Kit's séances? Do you agree with the way she justifies her work, or is she just taking advantage of people?

2. Is working with a medium a good way to find closure, or does it trap you in the past? Which of Kit's clients exemplify your position?

3. How does Kit cope with Zoey's long incapacitation? Is there anything you would do differently in her position?

4. Describe Tony Cabrini. What do you see as his dominant personality trait? How does that trait shape his actions throughout the book?

5. Kit muses that every grief is private, yet the words we use to define it are often the same. Do you agree with her? How can we support other people even if we cannot truly understand their grief?

6. Did you approve of David's methods of investigating Kit? What boundaries should undercover investigators abide by? Do you think those boundaries would have significantly changed the outcome between Kit and David?

7. Kit is uncomfortable with the increasing reality of her medium work. What strategies does she use to try to understand what is happening to her? Is there anything else you would have tried in her position?

8. Kit's acting career is a severe detriment to her financial stability. In her position would you still be auditioning? Where do you think she gets her ability to persevere? Is her determination good for her?

9. How do dating conventions and gender roles disguise David's suspicious behavior in the early stages of his relationship with Kit? How can we make dating more equitable?

10. Compare Kit to Alison Ingalls. Do you think they caught David's attention for similar reasons? What is the biggest difference in the way the relationships played out?

11. Tony threatens to take Kit in for "resisting arrest," and Barbara Ingalls points out that David's status as a detective protects him from the consequences of his affairs. Do you think these corrupt detectives are common? Do you think they would face appropriate consequences if they were caught misusing their power?

12. Do you think all the characters got the ending they deserved? If you could change the outcome for one character, whose fate would you change, and how?

A Conversation
with the Author

**Where do you usually turn for inspiration? How did you
decide to write about a not-so-phony medium?**

I'd wanted to write a novel about a medium from the
time I was living in England but until now had never quite
found a way in. Apart from the work of the Polish director
Krzysztof Kieslowski, whose films are filled with the shimmer
of the uncanny, a sense of an unspoken mystery woven into
a character's daily life, two movies in particular had inspired
me from early on: *Seance on a Wet Afternoon*, with Kim Stanley
and Richard Attenborough, and Nicolas Roeg's *Don't Look
Now*.

Based on a short story by Daphne du Maurier, *Don't Look
Now* is an ingeniously structured psychological thriller. Though
a medium features as an important character, what interests
me is the way it deals with how the living try to reconcile
themselves to the dead. In the case of the couple at the center
of the movie, played by Julie Christie and Donald Sutherland,
it's the loss of their young daughter that has broken their lives,
their marriage, their hearts. In joining her husband in Venice,
where Sutherland's character has been commissioned to restore
an old church, Christie's character comes to believe that she
can reach her daughter in her afterlife. But they are caught in

a tragedy that has been unfolding since the first minutes of the movie.

Kit recalls the film in remembering her initial encounter with Alison Ingalls, the docent at the Met, whose voice is so like Christie's. But what interested me in having a spiritualist—or someone who portrays one—is the relationship between the medium and the client. Persuasion is on one side of the equation, while the desire to believe is on the other. If one truly wants to have faith in reaching the dead, then it's possible to convince them that they actually have—especially if one has a few facts or impressions to hang a séance on. Although there are certain authors who have inspired me over the years, in general I rely more on exploring themes common to many of my books: time and memory, and how past actions can haunt the present, which is something I'll be exploring more explicitly in my next novel.

Most of the characters in the book could be classified as skeptics. Do you believe in the supernatural yourself?

Though I've had no direct experience of "seeing" the dead (other than when my mother appeared in a dream to me around the same time she died, looking forty years younger, which really doesn't count as supernatural), my wife's mother had had several experiences of this nature and took it all in stride. Nothing ever frightened her. When a relative suddenly appeared in her kitchen, she looked up and said, "Oh, you've died, haven't you." A minute or so later the phone rang with the news that he had indeed died. She had a number of similar experiences after that.

If you could visit a medium who was completely legitimate, would you go?

Definitely out of curiosity, though I'm not sure whom I want to contact. Although as I get older I've grown increasingly more aware of, and uncomfortable with, my own mortality, the religion I was raised in stressed life in the here and now, not afterward. And heaven and hell never came into it, so I'm not fearful of falling into the great fiery pit or ascending a stairway to heaven.

But death is the one great mystery common to us all—writers, rock stars, politicians—and no one can state with any certainty exactly *what* is going to happen after we take our last breath. Hamlet calls death, "The undiscover'd country from whose bourn no traveller returns."

Except, of course, in a séance...

Do you prefer heroes or villains as a writer? As a reader?

Villains are always far more interesting. Consider Shakespeare's Richard III: he's a kind of evil incarnate, ordering the murder of children, seducing a widow at her husband's funeral, and so on. Yet we can't take our eyes off him. Likewise with, say, Hannibal Lecter. Or John Milton's Satan, the most interesting character in *Paradise Lost*, even though the competition is stiff, what with God and Adam and Eve. I'll also toss in Patricia Highsmith's Tom Ripley, who would as soon kill you as look at you, and yet somehow you'd be flattered to be in his company.

And who was it who said the Devil has all the best lines...?

Evil requires style, for style is a means of seduction, and the villain has to work at it as meticulously as an actor prepares for a role. Dracula is a prime example, with his (very) old-world charm, that cape, and his inescapable magnetism. He can also bite and fly, but he would see those as merely perks of the genre.

What was the most challenging part of writing The Summoning? Were there any scenes that were especially fun to write?

The challenging part was in finding a balance between the thriller elements and the supernatural, so it didn't just become another ghost story. I find it's best to work in subtler ways, such as when Kit, in channeling an Irishwoman's daughter, feels the little girl's fingers in her hair. Or when she hears someone playing her daughter's piano in the dark predawn hours. Creepy haunted moments that would make anyone question their own sanity.

The séance scenes were especially satisfying to write. From the atmosphere of the little room with the table and the candle, to the words Kit has so carefully field-tested and worked into a script, to the whole psychology of manipulation: as though she were preparing a scene in a movie—something that comes naturally to this actor. There's the sense that at least Kit *seems* genuine, hopefully leaving the reader wavering between doubt and belief. And then she *becomes* genuine.

Or is she just a very skilled con artist…?

What are you reading these days?

I'm doing research for my next novel, a psychological thriller which shifts between 2009 in New York and 1969 in Los Angeles. So a lot of nonfiction, memoirs and such. I've also been

reading Eve Babitz, one of the most acute and acerbic observ-
ers of the Southern Californian culture of the sixties. Though
I remember 1969, largely from a New York perspective, Los
Angeles had a very different scene. The sixties everywhere,
though, weren't as sunny and happy as some have portrayed it.
There was a dark side to it that I was quite aware of, even in
the so-called Summer of Love in 1967. And then I'll mention
Manson and Altamont, and that pretty much wraps the decade
up in a shroud.

I found the late Michelle McNamara's *I'll Be Gone in the
Dark* fascinating, also pertinent to my next project, as one of
my two main characters is a successful true-crime author. I was
especially taken by the relation between McNamara and her
subject, and how what begins as a routine review of files and
police reports and maps becomes an obsession that engulfs her
life up until its tragic end. The book is as much about the author
as the killer she's hunting (and who was eventually captured not
long after her death).

Otherwise, as I really don't read much contemporary fiction,
I've been rereading novels that had an impact on me years earlier.
I also keep up in reading (and rereading) novels in French.

About the Author

© Sharona Jacobs

J. P. Smith was born in New York City, raised five minutes from the Bronx, and began his career when he moved to England, living with his wife and daughter in London, Lyme Regis, and Cambridge for over five years before his first novel was initially published there. As a screenwriter, he was an Academy Nicholl Fellowship semifinalist in 2014. *The Summoning* is his ninth novel.

He currently lives four minutes from the Atlantic Ocean on the North Shore of Massachusetts. Visit him at jpsmith.org.

Don't miss a single thrill from J. P. Smith!